THIS STRANGE AND PRECIOUS THING

Also by Esmé Ellis:

Pathway Into Sunrise
Clea and the Fifth Dimension

THIS STRANGE AND PRECIOUS THING

Esmé Ellis

Published by
Horus Books

First published in Great Britain in 2008
by
Horus Books,
Bath, BA2 5DL, UK

ISBN 978-0-953392-81-0

Cover:
Illustration by Esme Ellis, and Computer Graphics
by Robert Palmer.

Copy-editing, design and typesetting by
Mushroom Publishing, Bath, BA1 4EB, UK

For Ellis Morgan. Fly, little bird.

"....that awful Spanish moulding" by Robert Palmer

ACKNOWLEDGEMENTS

My grateful thanks to all who have encouraged and supported me in the writing of this book, especially to Lindsay Clarke for his tough and inspirational teaching during its early stages, Kevan Manwaring for some later-stages 'doctoring', and to Crysse Morrison for her invaluable editorial critique. Also to Martyn Folkes for his editorial support and exactitude, and for the interior design. Grateful thanks also to Robert 'Skip' Palmer who, with his computer skills and 'deviant' aesthetic flair, helped me bring my ideas for the cover into being.

I must also acknowledge contributions from the sources of inspiration which, in the inter-dimensional manner of these things, dropped onto my lap(top) or into my mind at precisely the right moment. In this respect, my thanks to Daniel Jacob for allowing a quote from The Reconnections which precisely echoed a passage I had just typed. Writing this book has been a test of discipline and trust, and here, especially, I offer my thanks to Saint Germain, who, on the many occasions that the narrative stalled, leaving me teetering on the brink of the unknown, awakened in me the discovery that I, too, had the wings to fly.

CONTENTS

'*I simply believe that some part of the Self... is not subject to the laws of time...*' C.G.Jung

'*Anyone who is not shocked by Quantum Theory has not understood it.*' Niels Bohr

Res ex qua sunt res, est Deus invisibilis et immobilis.
(That from which things arise is the invisible and immovable God.)
Attributed to the "Liber Platonis quartorum" and quoted by Paracelsus.

THE ISLAND

Sunlight flashed across the face of the ocean. The girl had waded out to where it was deep enough to swim, but the wind was strong, so strong that the waves were being driven across the bay slantwise to the tide. Swaying with the lurch of the water she waited, legs and stomach submerged in the cold Atlantic, while an Azorean sun beat down on her shoulders. Eventually the right wave came along; a vigorous, glittery wave. She dived into it and headed out to sea. An experienced swimmer, she kept her stroke going determinedly. At one with the motion of the sea and the rhythmic power of her limbs, the sensation was heady. After some while she turned onto her back and did a few relaxing stretches, getting her breath. The boisterous rocking of the waves was strangely reassuring, lulling with that same soothing effect new-born babies take to instinctively. Her breathing too began to take on the sea's rising, falling rhythm. Suspended between the swelling depths below and the arc of blue space above, she looked up.

Her gaze drifted lazily, slipping and curving down through wisps of cloud, resting for a moment on the pearl-pink tips of the mountains encircling the bay, before dropping to the coastline. But the landmark hotels and bars along the front had lost their familiarity. The current must have carried her quite a way down the beach—a mile at least from where she'd left her clothes. Alarmed, she made a rapid about-turn in the water, flipped onto her front and began pulling for the shore. As panic kicked in, the spurt of adrenalin gave her arms and legs new energy. But several desperate strokes later and with her stomach a tightened fist, she realised she wasn't making any headway. The element which had been her ally until now had turned against her and was forbidding passage.

Her thoughts raced. Oh God! Why today of all days? My first alone, with Simon gone. No-one knows I'm out here. She battled on, thrusting against the walls of water. But her limbs were tiring fast, and when she stopped, stretching down for a moment with her toes to test her depth, there was nothing below but a lot more water. Making it back was now in doubt, and there were mini people on the beach giving every sign of unconcern. Some line from Stevie Smith's poem about not waving, but drowning, suddenly seemed a bit too close for comfort. With the undertow bobbing her round like a cork it was a struggle just to keep her head up. Blasts of wind stripping foam off the tops of waves were adding insult and slapping it into her face. The elements were mocking her. She could definitely hear laughter. Buffeted and tossed about, she listened intently. Yes, there it was again! Each fresh gust of wind bringing her this incongruous laughter.

Another giant wave lifted her and she saw where the sound was coming from. Some jet-setting joy-riders were cruising further out aboard a high-powered yacht. To the accompaniment of their hysterical shrieks she watched as the yacht made a U-turn and headed back in the direction it had come. No-one had noticed her frantic waving. Instead, their manoeuvre was producing a massive wake, and it was rushing towards her. Realising she could do nothing now to avoid it, she surrendered to her fate.

But the mood of the elements seemed to have changed once more. The wave took her up. Like a child rescued by some friendly sea creature it lifted her onto its back and she found herself riding the crest as it curled towards the shore.

Yet if it had promised rescue, as the wave neared then thundered onto the beach, its boiling roll began to suck her down. She was tumbled into a mass of sharp grits and pebbles, and dragged under. She struggled to get her head up, but the sea held her fast. She had to breathe; but she couldn't. Her lungs screamed for air; there was none. It wasn't until she felt her knees and palms grate on the shelving beach that she found purchase enough to force up her head and gulp air.

At last, with firm sand once more beneath her, she scrambled, scratched and bleeding, to her feet, and with an inelegant stagger, collapsed onto the beach.

Finn too was having a little trouble with the elements. Without a physical body as such, and the atmosphere far too dense for his liking, he was hovering twenty or thirty meters above the beach. He spotted the girl lying face down, a little apart from maybe a hundred other bodies. But there was something different about hers. Not only was this body unique, to his mind, in not being positioned flat, as many others were, upon multi-coloured lengths of stuff, or bent into similar coloured support frames, but this one heaved and spluttered.

It had been so long since he had been conversant with the terms of communication used by the inhabitants of an Earth-like planet he was having trouble recalling the appropriate nouns and verbs. He would stay where he was for the time being, he decided, and let the conversion process take him comfortably step-down by step-down into this heavy atmosphere. The image of a rubber-encased, weighted down figure preparing to descend into deep water flashed across his mind-screen as he contemplated the process. A memory-metaphor from a previous lifetime, he supposed. After all, this same Earth had once cradled him, although, when he'd lived here the atmosphere was never as heavy as it seemed now.

Finn gazed at the girl, scanning her. Terms were coming back to him now. He could sense her body's distress, but he was making a distinction between Her and Body. She *had* a body, and it was this body with its animal intelligence that was distressed. He could feel

5

that. She was not distressed. Not in the same way. He felt a kind of exhilaration in the Her aspect. There had been an experience only moments before, and the brain was struggling to process it. He sensed a major disruption to the patterns of the emotional body. He guessed it was panic. The cause seemed to have been deprivation of air. She had never had this element—or the lack of it—drawn to her attention before in such a dramatic manner, and the brain seemed in chaos.

They're all staring at me, she thought.

They weren't. In fact, they had barely noticed. Everyone else was playing happy families on the warm sand well away from the water's edge, while the girl's lungs gasped and wheezed.

God, this is awful. All this puffing and panting... and my heart banging away, hammering at my ribs. So loud they can all hear. Oh God! I can't even turn over now. Ab-so-lutely knackered. Bloody mess I'd look anyway, all scratched, and seaweed down my front. Better just lie here 'til it all settles down, then I'll get myself back to where I left my clothes.

The panting slowly subsided, but the beating didn't. She waited. It was hot. The sun began biting and blistering her skin.

Getting myself burnt now, she moaned. What a sight! Back like a traffic light at red, blood all down my front. And this bikini. Feels like it's been done over with a cheese grater. What an idiot! At least Simon won't ever know. I'm supposed to understand about currents and tides. Winds and all that. He'd be screaming at me, "Look what you get into when I leave you alone for a minute." Or he'd be falling about. But if you hadn't gone off, damn you Simon, none of this would have happened.

She raised herself gingerly, sat up, and felt for her bikini top. It was still in place—just. As she tugged at the scrap of cotton a strange sensation shivered over her skin. Someone was looking at her! Stupid! she told herself, you've already decided you're making a spectacle of yourself. So what do you expect? Manoeuvring what was left of the bikini bottom into place, she glanced around the beach. Minimal and shredded though it was, this fragment of cloth would look better covering the parts intended, she thought. But nobody appeared the least bit interested. She was just so much flotsam—or was it jetsam? Yet the sensation of being observed from on high persisted.

There you go, she told herself, imagining someone 'up there' is interested in you. Doubly paranoid, now. All the same, why not sit here a bit longer, just 'til you get your legs back... and your breath. And you won't seem—what do they call it?—half seas over?—when you get up covered in mess and begin staggering back all that way. God, though! Was I lucky out there, or was I lucky? If that rogue wave hadn't come along! You'll be even luckier if your stuff's still there, with all those people about today. And not just your clothes, but your damn key. (She'd put it inside her sunglasses case for safety, rolled up in her pants, along with a screwed up Euro note.) If all that's gone, she told herself, you won't be able to get back into the flat, and there'll be more trouble. Security and God knows what. Police maybe. And you'll look even more stupid. Trust this to happen today, just when Simon's left for Amsterdam.

Aren't you glad no-one ever hears what goes on inside your head, Annya? This is gibberish, woman. No-one would think you were a together, intrepid correspondent from... Shit...! Someone up there *is* looking at me! Shit!

A rash of goose pimples ran across the top of her sunburnt, gravel scored and blood bedribbled skin.

Bodies, bodies. Bodies on the beach. He'd been away rather too long. So long apparently, he'd forgotten how ludicrous they could be. The small ones, children—at least the ones unencumbered by excessive upholstery—they had a kind of beauty. He watched. He was taking his time. The colours on this planet were so muted you had to—how to say it—get your eye in? On the planet he had just come from, everything was luminescent. Everything sparked, whirled, spun. Life-forms spiralled and wheeled, sending out spurts of electromagnetic energy into the atmosphere by way of communication. Intense, intelligent, vivid, and light they were. Even the mysterious blue ranges, the infras, Zedonites and Indragons—his favourites really—were light-filled. But the solar colours on Zurillian with their powerful frequencies of ultramagenta and rhosacandescence, gave you that buzz of energy which he felt was sorely lacking from his system at this moment. This was a belated homecoming. It would take time. These people had to use Time. He must get used to it too.

Eventually, also, he would need to find a way of creating a body to inhabit, as dense in matter as those he was observing now. Of course, as an Earth-born entity, he had retained his etheric anatomy with its vital organ connections, and from this it might be possible to reconstruct a flesh-and-blood form.

He studied the children some more and, focusing beyond their solidity, began to notice curious energy-shapes with colours swirling about them. He tuned in to the sounds the youngsters were making. Their harsh whoops and shrieks jarred his system. But at the same time the sound was causing strange tremors in his heart centre.

Laughter! I remember laughter. I *did* laughter a lot, he thought. These colours spinning around them are matching their mirth, changing from moment to moment, flaring out as they run and throw and catch. There are silver joy-waves rippling about them too, as they dig with hands or those crude, coloured implements. It's wonderful. They're constructing fantastic forms in their minds, and then attempting to reproduce them in matter.

A spiral of exhilaration escaped from his throat. He was beginning to enjoy himself. But, he was thinking, the older bodies, not so beautiful. He studied a bit more and saw that some of the adults had images in their minds too as they strutted up and down. Idealised body-images which their corporate solidity didn't reflect. On the other hand, some oddly proportioned, squat or scrawny persons had beautiful colours round them. It was fascinating.

The body he was looking at now, for instance. The one who'd caught his attention from the beginning. It seemed reasonably put together, proportion-wise, yet she, the owner, was mentally creating a self-image reflecting a starring part from a horror movie. Monster from the deep. She seemed to be conjuring up a sea-weeded, barnacle-covered nightmare. Her mind-pictures intrigued him. He was becoming so empathetic, he thought, that he seemed to be taking on her life-knowledge. He instantly knew 'horror movie', although such a term had been unknown to him until this moment. He was, he felt, right into her mind now—into her play—and was playing along with her. The game, in fact, was becoming so hilarious that his own mirth must be loud enough for her to hear. He was in danger of cracking up, and decided it was best to withdraw from her before his laughter disrupted her performance.

Finn had known sooner or later he would feel the call to return to his home planet. It was, they'd told him, written in—sacred contract. But that hadn't meant a lot to him at the time. In his own terms, he'd done a bit of surfing first—inter-dimensionally speaking. It hadn't seemed like running away, not to him at least, although his parents had tried to persuade him to stay around a bit longer. Too young, they felt, for him to leave home in that impetuous way. Maybe he'd inherited this trait from his mother, Cléa. After all she'd gone off on an interstellar cruise of her own.

HOO-HAA IN THE COUNCIL

If Finn's beginnings are a little hard to describe, that's partly because the language needed isn't one which can easily be written down. We haven't yet perfected the knack of conveying multi-dimensional and co-existent concepts onto a two dimensional page. Finn's own conception, for example, happened 'out of time' in an 'instant of cosmic passion.' This is not a metaphor. The event occurred while one part of Cléa's consciousness was abroad in what some would describe as the 'Beyond Earth Realms'.

While many people are prepared to believe that some part of the Self continues after death, non-physical existence is never a guarantee of sudden enlightenment. Wisdom diplomas, halos and wings are not handed out at the pearly gates. On the contrary, the *Near* Earth Realms which the vast majority of humans find themselves in post mortem, are not dissimilar to the world they have just left. Mass consciousness holds sway with its same old illusions and behaviour patterns. Cléa's case however was different. As ecstasy flooded her consciousness, and with her physical body clinging to her lover down on the physical Earth, she scaled the angelic ladder. On arrival at the Beyond Earth dimension she heard a voice announcing that a strange and precious son would be born to her, but also, and this may seem even stranger to us in our present century, it would be for her to choose the time, and in fact the *era*, when the actual birth would take place.

Yet, if the term 'Annunciation' itself has resonances of other-worldly intervention concerning miracle birth—messianic comings—it is by no means intended to imply that her child would be in any way extraordinary. Finn was simply an extra *ordinary* kid: one among many thousands of extra ordinary kids born around that time. That 'Time' being circa 2250, Anno Domini.

When, eventually, the Day of the Birth arrived, some centuries after the conception (if you count events in linear time) the Naming Day was set. It was decided that this would be an occasion of great celebration. Hardly surprising, since the people had waited so long. The thing would be made much of, and a great party was arranged. The wine—or its 23rd Century equivalent—flowed, and so thoroughly did Joy As She Flies unconfine herself that, not only did she unlace her stays, but ripped out the ribbons and flung them to the winds, so that the Ceremony of Naming became somewhat secondary and rather blurred in people's minds. No-one could quite remember what the actual name was supposed to be: Fingeld? Finnigal? or was it Finnegan? In the end the child became simply Finn—at least until his friends began teasing him with that silly Strange and Precious label.

As a child, Finn had been enthralled by accounts of his mother's initiation. She'd crossed over from the Fourth to the Fifth Dimension around the cusp of the Twentieth Century, and found herself alone, in an unmapped and unexplored territory—a new reality where the ground of existence, the solidity, which until then had been taken by the majority of humanity as immutable, became fluid and changeable. This had been disconcerting to say the least, until she learned its ways. But in discovering the strength of her inner spirit, her path unfolded and led, not only to her meeting with Grayling, but to the flowering of her creativity and to the realisation that she had the power to shape and steer her own reality.

With both his parents regaling him with stories of their pioneering, Finn, even at an early age, began to be aware that they were regarded as heroic figures. A fact which made him feel he had something to live up to. Some of the adults tended to see *him* as special too. But the little boy, hardly more than a babe, didn't know how to *be* special. Enlightened as his parents were, old-fashioned pride often swelled their bosoms, and they caught themselves thinking aloud at times. Maybe that's why little Finn attracted some teasing from his playmates.

'I don't know what you think, Cléa my dear,' his father, Grayling would be heard to say, smiling benevolently, 'but it seems to me this child of ours is a one-off.'

'Quite agreed,' whispered his mother. 'Something of a phenomenon, I'd say. Just look at him now. Those little legs running away with him before he's managed the art of walking. I used to watch him in his cradle. His kicking was in phase all right, but even so it didn't quite follow the development graphs for his age. Even as a new born his limb movements seemed conscious and deliberate rather than instinctive, as if he was kicking *something* rather than just kicking. And speaking as one who had that kicking going on inside her for a thousand years, I should know.'

'Now you're exaggerating again,' her husband told her, his eyes smiling. 'You weren't gone all that long, darling. And I should know *that*, if anyone does.'

Even with his reputation for kicking out and running wild established, Finn's precipitous departure from the planet at such a tender age had taken everyone by surprise. Luckily he'd done a period of basic grounding in the Academy of the Universal Family, his father's learning establishment, first. This had been in its early days, founded, as it was, around the time of his birth, and still in its experimental stage.

Watching today's kids at play on the beach, Finn smiled as he thought about his schooldays again. Parents and children all mixed up together. Animals too, he recalled fondly. The flesh and blood, hairy sort, along with the appearing and disappearing, shape-shifting kind.

Then there were the Archetypes, who also, you might say, came and went. And of course there were the Tutors—Chiron, and that Doctor Mandelbrot.

Mandelbrot had been assigned to Finn from an early age.

The good doctor had also appeared one day. He'd transited from the Fourth Zone like Finn's mother. But unlike her, Mandelbrot had found *his* way in through a hole in the fabric, though not in the sense he was consciously looking for it. He'd happened on it accidentally. But, as he'd struggled to explain on making his sudden appearance on the lawn one day, blinking and very shaken, 'Accident' was what he was currently working on. Happy Accident. Serendipity.

Mandelbrot's entry into an unrecognisable world, and his appearance in front of a group of extraordinary 23rd Century strangers, was as mind-blowing to him as he imagined his sudden arrival was to them. So mind-blowing that he continued to babble unintelligibly for some minutes.

'Yes, Accident, you see,' he blathered. 'It's a thesis I'm working on. Currently. My thesis, as well as my manner of travel, so to speak. Because, you understand, this is the area I'm researching at the moment. And 'The Hole' is what *happened*. Eureka! *Happy Accident!* So there we are. It's all to do with the fabric, you understand—the time/space continuum. And I *happened* on the hole. So, natural I should investigate it. And, happily for me, and hopefully for you as well,' he burbled on, flapping his hands and looking as baffled as they did, 'here I am!'

In appearance, Mandelbrot looked like one of those old fashioned philosophers—elbow-patches, beard with a touch of grizzle—and not everyone took to him at first. The common agreement was that this *uitlander* who'd arrived without referral or credential would pose too much of a risk to be entrusted with the position of tutor to the little boy. But the two seemed to have bonded from the start, and Finn's father announced one morning that Mandelbrot should be appointed as he was right for his son. Cléa was absent at the time, otherwise she might have had something to say about it. When it was discussed in Council everyone was against it, except Grayling. They felt that Cléa should be consulted, and the decision should await her return. They felt that there was something odd about the doctor, too much of a wild card, and that being his mother it would be Cléa who'd know what was best for her son.

But Grayling only listened and smiled.

'Mandy,' the little Finn said one morning, a while after the tutor's engagement had finally been sanctioned. 'I did a dream last night.'

'Nothing new in *that*. Aren't you always dreaming? You dream in class, don't you? So what's the big news about a dream at night?' Mandelbrot asked.

They were taking a walk before breakfast and the start of the day's teachings. His tutor was accommodating his large strides to the little boy's much shorter ones. They'd established this ritual, walking in the woods, idly chatting. It was their sacred time together when Finn could say what he liked without anyone else being present. But as it happened, on this occasion, they weren't quite as alone as they thought. Cléa, his mother, was there; or perhaps present in spirit might be a better way of putting it. Precocious her child might be, she felt, yet in many respects he was as immature as any three year old. She was keeping an eye on him.

Unaware of her presence, Finn seemed hesitant. Something had happened for the first time last night, but he was wondering how he knew. He'd always seemed to know that there were happenings, but now he was discovering 'first times'? 'Well. But...' he said.

'Come on, spit it out,' Mandelbrot told him.

Finn's face screwed up. 'Well, it wasn't *that* sort of dreaming. It was, I went to see Ma. At least, I *think* that's what it was,' he said at last.

'Oh? But, we've talked about that a lot, you know. She's been to see you a few times, hasn't she? Sleep-visiting? You told your father, and he verified it. He often sees her like that, and she's always sending you messages and presents, and things from her world.'

'Yeh, but...' He was reaching inside, trying to find what he meant. 'It wasn't her,' he said slowly, 'visiting me. I—went—to see *her*. I *went* where she is now.'

'And?' Mandy looked duly impressed, but waited for more.

'Well, that's different, isn't it?'

Cléa smiled and looked pleased. Her child was learning fast. She blew him a kiss.

'Yes, it probably is,' Mandy agreed. 'But what do *you* think? Was she surprised? Did you talk?'

'She said it was just about as brilliant as when I took my first steps on the ground. But then we talked about what they're all saying. You know, in the council and that, about whether you and me—you know, whether you are the one who is really my tutor. If you're right, and all that stuff. I went to see her about all that. You must know what they're saying. About how I'm too young and you might put ideas in my head.'

'And you don't *have* ideas in your head? I thought that was the problem.' Mandy chuckled.

'But they think... Well, I heard someone saying I need reignin' in a bit. What's that mean, Mandy? And, maybe I need an old bit of *disup*, or something.'

'Would that be 'old fashioned discipline'?' Mandelbrot looked at him down his nose, and raised his eyebrows.

'Yeh, I guess that's what they said.'

'And, what does your Da say?'

'He doesn't. He says he'll talk with Ma. Then they all talk, the council, and go on and on about it. You know. Anyway. You're *there*, aren't you—while they're talking? So you know what they're saying.'

'Yes, I'm there, but I can only put my chips in once, and of course they think I'm biased. Your Da holds the ring impartially, and then smiles and goes off to consult your Ma. And apparently she has the final word, because she is the woman, for one thing, and because she has the advantage of being in inter-dimensional space.'

'My Da's inter-dimensional too, you know.' Finn stuck out his small chin. 'More than all the others,' he said, his face growing pink. 'He's *multi*-dimensional. So why can't *he* say?'

'Because,' his tutor explained with a sigh, 'your father's contracted to be here where the students are for the education project. So he has to *contract* himself. Get it? And play by the rules. See?' Demonstrating, he went into a performance of shrinking man contracting himself into a kick-ball shape, elbows squeezed in and knees bent.

Finn shrieked with laughter, and joined in the game by kicking the fantasy ball back. 'But,' he said as a thought struck him, 'my Da *makes* the rules. So why can't *he*...?'

'Hold it Finn! Hold it,' Mandelbrot wheezed, unfolding himself and with difficulty standing up again. 'Too much like philosophy for this early in the morning. And—hey, can you smell *that*?' They were in sight of the kitchen door by now. 'You hungry or what? Didn't you choose the breakfast menu today?'

Finn had to wait until the next morning before he could bring the subject up again.

Cléa withdrew from the woodland with the smile still playing on her face. She'd been in the habit of dropping in, so to speak, keeping an eye on the progress of her precious son's education—that word education being employed in its very broadest sense, as her eyes took in a very wide angle indeed. Watching the unfolding events on Earth from her multidimensional platform, Cléa was aware of time-frames merging, separating and coming together again. Who knows what intricacies of destiny her eyes saw, what alchemy at work? Noticing perhaps the significance of her son's growing attraction to his little girl-friend Li-Ona. Or looking deeper, had they glimpsed the fateful consequences for herself and for the Finn grown to manhood, who, journeying backwards in time, had already encountered Annya?

'Enjoy your breakfast then?' Mandelbrot asked as he and the boy set out the next day.

'Haven't had it yet, stupid,' Finn replied happily.

'Stupid yourself. I meant yesterday. You chose the grub, didn't you?'

'Grub? We didn't have grubs, Mandy. It was bargers and squigey dip.'

'Oh, don't mind me, Finn. That was just one of my Oldy Worldy names. I forgot you hadn't heard it before. So! You had bargers, did you? And did they live up to expectations?'

'Fantasma-*goric*! Pluto and Li-Ona made 'em. But it's my turn tomorrow.'

'So, does that mean we won't be doing our walk in the morning then? Want me to give you a hand in the kitchen instead?'

'No thanks, Mandy. Li-Ona's going to help me,' Finn said brightly.

'Aye, aye! I see,' Mandelbrot intoned.

Finn knew he was being wound up again, but fell for it anyway. 'What? What do you mean?'

'I mean, I see with my little eye,' the doctor grinned.

'*What* do you see, Mandy? What do you mean, *see*?' he demanded, squealing with irritation.

'You and Li-Ona. That's what I see, Finn my boy.'

Cléa's eyes must have seen too, as she smiled again.

'You. You're err—kinda sweet on her, aren't you?' Mandelbrot was saying, as tactfully as he knew how.

'You're not to ask. I'm not. It's not fair,' Finn spluttered.

'Reprimanded, Finn. Forget I said anything. All unsaid. Clean slate, begin again,' Mandelbrot promised, hand on chest, but with an unconcealed wink.

THE INTRUDER

Still hovering some metres above, Finn followed the girl along the beach. He'd watched her stagger to her feet and now she was making her uncertain way over the sand. Wonder if she's got a name? he mused idly. Well, of course, we all of us have names, but I wonder if hers has that... There's something there, some resonance. A frisson of some kind, as if I should know... He searched his memory without coming up with anything. 'How bizarre,' he thought, 'if it turns out I'm looking at one of my ancestors right now.'

The day was moving on, heat beginning to dissipate. The fire-red ball in the sky looked about to sizzle into the sea as the girl finally reached the spot where she'd left her clothes. He sensed her growing dejection and felt concern. She glanced up, shivering, but her mind, seemingly occupied with concerns at ground level, didn't wander in his direction this time. Then a sudden rush of cool air caught his attention as it began sweeping particles of tawny dust into the faces of the last few sun-drugged bodies stretched horizontal on these strange support frames causing them to stir themselves and sit.

Up and down the beach as far as he could see were these ranks and blocks of colour; ultramarine and vermilion against the flat ochre. Most were empty of occupant, but here and there small groups of people, standing upright now, were rubbing their skin. Some were bending over, shaking materials free of particles, folding and packing items into receptacles, pulling footshapes onto feet. These beach visitors, it occurred to him, were feeling the call to herd for home.

Annya had wasted too much time wandering up and down the beach, searching without any luck. This *was* the place where she'd left her things. She was sure. A youth with sprawling legs, finishing off a last smoke with his mates, grinned at her. Not certain what it meant, she went over. 'Don't suppose you've seen, er, my towel and stuff?' she asked. He continued grinning like an imbecile. 'Or anyone taking them away, maybe?'

Her unease grew. Insolence was spreading like butter across his red and pitted face. A wave of anger flared inside her, but faltered before making it into the F.U. she longed to spit at him. An inconvenient prickling had started at the back of her eyes. She turned and began the walk back to her apartment.

The wind, which was gusting now, would, she hoped, cover the fact that her eyes were streaming with tears, though nothing would hide her barefoot, dishevelled retreat through the streets. She stopped to wash off the blood as best she could in the beach shower, then climbed the steps to the Avinda. But she was wet without a towel, her bikini definitely the worse for wear, and her grazes smarted.

Strangely enough, after the first few minutes trudging self-consciously past ice cream parlour windows, bars and fast-food diners with her distorted reflection constantly thrown into her face, a curious sense of protection descended on her, wrapping her like a warm blanket. As she left the front and began to make her way up the steep, narrow alleys, sheltered from the wind and still warm from the sun, no-one stared. It was as if she was invisible.

She reached the apartment complex at last, but it was late. The office was closed, so the concierge wouldn't be back until morning. Without her key how was she to get in? Limping up the hibiscus-lined path to her door she made for the plastic chairs that graced her square of patio, and sat down.

The light was beginning to fade, and the chair felt suddenly hard and cold. She'd sat there long enough, and now her bare feet, bruised from the cobbled alleys, were beginning to hurt too. Lights were being switched on in other apartments; laughter, music, cooking smells drifted towards her. But the two adjoining apartments remained quiet and dark. Her immediate neighbours weren't yet back, and who knew when they might return.

She'd got to know them slightly—friendly northerners. Glaswegians on the left, folks from Cheshire on the right. Runcorn, had they said? Anyhow, these were a hearty young couple who hiked in shorts all over the island—up and down the mountains, whereas the Scots were elderly—came several times a year. Comfortable types. They'd have invited her in, she thought. A drink, maybe. Offered her a towel. Warmth at least. And maybe someone would have suggested climbing in through the window. But she'd already given that a try, as she'd tried the door. More as a matter of course than with any great hope. Everything was locked securely, just as she'd made sure it was before leaving for her swim.

She hadn't got to know the other people in the complex, and now it was a bit late in the day, she told herself, to go knocking at doors cap in hand—except there was no cap, nor shorts, nor tee shirt, for that matter. She had to get some clothes on.

Better get on with it then and phone. Get the guys in uniform over and pay whatever.

She stood up decisively, but instead of making for the far end of the complex where the emergency phone was fixed to the office wall, she turned back towards the apartment and, as if on automatic pilot, reached for the handle and pulled it down. Warm air met her.

The door, which was definitely fast locked when she'd tried it a few moments ago, had opened on a stifling room.

Annya's mouth dropped open. What the hell! I must have

wandered next door by mistake! She put her hand to her head, puzzled and anxious. They all look so alike these properties, inside *and* out. That's the trouble with these quick-build, breeze-block things. All built to the same design. Lots of glass that doesn't open, so the interiors heat up like ovens and go on slow cooking, even when the temperature drops at night.

It was easy to forget, surrounded as they were by the cooling effect of the Atlantic, that the Island was on the same latitude as Kuwait.

But if this is next door, she thought, I couldn't have climbed over their flower bed and not remembered, surely. Must be that sun. It must have got to me, lying on the beach all that time getting my breath back. Come to think of it, I did feel a bit woozy just now—sort of blanked out for a moment. This one's got to be mine! I'd better go in and see.

Feeling like an intruder, she stepped over the threshold. It was dim inside, yet this was *her* room all right. Similar they might be, but this was definitely hers. Her sofa, her table. She went round touching everything just to make sure, then opened another door.

There was her bed—just as she left it. Undies all over, hairbrush on the floor. She pushed another door. Bath, shower, bidet, taps. She turned one on and it trickled, hiccoughed, then gushed into the basin. And there was her treat, the treat to herself, the luxury soap she'd unwrapped that morning.

'My soap, my soap!' she squealed, pressing the fragrant cake to her nose.

So I *must* have left it unlocked. She shook her head as if the mystery was some insidious gremlin sticking to it. No! I'm absolutely sure. Oh hell, what does it matter! Come on, she told herself irritably, let's get some air in here.

She went round opening all the vents. A sweet smell of evening breeze wafted in. She breathed it deep into her lungs, then collapsed onto the sofa. 'Oh, boy, that's better!' she sighed, kicking her legs in the air and thumping down on the cushions with her feet, rapping out, I'm home! Fantastic! At last! But before any sense of relaxation could take hold she was leaping to her feet again.

'Holy shit! I *know* it was locked. How in the blazes...'

'Annya, Annya,' she moaned, her fingers tugging at strands of hair. 'Pull yourself together, my girl. What's your problem? The main thing is, you're inside. Quit worrying. Everything looks OK. Doesn't it?'

She sank back on the sofa, stretching her grazed legs, then poked her feet into an old pair of espadrilles she'd kicked off that morning.

It was a fact. Nothing in the room gave the impression of being other than Annya's casual normality. Magazines, bottle tops, check-out receipts and a plate with crumbs littered the coffee table. Among the jumble of stuff sat a small china vase containing flowers from a prickly pear. They'd been fully out, but now, twisted into tight spirals, they seemed to have dripped syrup onto the table as they'd closed up.

She got her fingers badly spiked when she'd picked them yester-day. She'd tried to slice them off the plant with their kitchen knife. Simon—she could see him now with tweezers poised—he'd been laughing and called her stupid as he tried to pull them out. Her fingers were smarting still.

She dipped one of them absently into a drop of the sticky nectar on the table and licked it. 'Simon,' she murmured. Glancing vaguely round the room she began mentally ticking off the objects. All of them seemed undisturbed and reassuringly in their places. At last she was beginning to relax. Her gaze fell on a glass ash tray among the rest of the stuff on the table. There were her rings in the bottom, and the watch she'd taken off before setting out for her swim. She began idly swirling them round and round in the dish. They made a pleasantly musical clink. One of them, a gold signet, felt heavier and chunkier than the rest. Simon must have forgotten it. Absent-mindedly she tried it on, one finger then another, until she found the one it fitted best. If only I could have more of him around me, she breathed. At least no-one's found the rings—whoever it is that broke...

Broke in! A strangled squeal escaped from her throat. She spun round, darting a look behind the sofa. The wall safe! My currency and credit cards.

She was on hands and knees yanking the safe door. But that too seemed locked, just as she'd left it.

The safe key! What if they found it. It should still be where I hid it, on top of the wardrobe behind that awful Spanish moulding.

She dragged a chair across the room, climbed up and reached, feeling for the key. Which end did she put it? Fingernails frantically scrabbling dust and dead insects, she couldn't feel a thing! Then, with a yell of relief, she got it.

Carefully lowering herself from the chair with the tiny key clutched in her fist she caught sight of herself in the wardrobe mirror. Objectively, the image was that of a shapely-slim, fair, good looking young woman. What Annya saw, however, was only there for a second. A blurred reflection of her familiar and disappointingly ordinary face disappearing as a blinding flash of light ricocheted into her eyes. It was so sudden, it was impossible to tell if the light came from somewhere in the room, or from outside. Dazed, she grabbed the back of the chair for support. Her reaction had been immediate; someone was out there with a camera. She spun round to face the window.

Oh, God! I'm still in my ripped bikini, and the door's open. What the *hell's* going on!

Only there was nothing to be seen. All was dark outside and unusually quiet. She leaned her hand on the mirror as a wave of nausea swelled round her head. Her damp palm misted the glass. Snatching a cotton cover from the sofa, she threw it round herself, and ran to slam the door shut.

Christ! Of course. There's still no door key. How the hell am I going to lock it?

She dashed back, grabbed the chair and jammed it under the handle. She'd seen people do that in old movies. But would that keep intruders out? She doubted it. Yet she couldn't manage to drag a heavy sofa-bed across to the door by herself. At least she'd got the safe key. Then she suddenly remembered, she still hadn't checked if everything was OK inside it.

She doubled back to the sofa and crouched down behind it, her heart racing into overdrive as she wrestled with the key. The safe lock wouldn't open. It was stiff, and her sweaty fingers ineffectual. She gritted her teeth, determined not to let panic get the better of her. After a long couple of minutes the lock turned and the door finally swung open.

The sight which met her should have allayed any fears. All her cash and cards were there. But instead of reassurance, what she saw turned her legs to jelly. The door key which had disappeared from the beach lay brassy and unmistakable—on top of the wallet. She examined it in her trembling fingers. No doubt about it. There was her personal code, plus the apartment number impressed on its pale green tag.

There was no logic to this. Had she had a lapse of memory and gone out without locking the door? In which case she must have placed the door key in the safe, locked it, climbed on the chair and hidden the safe key on the top of the wardrobe, and set off wearing nothing but a bikini, barefoot, no towel... This was plainly ridiculous. To have forgotten such a pantomime of absurdity, there must have been a hole in her head as big as... Simon, then! But she'd seen him off to Amsterdam yesterday. Could he have boarded another plane and flown back just to set up this elaborate caper? Peter Balcon—the Amsterdam office. He'd phoned a couple of days ago—told Simon the news—they'd given him this Middle Eastern assignment. The one he'd been wanting all these months. She'd heard them discussing it. Simon was over the moon. Why would he mess up his career for the sake of a schoolboy prank?

I'll phone Peter in the morning and see if he can throw some light on it, she decided.

Mystified as well as shaken, Annya made up her mind there was nothing for it but to focus on the positive. Enjoy the fact that she was at least home and dry. She had all her cash. Had the key, and could lock the door now. That was it, she'd run herself a luxurious bath, change into something loose—pamper herself. Fix a nice meal, glass of Rosso. Candles on the table maybe, then an early night. Sleep would do wonders. It would all seem different in the morning.

She poured her wine, and, glass in hand, went into the bathroom. She turned on the light and began running water. Tired out all of a sudden she flopped down on the stool. The warmth of the steam was soothing and relaxing. She reached for that expensive bubble-bath. On the shelf by the foot of the bath lay a neatly folded towel. On top of the towel was her sunglasses case, and beneath, also neatly folded, lay a pair of shorts and a tee shirt. The very ones she had left on the beach.

Annya leapt to her feet and spun round, colliding with the wash basin. The bathroom mirror was filmed with steam, but through it Annya's blurred white face, its mouth wide open, stared back at her. And peering over her shoulder, reflected in the glass, was a radiant and utterly extraordinary male countenance.

BALL GAMES

'When you found the hole, Mand, what was it like?'

'What do you mean, *it*?' Mandelbrot asked. 'What was *what* like?'

'The hole—and all the rest of it.'

'Oh, Jeez! Ask me another, lad. I'm not up for all this—this early in the morning.'

'All what, Mandy? What you not up for? It's just a question.'

'Just a question! And you want the answer to All an' Everything before breakfast, huh? The Universe an' how do I get off it, before I've had my orange juice!'

'No, not all of that, for Jeez sake! It's just a question, Mandy. That's what you here for isn't it? Answering questions?'

'Whatever gave you *that* idea? And don't say, Jeez. You don't know who the big Jee is.'

'*You* say it.'

'I know. I know who he *is*. I'm allowed to.'

'That's what I'm saying. You *know*. You know things, and that's why you're here. To answer questions.'

'We've gone into this before, my little Strange and Precious. You ask what you like. Anything. But if I don't feel like it, I don't have to answer.'

'What's the hole like? That's all I'm asking. What's so complicated about a simple hole?'

Simple? Mandelbrot took a breath. 'OK. OK then. Pin back your ears and listen carefully. I was over there, and then bingo! I was here. There I was—then I wasn't—because I'm here. You getting this?'

"Course.' Finn nodded with an irritating air of assurance. 'Can you get back though?'

'Back? What! back there? I don't exactly want to, lad.'

'But could you? Cos I'd like to come with you. Can you take me?'

'Wouldn't like it. Believe me, *you wouldn't like it.*' Mandelbrot was emphatic.

'Why not? I might, mightn't I? I want to find a hole. If you won't tell me what it's like, what it looks like, how'm I going to find my own?'

'Because we all have to find our own. And so I can't tell you. Telling you about mine wouldn't be any good.'

'You're not helping, Mand. It's not fair. What's the hole *in*, so I can look for it?'

'OK.' With a sensation of inevitability creeping up on him, Mandelbrot clutched his throat. His words were being drawn from him as surely as hooked fish from water. 'OK. If you must know, it's in the fabric.'

'What fabric? What's fabric anyway?'

'Reality, my strange and precious one. Reality is fabric. Fabric is reality. And your reality *here* is far easier to live with than where I was on the other side. So that's why I don't want to go back, and why *you* wouldn't like it.'

'Well... OK, so if...'

'Get that aroma, Finn. That's breakfast on the air, or I'm a grilled herring. Can't you smell...?'

'You're not getting away with that again, Mandy,' Finn squawked. 'There's a juice bush right behind you, anyway. Grab a piece of that and have a chew. Chew a stalk. Look! Some munch-nuts. They're fab-u-loso. Get me some, too, while you're at it.' Mandelbrot had once asked him what the twigs tasted of, and was bewildered at Finn's description. It reminded him of one of those pretentious wine experts back in his own times blathering on about floral counterpoints and hints of citrus, with undertones of liquorice and pencil-sharpenings. He'd only managed to discern the pencil-sharpenings himself. 'So *if*, Mandy,' Finn was saying, between shlushings and chomps, 'as I was saying, going back to where *you* were—and like you say, I maybe wouldn't like it, but that's for me to find out, yeh? Then I can go the *other* way instead. Can't I?'

The other way! The only other way from back, as far as Mandelbrot knew, was forward, future tense. Whichever way, this was bad news. This is where I lose my job again, he told himself, and I'm still on probation as far as the Council are concerned. 'Talk about out of the frying pan,' he muttered, thinking of the situation which had led to that precipitous ejection from his own previous reality. 'How did I know this was where we were heading with this conversation? OK, Finn. All in good time. We all have to abide by contracts, like I told you, otherwise...'

'You want me contracted—like a kick-ball—like Da? *That* what you want, Mandy? Well, *I* want to bounce. Make me into a ball then. Do that. Go on, and I'll bounce away.'

'I do believe you will. You're getting there, Finn, fast enough in spite of all my efforts,' Mandelbrot said, under his breath. 'Only it's my job to hold you back, as long as I can.'

This darn precociousness. He really is too young for that malarkey, even here. Even in these parts there's some growing up to be done before they get into... Well, that sort of stuff.

It was late, and a be-jamma'd Mandelbrot was perched on the edge of his bed, one foot bare, talking to himself. "Bargers and squidgydip." Says the same thing here as it says back home. "Where can I find a hole of my own, Mandy," for Chri'sake. You know what good ol' Doctor Freud would make of all that. Takes some getting used to, I know, the way these kids are. Years ahead of ours, maturation-wise, in their heads. But even so... Same old symbolism, reaches right through to this reality too, or I'm a Dutchman. Well, what if I am—or half a one, at any rate—or was, back there, before. He's gotta be watched, that young'un. That lovely little Li-Ona, all sweet and pretty. Well, maybe she's not so innocent either. Bless me! I don't know! Better keep my eye on her too, he muttered.

Not really my field, this stuff, anyway. Kids and premature stir-rings in the pants department. Definitely not my scene. The wife now, Lucy... She now... He was yawning. Only...

He yawned again, his mouth opening so wide his jaw could have jammed. It stayed that way as he drifted into a reverie, sock in hand.

Maybe I *am* too old. Maybe they're right. It *is* a long time... Lucia mia. Here on this lonely bed, and where might *you* be right now, Lucy. Which hole did you go through, my darling? Which sky are you float-ing in tonight, Lucia mia? Gad! I miss you. Being there... talking to you.

His mouth snapped suddenly shut and he sat upright, dropping the sock. One of the kids was screaming. High pitched and penetrat-ing, it seemed to be coming from the cub's dorm.

Now, that's a sound you don't hear in these parts too often. One of 'em having a nightmare? The scream crescendoed. Blue murder, that's what that is! Who's on duty? Where's Kiri? Is she on sleep-watch tonight? Jeez! Gad! It's *him*. That's our Strange and Precocious all right.

How Mandelbrot knew—how came he on this piece of esoteric wisdom—perplexed his superannuated brain. His mind sought illu-mination, and alighted on a field of sheep.

Ba, bah, stupid bahh. Must be a hundred... five hundred... No, a thousand at least. Gad! I'm counting 'em now. All those sheep, and they all look alike. Yet one lamb gives a bleat, and no matter how dis-tant from its mother, nor how indistinguishable its voice from all the rest, one unique squawk hits the button. A mother knows her own!

He winced and rubbed his navel. Better get myself dressed again and see what's up, he grumbled.

The Campo was a good-sized meadow, bordered, on the far side, by trees. The same woodland in which Finn and his mentor took their morning strolls. Recently cut grass was lying around drying in the sun, and the kids had streamed out of the school-house earlier that day like a string of colts penned up for the winter. The grass had smelled wonderful, and they began picking up handfuls and throwing it at each other. A group of them wandered off to play ball in the far corner, and Finn had gone over to join them. Little Jaspa and Li-Ona had formed a twosome and begun tossing their ball to and fro and up in the air. It was a labyrinthite coloured ball, so as they threw it higher and higher it sang with the vibrations and changed through a range of blue-metallic greens. As it caught the sunlight it sent flashes streaking across the sky. The two children screamed with joy. They were getting better and better at sending it up high and catching it.

Finn stood watching. Once or twice he jumped up and tried to snatch the flashes. Little Li-Ona smiled at him and laughed, and her eyes seemed to beam the flashes back. They're labyrinthite too, like the ball, Finn thought. Jaspa laughed too and clapped his small hands. Li-Ona threw the ball to him again, and Jaspa jumped in the air and caught it. He threw back.

Suddenly Finn leapt sideways, making a twist in the air which knocked Jaspa off his feet, and snatched the ball mid-way on its trajectory. Instead of returning it to them, Finn deliberately placed the ball on the ground, took aim, and kicked it way into the woods.

It sailed up and over the trees and out of sight. Jaspa began to cry, and Li-Ona ran and put her arms around him. Finn felt a sickening new sensation. The feeling was burning in some low place inside—a deeper place than he'd known existed. It felt like something black and churning, a heat which oozed and welled, making his face change. He wanted Li-Ona to put her arms round *him*, not Jaspa. But she looked into Finn's eyes, and Saw, and her own face changed.

'Why did you do that, Finn?' her voice said, but it was a different voice; changed, like her face. 'Where's the ball?'

'It's gone,' he told her coldly. 'Lost.'

'No, Finn. No. Get it back for me.'

'It's gone,' he repeated.

'I don't understand. How can it be gone?'

Something else she didn't understand either, a salty prickling in her eyes, and she felt she wanted some big arms around *her*. 'Finn,' she said, bewildered, 'things don't get lost. You know that. Call it back.'

'No. It's gone. I told you.'

His burning wavered and swelled—molten inside—and he turned so they couldn't see his new face. He turned away and ran: the hot, black wave pursuing, getting bigger all the time. He ran, and ran.

He ran as far as the cub-house. There was no-one about, so he went into the dorm and hid in his nest. Kiri came a while later and called him. But he lay still, not breathing, and she went away. He didn't go for supper. No-one seemed to have noticed, because the buzzer didn't go, and they didn't send out a search for him.

It got dark and the kids trooped back in twos and threes. He heard them thumping and jumping about, but he tried not to hear. Kiri would call them to bed soon.

The moon came out. Under that cold luminous eye he fell asleep.

The white marble 'I spy in the sky' turned on its axis and spun. Spun and spun, and grew bigger. It peered right into him—a marble ball racing after him, spinning and bouncing. And he ran before it so fast he was flying. But it grew bigger. Faster and faster it spun, whirling all round him until he couldn't see for the whirr of it. It was winding him up and swallowing him. He could feel the suck of it.

And then he *was* the white ball shooting across the sky, all burning and aglow. Faster than it was possible to see, leaving no track or trace.

Suddenly he catapulted through the fabric, through the net, and The Sound erupted. A raging, ear-splitting roar circling round and round. But he was trapped, motionless inside the ball—the unblinking eye at the centre, torn between terror and exhilaration.

He couldn't move. He couldn't see. Nothing existed but The Sound rising to meet him as he plummeted through the layers. Through circle after circle he was dropping down, re-entering the planes and arenas of existence where the cycles of life were forged.

In the Beginning was this Roar, the wail of birth and death with everything exploding out of nothing. The Big Bang, the Great Shattering when Unity broke into an infinity of fragments and flung them to the edge of space.

Through mists he saw ancient stones dancing, forming themselves into circles. He was falling to earth, and the World again was gathered in the Arena, waiting for him.

The roar climaxed as he thudded to a stop.

A boot tapped him into the mud of the stadium. A hand steadied him, and the sound ceased.

The player's feet began stepping back one at a time. His ankle ached and his calf muscles strained.

The player was beyond exhaustion; his mind one-pointed, at the dead centre where the foot would angle and connect. The dead centre of the spinning Earth.

Ninety minutes, plus injuries, and no decisive score. The afternoon scorched on. Throats were dry. Extra time and still no score. The whistle shrilled. Thirty minutes more, then the shoot-out. The last kick now, and it all depended on one man. All eyes fixed on his foot as he took his run-up.

His boot connected. The ball flew, the keeper dove, and a white sphere curved away from the desperate, splayed hands. It smashed into the back of the net, and through the fabric. An insignificant white marble shooting through the blackness of space towards infinity.

The space between everything was black and terrifying.

Cléa heard his screams piercing the night. She wasted no time; she flew after her child and caught him, wrapping her arms about him, cradling him. And he climbed onto her lap and snuggled up. Tenderly Cléa held her son and rocked him. 'Mother's here, little precious. Mother's here. Always here. Always always always.'

The trees next morning seemed more solemn. Finn said nothing. It felt to him as if, entering the wood, they had intruded on a deep and silent communion. It was like when his father sat alone in his meditation space. The stillness then was so powerful, it was almost intimidating. Not forbidding, exactly. But it had a majesty, a sacred presence of its own.

Mandelbrot seemed to be in tune with the morning's silence. Even though these trees were much evolved from those of his own era, they had roots, and so did he. Though tree-root networks went further back and deeper even than his. He knew. He'd delved into tree law, ancient knowledge from his own era, before taking that header through the gap. And today it felt as if the trees were creating a pool of quietness, that they'd gathered into a group. He felt they'd congregated for a purpose—maybe to assist in the lesson that he and the boy were in the midst of right now.

Mandelbrot had learned that if you listened well at these solemn moments you might pick up a signal, a nugget of wisdom or a vital piece of guidance. You never knew what would pop into your mind. It might be the answer to the mathematician's knottiest conundrum, a long sought alchemical solution, or a seemingly banal remark. But it wasn't yours to judge; only yours to trust and apply.

Problem is though, he was thinking, what to say to him? The boy's had a fright, but I've no experience to fall back on. Not with kids—even normal ones—not having any of my own. So how on earth do I handle this one? Seeing how young Finn goes way beyond any precociousness I ever came across.

He'd no idea what he was about to say, but the silence was becoming edgy, and it was obviously up to him to throw in the first pebble. 'You gave us quite a scare last night,' he said, suddenly.

Finn glanced up, then away again. He'd been strolling, staring at the ground, but Mandelbrot felt he wasn't particularly avoiding his eye. He was just allowing himself some time, more of the quietness. So they walked on a bit, until Finn looked up again of his own accord.

'I was scared, Mandy,' Finn said at last.

'Want to talk?'

'Mmm—maybe.'

They walked on some more.

'You know, it was like something came into me, Mandy. A sort of thunderball... a zagg of lightning.'

'Not sure what you mean, lad. Came into you? Talking about that dream, are we? Or something else?'

'It felt like power. You know, Pow! Like that!'

'Hmmm! Power? You sure? You know what power is? Must do, I suppose, if you can put a name to it.'

'That's what it felt like, Mandy, but it was really scary at the same time. Much bigger than me. Much stronger, you see. And it kind of hurts. Like it burns. Goes off.'

'Goes off?'

'Yeh. Sort of 'splodes and shoots you off all over. Stars coming out of your bum. Your arse, like you was a pulshun or something.'

'Pulshun? What in god's name's that? Ah!' And he stopped in his tracks. 'You mean propulsion, a missile. That it? That what you mean? So that's what power feels like, is it? Big words, Finn, propulsion and that, but a bit oldy worldy for you, I'd have thought. Where'd you get hold of 'em?'

'Ma. She told me.'

'Oh!' Mandelbrot sounded surprised. 'So you saw her again, did you?'

Finn, ignoring the question, asked, 'Was that how it felt when you whizzed through the hole, Mandy?'

'Can't say it was. I think this thing with you last night must have been something rather different.'

'That means you know what it was, then. Wish you'd tell me then, Mandy.'

'Not sure I *do* know, lad. But I can tell you I didn't get sparks coming out of my bum.'

They walked on some more, and in a while Mandelbrot dropped in another pebble. He hadn't quite got what the boy was on about yet.

'You say your ma told you—those words I mean? You been visiting her again, have you?' But still Finn didn't answer. The trees were still gathering round them so that the pool came with them wherever they moved. The trees, it seemed, were still in conclave, weaving their wisdom.

'You're not saying much, Mandy.'

''S'right,' Mandelbrot agreed. 'I'm listening.'

'What do you hear, then, Mandy? Is it those trees? Are *they* saying something?'

'I guess they are, but I just can't hear them well enough. I'm a bit deaf. You listen, Finn. Maybe you can hear 'em.'

'They're whispering, I think. I can't quite hear either. There's no words.'

They walked some more.

Suddenly, as if he'd just woken up, Finn chimed in brightly, 'Ma caught me, you know. Saved me, just as I was being kicked out of play.'

'Your ma! Saved...? Out of play! Gad, S an' P, I only know one kind of out of play, and that's back in my old 3D world. Don't tell me you were at a football game?'

'That was it. That's what Ma said anyhow. World Cup or something. She seemed to know. She saved me, anyhow. Best save in the World, it was, and they cheered like crazy. You could hear it all over, cross the whole universe.'

He fell quiet again, head down, twiddling pieces of twig and chewing the juicy ones now and then. It didn't look as if a proper breakfast was on his mind this morning at all. Mandelbrot's guts were rumbling, but he broke off some boring looking twigs and chewed too.

Glancing up, Finn said, 'It was quite scary though. Ma... after she caught me... she... well, I sort of got onto her lap, Mandy.' He looked into his tutor's eyes.

'You want to tell me then?' Mandelbrot asked softly.

Finn nodded. 'She sang me a song, and rocked me, and... Well, I curled up into a ball again and she... I just seemed to melt into her tummy—went inside, dissolved into the dark. But that bit wasn't scary at all, Mand, it was...'

He couldn't finish. There weren't any words to say what it was. But there among the trees they both seemed to know. In that moment on his mother's lap he had gone into the warm, dark earth of non-being which only Cléa, the mother, could provide.

'And I've grown a bit now I've come back,' he said solemnly.

'Yes, I can see that,' his tutor agreed. 'But have you grown up? Can't have you shooting off again. Not like that. My poor old knees and liver wouldn't stand it.'

Finn held up his small arms for Mandelbrot to receive a kiss. And the big man scooped him up and hugged him.

THE PROFESSOR'S TIME MACHINE

Out of the frying pan!

Mandelbrot, perched once again on the edge of his bed, was musing over his predicament. How he'd managed to get from There, the 3D+Time dimension, where he'd been on the verge of being fired from his job, to Here, and how he'd exited in the nick of time through a hyper-dimensional slot. 'Could say I fired myself,' he chuckled.

He'd become fascinated by higher dimensions and particle physics, with their place in the understanding of the fundamental structure of life, and gone on to experimenting with theories of relative reality. Back as far as the Seventies, he'd been doing research into quantum theory and practical shamanism. Then he got the idea of inviting a group of his students to try out a few simple experiments in side-stepping time and identity. This must have been where things started to go awry. Yet it seemed a fun thing to do at the time. He was never a man obsessed with formalities. More on the student's side when it came to college rules and regs. But you have to remember, he told himself, how volatile things were in those days. Student take-overs, Red Brigades, and all that. But we were just a bunch of kids, and yes, I suppose I include myself in that. Kids with a sense of adventure. Ready to give anything a go if it broke through barriers, blew up a load of conventional belief systems. Our explosives were in our minds. I expect this is what put the fear of God into 'em. The Hierarchy. The Control.

He'd never expected things would go this far out of kilter. They'd had some unexpected results. A few of the students experienced bouts of acute disorientation, while others reported mild but troublesome symptoms suddenly lifting—apparently healing spontaneously. That young French undergraduate with the headaches, for instance.

'Not as a result of the experiments, you understand.' (Mandelbrot was going over what he'd said to the Dean of Faculty.) 'His problem,' he'd told him, 'Marc Larré's problems started well before we began the experiments. He'd already sought help from the college medic, and she'd given him the usual painkillers. But his headaches persisted. Next she suggested they were due to looming exams, or girl trouble, and was there anything he wanted to talk over. He could make an appointment. But you know what they're like, Dean, he ignored the suggestion. But apparently—he wasn't in our faculty at the time, but he got to hear about me from another student...'

'My information,' cut in the Dean, 'is that Larré was told about a small group of students who were trying out unorthodox exercises under Professor Mandelbrot's supervision. So unorthodox that Mandelbrot failed to obtain permission, and was conducting experiments in secret.'

'Oh, this is ridiculous,' Mandelbrot snapped. 'You make it sound like I'm performing satanic rites in an opium den. I'm doing nothing of the sort. It began informally, a tutorial in my rooms. A handful of students, nothing more. But it escalated, created a lot of enthusiasm. That's what it's all about, isn't it, creativity, stretching minds? What's university life all about if it isn't the joy of seeing your students enthused? Marc was intrigued, asked if he could join us.'

'It's our job, and it should be yours,' the Dean thundered, 'to steer our students in the right direction—onto the right course. Joy comes way down the list. Performance, results, degrees. We have our reputation, we have our finances to think about. With all this political unrest, we are under suspicion, *and* we're under surveillance. I don't suggest you were dancing naked under the moon, you fool, but rumours *were* flying, and you were drawing attention. I was getting memos. You put me in a very difficult position, professor. I have to tell you...' and so it went on.

Our professor gritted his teeth. Whatever it was that had drawn the young Frenchman—the chance to skive off lectures most likely—once enlisted, Marc threw himself into the fun and games of the research. And this is what Mandelbrot believed in: wholehearted commitment to discovery—whatever the cost. But he could see he was getting nowhere with the Dean.

Should he have told him how by chance he'd invited the students to work on any personal health problems they might have. Marc hadn't come expecting a cure—Mumbo-jumbo healings were definitely not his scene—but he'd agreed without hesitation. I suggested they allow themselves to enter a semi-trancelike state, and separate mind from body. Under my careful direction, Dean, he would have stressed. But a sign had already flashed up in his head: *Forbidden Territory.* Territory he'd be mad to invite the Dean to share.

Pity! This arse-licking woodentop would have learned something extraordinary. Mandelbrot mused on, recalling fondly to himself. If it hadn't been for these excursions down forbidden paths, none of my students would have made the life-changing discoveries so vital for mankind's advance—and I wouldn't be here today.

Small steps at first. I began by showing them how to visualise their symptom as symbol. Explained the art of seeing the image-metaphor within the magnetic field surrounding the body. Or if they were more comfortable with psychological terms, within the defined space of their personal psyche. I was impressed. They got the hang of it in no time. Even our prize sceptic Marc managed to become receptive and allowed himself to drift into a semi-hypnotic state. But I made sure he retained enough alertness to reassure himself I wasn't introducing ideas of my own into his mind. Other, of course, than the suggestion that he could trust his own mind to allow 'whatever might happen to happen.'

He'd volunteered for guinea pig on this occasion, so we gave him the sofa. He got comfortable and started to relax when... I can see his look of amazement now as he saw his headache advancing towards him, a strange composite of lump hammer and drum-kit. He described how it came at him with a series of deafening thumps, grinning and baring its teeth. He was terrified. But we supported him, and the headache was slowly transformed into something more co-operative. We monitored him carefully, but as the weeks passed there was no return of his symptoms. (Mandelbrot was back explaining how it was to the Dean.) Not a sign, he would have told him with just the right touch of understatement. But he could imagine the man's reaction. The other students were impressed though, I can tell you.

Unfortunately, certain other experiments didn't go so well.

(The Dean's presence loomed closer, his eyes diamond-sharp points. 'See me in my rooms, old chap. Eleven suit you? Just a chat.')

Of course we went through all the usual—gentlemanly pleasant-ries, drinks and monographed cigs—but the nitty-gritty up-shot was, *desist from further dodgy experiments—or resign.*

But such was my magnetic personality that by now the students were hooked. Began coming to me privately, asking if they could carry on—on neutral ground, outside college walls if necessary. I had to do some serious thinking. 'I'm suppose to be teaching you guys philosophy, and the hierarchy feel that these psychedelic trips...' They were affronted. He could hear their voices as clear as if they were in the room right now.

'Hey, come off it, prof! We're not smoking stuff, or any of that crap. At least, not while we're with you,' they argued.

'I know that, chaps, but the powers-that-be suspect me. I seem to have acquired some sort of reputation... Some past life, maybe. Seriously, some shit's got it in for me. A lot of dirty politics behind the scenes in a place like this, you know. They want rid of me before I get that promotion. Easy enough to concoct a plausible reason when a few of you start going AWOL with a bit of mental delusion—insta-bility—OK, let's face it, downright schizoid paranoia. Anyhow, we've gotta cut it out or I'll lose my job.'

'But,' they were protesting, 'can't you tell 'em what you're teaching *is* philosophy. Besides, that episode with the alien implants projection phenomenon didn't last. It was only temporary. Chris and Jen did get carried away, somewhat. Got a bit over-enthusiastic with their visualising technique, maybe. But we learned a lot from that. We're not arsein' about, prof. We're serious.'

And so they were, he recalled. I only had to drop in a suggestion here and there, but for the main part it was they who set the pace. The nature of consciousness; the existence or non-existence of the soul. It all came from them. They lined up the fors and againsts, behaviour-ists versus the ones who rejected mechanistic or reductionist theories. What is Soul? Where is it located? Of what is it composed? Show it me, the rationalists challenged. Meaningless questions, shouted the other side. You might as well ask, Where's a Mozart Symphony located, or What stuff is Easter Monday composed of? These are concepts—not in space at all.

'Ah! But I may have experienced that Symphony just as you have. *Therefore*, smart arse, I can verify its existence.'

'But how can you prove you've had the same experience as I have, dickhead? Or for that matter the same as a primitive from the jungles of Borneo. His experience of Western music is a meaningless surge of sounds. Yet we can both call the experience Mozart's Symphony.'

As to identity. Who am I? What am I? Am I comprised of my memory? If I lost my memory, would I still exist as a recognisable entity? Could I say, 'This is Me, this is my world,' if my memory had disintegrated? How would I make sense of my perceptions? My world would be chaos.

45

It was out of these questions, my dear Dean, that some of our most advanced and interesting experiments came. We would explore 'self' and 'not-self'.

SIMON AND THAT PROPINQUITY THING

'Correspondences International. Balcon here.'

'Peter?'

'Hel—lo-o-oo... Annya, isn't it? Hi, Annya! How's things—what can we do for you?'

'Peter, I...'

'What is it, Annya? You sound...'

'No, I'm OK Peter. It's just... Is Simon there? Have you seen him?'

'What's the problem? I've seen him, yes. He came here right from the airport.'

'Is he there now? I mean is he still with you—in Amsterdam?'

'No, no. He stopped over just the night, picked up his brief and then caught the flight to Damascus.'

'Are you sure? He didn't catch a plane back here, by any chance?'

'What! Back to the Island? No, of course not. What's going on, there, Annya? There's only one flight a week out there—you know that. He couldn't possibly. Are you in some sort of trouble? You sound... He's in Damascus. He phoned in a report last night. Annya! Annie...'

She'd put the phone down.

Good old Pete. She'd expected him to be at his desk by seven-thirty, and there he was. But as far as the reassurance she'd hoped for...

Annya hadn't dared to sleep, and her head throbbed. Last night had been spent with all the vents closed, and the door double locked.

She and Simon usually left it ajar a few inches for air—but with the chain across, of course. Assailed now by every imaginable possibility, she was sure that by securing the door against intruders, she had locked her spectral visitor in with her.

So, Simon had gone. Why had this nightmare happened the day after he'd left? Had someone planned it? Were they waiting? Watching? Worse still, could it all be her imagination? No-one was going to help her with *that* one though. Apart from a chatty acquaintance with Rosa who owned the bodega, and a friendly, but business-like, relationship with the people who ran the holiday complex, she knew no-one out here. You couldn't just walk up to a stranger and say, 'Look, I think I might be going mad. I've had this visitor, the invisible man, and he's trying to scare me out of my wits.'

Simon, damn you. Leaving me to cope alone. If you'd been here, none of this would have happened, she thought, not for the first time. Why can't it all go back to where we were before you buggered off? Oh God, I didn't mean that, love. You were shit-scared too, weren't you? But you managed to act like it was just another job—hell of a lot braver than how I'm being now.

Her friendship with Simon went a long way back. He'd been at school, and then University with her elder brother. He was family, almost. This Easter she'd been mooning around at home at a loose end, and Simon, visiting their house at the time, had invited her to spend a few weeks with him on the spur of the moment. He planned to give himself a longish break out at the Island. The apartment belonged to him, though he rented it out sometimes. He casually mentioned there might be an urgent call for him—press agency—but if he had to leave in a hurry, the place would still be hers until the next batch of holidaymakers arrived.

'Annya's driving me nuts with her drifting and dreaming,' her brother had sneered. 'One minute she's Martha Gellhorn, next she's bloody Kate Adie. But does she get herself together and get herself some serious training? Like hell she does! So, please Simon, I hear you're some sort of a journalist, do me a favour will you? Take her away and knock some sense into her.'

It sounded too good to miss, and with nothing more urgent on the horizon, Annya jumped at it.

Simon knew the Island well, all the coves and harbours the tourists hadn't yet discovered, and their first few weeks flew by. But there'd been times when she'd begun to feel uncomfortable—conscious she might still be carrying around that ridiculous kid-sister complex. Always awe-struck by what she perceived to be his talent and glamour, she'd become sensitive. Her own twenty-odd years should have amounted to something by now. But her discomfort went beyond that. Living this intimately for the first time, their relationship had begun to change, and she'd become aware of him in ways that had never intruded on their friendship before.

They'd be in the kitchen together—he did an expert paella—and she'd suddenly notice his body, and how the warmth from the stove seemed to be releasing the pungent scent of that peculiar belt round his waist. He'd been after some crowd-shots that Sunday in the market, and they'd happened to stop and chat to an elderly African manning a stall. Simon bought one.

'A bribe,' she'd asked later, 'for letting you take his picture?'

'What? Buying this?'

'I've never seen you wear a belt.'

'I don't usually, but all these twisted thongs and knots. They were all different, didn't you notice? Different skins, but with these weird individual patterns too. He was telling me his kid brother hunts the animals—spears them. Then the old man works some magic into the leather. I didn't believe him, not a word. But I liked him. Tells a good tale.'

49

'It's warm,' she said, fingering it. 'It's soft when you're wearing it. It moves and stretches. Like skin.'

'It *is* skin. I told you.'

'It smells exciting,' she said, *sotto voce*.

And then he'd kissed her. A peck on the cheek, but his hands stayed on her shoulders, holding her firm so she couldn't move away, and then pulling her into him. She tried to put her hand to her face where he'd kissed—it had started to redden—but she awkwardly missed. His arm was in the way.

'Simon?'

And then his mobile rang. Pulling it from his pocket, he snapped, 'Lennox here,' then an abrupt, 'Oh!' and went into his bedroom and slammed the door.

The tone of his voice came through the wall, sharp and fast, rising and falling. But, although she strained her ears, she couldn't decipher the words.

Then she heard him pacing, opening drawers, shutting cupboards, and when he emerged he seemed, for a moment, like someone she didn't know. But he'd come and put his arms round her. Big brother again. 'We've got just one day together, now,' he said.

'One day? You're saying *what*? That call? Was that Amsterdam?'

'Yep. Sorry. It's the one I've been waiting for.'

'But... Already? It *can't* be, Simon. We've not been here five minutes.'

'I did warn you, love. We've had two or three good weeks, and...'

'And, *what*?'

They stood, both saying nothing, not moving. Then she said, 'Where, Simon? Where're they sending you?'

'Can't say, love. Orders from on high. Secret Service, and all that.'

'Oh, come on. Do you have to be so mysterious?'

"Fraid so. Scout's honour and hope to die. Truly though, Anns, they didn't tell *me* till now. I had a good idea what was in the wind, of

50

course, but... Hey! Look, I know a place, been keeping it for you. Not the bodega this time, but we can eat. Terrific tapas... Just the locals. They just keep bringing the plates. You don't order. They do their own thing—no menu, but it's the best. Then I'll take you to my secret rendezvous and seduce you. There's a hidden pool too. In a cave up there. It's ice cold and blue as blue. We can jump in, splash about till we get our butts froze off. Then I'll warm you up. How about it?'

'What's come over you, Simon? What *is* this, all of a sudden?'

'I just want the day to be special. For both of us. Don't you?'

'Let's just play it by ear, shall we,' she said.

'What you talking about?'

'Well, you know, it's... What would happen to us?'

'Don't know what you mean. Happen?'

'It's... I really value what we've got, Simon—what we've always had. We'd never be the same again.'

He'd gone quiet. Sulking, she thought, but... 'Anns, love,' he said, suddenly measuring his words, 'there's a lot of history in this, isn't there? All my stuff on the one hand, marriages, affairs...'

Marriag-*es*? Plural? She hoped her face didn't register the shock. 'I'd no idea.'

'OK. Wishful thinking then on that,' he said.

But now she wasn't sure. Wasn't sure she'd *ever* known him. 'And you've always known about Sondra,' he was saying, but she wasn't altogether listening. Of course she knew about Sondra, but... 'The odd few might-have-beens...' his sentence trailed. 'Anyhow,' he said, picking up again, taking a step towards her. And she thought for a moment he was about to put a brotherly arm round her shoulder again. 'There's, you know, this other stuff. Me, knowing you since you were that little teenage scrawny. Like you were my sister for a long time. And now, out here, just the two of us. It's all... Well, we're into new territory. But it's that old propinquity thing, I guess, casting its shadow.'

'Christ sake, Simon. You're sounding like a lawyer now. Or something from the Old Testament.'

She wasn't really sure what the word meant. Propinquity. He was standing, their bodies all but touching, looking at her, with that scent of his shirt in her nostrils. He'd left it half undone. Nothing unusual, he wore his shirts that way often. But now she caught herself counting the buttons all the way to his waistband, imagining her fingers unfastening the last few, loosening that belt, sliding down his warm skin. She quickly pulled her eyes away from where they had strayed, and up to his face. His lips, a fraction apart, were smiling, so she could just see his tongue pressed against his teeth. He was teasing as usual. But when she checked his eyes to see, they were serious, gazing into hers with an intensity that made her heart stumble.

It means, "this close", that word, she thought. And her skin flushed, though she was shivery inside.

And then their last whole day. Setting out together for his hide-away in the hills, the place he'd been storing up, there had been that hint of awkwardness. It may have been tension about what lay ahead for him, as much as anything else. But suddenly he didn't want to talk, keeping his anxieties in check. She'd kept her own feelings on the subject to herself too. Simon Lennox, prize winning photo-journalist, was one thing. But as to this new mission of his... All she knew was he'd been assigned to a team heading for some Arab State. And she wasn't given that information until she'd been driving him to the airport the following morning.

And what a day *that* had been!

But now today. She'd marked it out. It was meant to be the start of her self-improvement campaign, time out with herself, and a belated opportunity to get her life together, yet it had disappeared into a black hole of self-doubt. Well, she wasn't going to let it defeat her. She would force it back into something like normal. She wouldn't be spooked. Not by anyone. Especially that face in the looking glass.

OK Annya, begin at the beginning, she told herself. Breakfast. Hot, crusty bread and croissants from the bakery, bananas and yoghurt, swirls of honey. Then you can eat it out here on the patio and enjoy the view.

Studiously avoiding the mirror, she went indoors to check out her linen skirt and rose-coloured, strappy top. This early in the morning the queue at the bakery would be composed of middle-aged Germans. She only knew a few words, but enough to know they'd be slagging off 'dei Englander'. So slovenly, my dear. Lager louts, the lot. And their dress sense! Ach! did you see those two? Underwear spilling out, top and bottom. And yesterday, that Irish bar! Vomit all over the pavement! Annya would wince, but secretly had to agree with most of it. The Brits usually sloped out of their apartments around ten looking as if they'd slept in their clothes. Even so the sniggers riled her and did nothing to improve her view of Germans. If one of them deigned to smile at her, she'd beam back a 'Guten Morgen.' But she was never sure. Were they taking her for one of themselves, or assuming her the so dumb Englander that their insults sailed past? She pictured them with pointed Brunhilde breasts and horned helmets, massing on the baker's doorstep, banging on the door as always a good fifteen minutes before opening. She allowed herself a smirky smile, then noticed it was eight already! She'd better get her skates on.

Back home again with her canvas bag full of goodies, all was quiet; the Brits on either side were still abed. She went inside to make some coffee. If nothing else, she would have a terrific breakfast today.

She carried the steaming jug out onto the patio. It was the distinctive brand Simon had selected, and its aroma curling through the air was conjuring him up. She began setting everything out on the table. Fresh orange juice, a pot of English Seville marmalade. Even those damn Germans couldn't better us on marmalade. Blue butter dish, that lovely olive-wood board, another find from the Sunday market. She piled it with warm croissants, arranged bananas in a bowl. Even though they grow here, Simon said, they export the best. She tilted the big yellow umbrella so the sun wouldn't get in her eyes, and took a breath. It felt like the first that day. The luminescence of morning was still shimmering across the sea.

So, Annya! She could almost hear him, sitting the other side of the table, legs sprawled, hand round his cup, reading. *What are you going to do with yourself then?* The skin in the soft crook of his arm, hairs on the back glinting gold. His absence was making him more present, more sensual, alive—necessary.

Usually they had a swim. But today? *Well! Maybe leave that one alone, don't you think, Annya?*

He wasn't here though. No-one was here. She was alone. Alone with these inexplicable events.

What then? she asked herself. A drive into the mountains, a bite to eat in their favourite bodega—space and solitude. That's what she needed. Or was it? Wasn't it answers she needed? And someone to talk to? But who? Either these things were real, or if not, then some-one was suffering from serious delusions. A possibility she didn't wish to confront herself with. But she would admit she was scared.

Two facts she could take on board. Alone and scared. The space they'd shared had been violated, and calling the police was no solu-tion, and spending another minute in that room—impossible.

She'd eaten very little after all. Stacking the dishes she took the remains into the kitchen. The Opel they'd hired was out in the street. Gathering a few things into her bag she carefully locked the apart-ment door, double checking the key was in her bag, then went out to the car. She switched on. Her hand reached to stroke the fabric of the passenger seat. His impression where he'd sat when she'd driven him to the airport yesterday was still there.

* * * *

54

Packed streets left behind, the engine cruised up the rutted, twisty road into the hills. Her spirits lifted with the altitude. As the volcanic peaks loomed closer a dual sense of awe and peace settled on her. It was virtually uninhabited up here; a landscape scorched and treeless, apart from the odd, solitary palm. But today, for some reason, she felt part of it. Details Simon had pointed out to her were no longer abstract features. She could feel the pores of her skin absorbing it, making it her own reality.

The road changed direction and, climbing still, headed into the wine producing region, a blackened waste of volcanic ash. Where violent nature had blotted out, human ingenuity over time had nurtured the tender green tips of life. Single vines, sheltered by half circles of lava walling, each in its saucer-shaped bed of picon, flourish defiantly. By day the ebony granules bake, then moisture from the evening mists condenses and filters down to the roots. Drinking a glass of this land's extraordinary wines is to sip power from the volcano's rim. It was perhaps Annya's anticipation of this which caused her to spur the engine on.

Every so often now a small figure appeared in a field silhouetted against the dark ground and the blue emptiness of sky. You'd wonder where they'd sprung from with no building visible for miles. Hoe in hand, each addressing a vine, brilliant, lime-green against the scoop of ebony, these lonely tillers of the land were evidently original island stock. She could tell by their dress; a woman's outsized hat held down by swathes of cotton, fastened beneath chin, and draped around shoulders served for protection against the desiccating winds. Up here, Annya felt, everyone, herself included, was rooted into this land.

The gradient grew steeper, bend succeeding bend. Then a sudden flush of roadside green augmented by a sunburst of flowers and iridescent butterflies caught her by surprise. One of the minor miracles, apparently, which happens in these highlands after a rare overnight shower.

At last she reached the spine of the island, a compacted single-track causeway of volcanic granules. It was level going now, but with the surface raised above the jagged scoria by, in some places, fifteen inches—a slight misjudgement, and there would be no getting back on the road. With eyes focused on the crumbling edge she missed the turn-off to the bodega. Nothing but a dust-track, it had always been difficult to find, but she'd driven a few miles past before noticing. She pulled off at the nearest passing place and doubled back, and this time spotted it more easily. Cursing herself for the wasted time, she was surprised that it was only eleven-thirty, too early for lunch, when she finally arrived at her destination.

Engine idling now, she allowed her eyes to sweep the gold dusted, indigo shadowed circle of peaks which guarded the horizon. Her disturbed night must have caught up with her, because a deep wave of fatigue suddenly overcame her. No-one else had parked here yet. In fact no-one seemed to be around at all, so she put her car into the shade of a couple of straggly fig trees, opened all the windows and sank back into the seat.

Wave after wave washes over her, and she is sinking. Struggling to breathe, making no headway against the tide, wave after wave of fear forcing her down, drowning her in panic. Dark waters beneath, fathoms deep, bottomless. A tornado shrieking in her ears, but without air to breathe, she is fighting for life. Swallowing water, gulping salt, her lungs scream, but she manages to force up her head, and looking to where the sky should be, her eardrums begin to oscillate. They're ringing—and the doors of dimensions are springing open. Symphonies of strings and superstrings begin to vibrate. The whole sky is alight with infinitesimal particles; electrons, selectrons, hydramezons, capamezons, delta particles, all vibrating, resonating in hyperspace, and she feels her head will burst. And out of the great sound hurtles an incandescent ball of fire-red, shooting out of the void, rushing down through the air, crashing into the sea. She sees it bubble and foam and spin and begin to form a crater with walls of water. The walls mount higher and higher and swell into a mountainous wave which sweeps towards her. She feels her skeleton dissolve; legs and arms become seaweed. Then, suddenly, she's riding the wave, up, onto its crest, she's surfing its energy as it powers towards shore.

From the sky above a strange, radiant face gazes down.

A crunch of gravel and a door slammed shut. The shade had shifted and a blazing sun was streaming into her face. She woke with a start. Another car had pulled up alongside.

GAIA

Finn, meanwhile, had been overflying the island, sensing out the georama. He'd risen with the thermals as they took him away from the coast, and was hovering over the mountainous fire-fields of the hinterland, within touching distance of its peaks.

Now he was beginning to get his eye in, the softer colours of this island landscape felt increasingly delicious. He longed to taste them through the soles of his feet, and draw nourishment from the earth. He badly needed to replenish his own energy which was rapidly becoming depleted since he was no-longer part of the vibrational atmosphere of Zurillion.

The planet Earth he'd flown as a rebellious adolescent, long ago, was a world of verdant woods and flower-banked streams. But the terrain he could see below him now showed no trace of vegetation. Yet this oxidized land of dunes and ashes, of twisted basalt and fantastically sculpted scoria, filled him with awe. Those velvet-soft peaks which had thrust heavenwards through Earth's crust on that fateful day when her core erupted, were sublime. He'd almost risk alighting for a moment—the briefest contact only with one of those rounded cones beneath him—but it seemed to defy him with its purity. Something terrible lay beneath the surface, he was sure, yet those breasts—which he was almost touching now—seemed virginal. Smooth, iron-red and yellow mounds of powdery ochre, creamy pumice roundels glistening like pearl in the sunlight, called out to be kissed. Yet among them protruded devilish hornillos and jagged egg-shell craters which had blown their tops with unimaginable violence. A world of such contradictions was perplexing.

Yet the barrenness of this raw earth didn't speak to him of infertility. This was a primordial world—planet Earth as she had been at her inception, burning and twisting into shape. Contorted in the metallic pains of creation. Birthing. Creating life out of herself.

How terrifying these mothers are, he said to himself, quietly. Unbearable in their beauty and their unutterable peace.

Then words came to his mouth and he shouted aloud. 'O Goddess. O Mother. Oh Earth, my home, do you command my return?'

Without warning a hurricane of an answering voice erupted from the ground, the force of it hitting him backwards. 'Earth child, welcome,' it roared. 'Softly I command, and I embrace your feet with a kiss.'

The last thing he'd expected—a reply! With a series of ear-splitting reverberations a blast of hot wind tipped him off balance so that he almost struck his head on the nearest peak. Were those volcanoes about to shoot their tops again?

He was not sure who or what had addressed him, but if this god-almighty, sky-rending, thunder of a voice was its idea of *soft command*, then heaven help him if it ever lost its temper.

'Welcome again, precious child,' the hurricane thundered. 'You are right to address me as mother. Here I lie, at your feet. Goddess Earth. Some call me Gaia. Welcome home Finn. I will try to speak more softly, little one. I didn't mean to shock or upset you, but I don't know my own strength sometimes.'

Finn, still struggling to keep his balance while the air whipped about him like a spinning-top, gazed around in alarm. Below him, fields of black lava, solidified many centuries ago, were heaving and rippling. It looked for all the world as though the goddess was giving her blanket an early morning shake. Indifferent to his alarm, or apparently to her own violent contortions, Gaia went on...

'Your sacred contract, Finn, has drawn you home. Let me congratulate you on your timing. You have come to fulfil an urgent undertaking, one to which you agreed to dedicate this lifetime, knowing that you would be called to return at precisely the right moment.'

Still stunned, Finn nevertheless had a faint recollection that at some point during his protracted trip around the Galaxies he had been present at a Grand Council meeting with the Lords of Karma, and some such undertaking had been consented to. But the precise nature of what he'd agreed escaped him right now. 'May I be permitted, O Majestic Mother...' he began. But the voice interrupted him.

'Gaia is my name.'

'Gaia then. Mother Gaia, may I ask you a question?'

No thunderbolt, no hurricane, in fact no reply at all. For a moment all was quiet, so he felt it was perhaps all right to carry on. 'Would you please give me a clue here. What exactly... this task... what might it involve?'

'Drastic changes,' came the reply.

'Oh! And?' he asked, feeling it might be disrespectful to quibble.

'Humanity, Finn, the race to which you belong, is at a crisis point in its evolution. An upheaval of immense proportions is imminent. But from the beginning my relationship to humanity has been symbiotic. I also am in crisis—a deep inner crisis of change. This is why you have returned. Yet even I can't say exactly what this task of yours is.'

'Can't?' Finn asked, astonished. 'I don't understand.'

'But you do, Finn. On this Earth where you were born, life is governed by my rhythms and seasons. Day follows night, winters go and summers arrive. Human consciousness also changes and evolves, and my awareness, though different, moves in step with humanity's. Yet for both of us, some things will lie in the dark soil of unconsciousness until the sun's warmth awakens them.

A mother always senses the quickening in her womb, although, until the infant is born, she may not know precisely what features it will have. I have given birth to every kind of being—monster and saint. I nourished the most depraved of men and nurtured the greatest wisdom. I don't judge; I love without favour, even when those I give birth to appear bent on destroying me. And this is where we stand at present. This is the crisis, and this is why you are summoned. So, although I sense that your task is immense and important, I am in the dark myself about its final shape, because that is given for you to discover.'

The turbulence had all but ceased, as had the tremors in the ground. A chance for Finn to air a few questions. But so many thoughts were clamouring, half formed in his mind, including the obvious—why given, and even, by *whom* given, for me to discover?—that none came to his tongue fast enough. She was already into her stride again, although the numinous voice had moderated itself considerably now, and almost assumed human proportions.

'But one thing, Finn,' she went on. 'I do feel that a certain young female is linked to your destiny. I have watched you ever since your return, and you've been paying a lot of attention to the contours of my body. But you have also shown more than a fleeting interest in this young woman. She seems to hold a strong attraction for you. Did you see her beneath you, just now, as she fell asleep inside her mobile vehicle? Or weren't you quite as observant as you think?'

'I can't think who you mean,' he muttered, 'unless it's that girl I spotted on the beach a while ago. The one who thought she was in danger of drowning.'

'Yes, that's the one,' she said. 'I believe you organised a rescue party for her. She is below you at present, dreaming inside that pestilential wheeled contraption. I happened to notice signs of sexual interest coming from you—all quite natural—no need to blush and look skywards. But I think you were feeling drawn to her once again. Is that so? Did you see her?'

'No. Not exactly. But you may be right. I guessed she wasn't far away. It's just that my focus was on the larger picture, the landscape.'

'My body, Finn? Is that it?' Gaia inquired.

'To tell the truth, Mother, it's becoming urgent for me to connect with your energy. This etheric atmosphere is suddenly not sustaining me as it did. I'm beginning to feel a trifle insubstantial up here, and it was your body that drew me. So I guess with all these things going on, I didn't spot her.'

'Things, Finn? Going on?'

'Anxieties, then. Surely you understand, this etheric body of mine is fine for extra-terrestrial travel, fifth-dimensional existence and such, but if this contract includes me coming down to earth—becoming a true earth-being again, then shan't I need something more biological, neurological, physical, perhaps? You should know, if anyone, Mother. Your stock-in-trade, eh?'

'But anxiety, Finn? This is something peculiarly human, I think. Not something I experience myself. I confine myself to providing the building blocks of physical existence, and the conditions which nurture life. All of life feeds at my breast. Your instincts seem to be in good working order in that regard. Instinct. Now that is something I do understand. A powerful—er—life-tool.'

'Survival mechanism?' he suggested.

'No, there you go again. Mechanics belong to your sphere. But sexual attraction, male to female—very much my department. And this is where we came in. This girl, Finn. Do I detect some reluctance to get back to the subject?'

'Well, I admit, there were certain sensations I would associate with the human female coming through to me.'

'This is what I thought.'

'Can I ask why you bring this up, Mother?'

'Don't you have your own thoughts on this, Finn?'

'Maybe, but I would like to keep them to myself.'

'I will speak then. Although I shall still pose a question. Why does she draw you, Finn?'

'OK. You win,' he conceded. 'Well, I feel, or you could say some instinct tells me, that she may be a former incarnation of my heart's love, Li-Ona.'

'And why didn't you want to speak of that?'

'Because—well, for one thing, it's incomprehensible.'

All had now gone quiet. Obviously she was waiting for him to say something further. 'Well,' he began, feeling he had to throw some offering in, 'if she *was* an earlier incarnation of my beloved Li-Ona, then wouldn't I have some sense of remembering her from a previous lifetime? You see, I do have a powerful sense of *knowing* her, yet I don't remember a life with her. And this perplexes me.'

More silence.

'How is it possible to know someone and yet have no recollection of them? Please can't you help me out here, Mother Gaia. Don't just leave me hovering like this. I feel stupid.'

'Dear me, Finn. In spite of all this universal education you've absorbed during your travels, are you saying you've not yet learned that calling yourself stupid *is* stupid? You've simply come to the boundary of what you know at present. Of course it often feels like the edge of a precipice, but this is where mankind has stood a million times before. And standing there is the least stupid position in the universe. Because, Finn, hasn't it proved something important to you?'

'It has?'

'What you have proved, my boy, is your mastery of the art of stepping into space and discovering that, at the last minute, you have wings. Isn't that so?'

'Well, I...'

'The universe,' Gaia went on, 'presents you with a conundrum. More often than not, when we're faced with the unknown it means we are about to break through into an entirely new dimension. No outside cause has brought us here. We have contrived the situation ourselves. We've arrived at the threshold of a new phase of our creative powers. God-sized... no, better still, Goddess-sized steps are about to be taken. Yes?'

'I suppose, if you say so.' He had to admit it all sounded familiar. When his father and Mandy had discussed similar mysteries in front of him as a child they'd fired his imagination. It had even been a factor in his own impetuous flight into space. Yet once he'd mastered the knack, transporting himself to whichever destination he chose to envisage, he'd found it so liberating that he began to see himself as this ever-youthful god, venturer through the planes and dimensions, welcomed, on whichever planet he deigned to touch down, like an honoured guest. But now, faced with these laborious Earthly demands, he didn't feel so keen on this particular adventure. He certainly felt this pull towards the girl, but exactly how he should go about relating to her, or in what sense appear to her, was quite a challenge. He was turning it over, still muttering to himself. 'How is it I seem to know her, and not remember her?'

'Is this a dialogue, Finn? Am I included in your thoughts?' Gaia interrupted.

'I have the strong suspicion that you do know, Mother. But do you have to keep it from me?'

'I 'know' all things, Finn, yet much is still hidden from me, as it is from you.'

'This is a tad too cryptic for me, mother Gaia.'

'We are part of the mind of Creation, Finn. The manifest, *and* the unmanifest. If All was known in advance, how could it be "creation"? It would be "The Created", something done and dusted. Yet you already understand this too, do you not? I can tell you one thing, however— you and the girl are bound together in your destinies, and you have returned to be united at this time for a great purpose. Allow it to unfold.'

65

BODEGA PAPAGAYO

She should have brought a sunhat, this light was intense. Annya clambered out of the car, steadying herself with one hand, shading her eyes with the other. As she ploughed through the dusty grit towards the now open doorway her tongue felt like a cinder. Bodegas existed for one thing only—to sell their wines, but all she wanted now was a long, cold drink. Several.

Stepping inside, the contrast was so stark that at first she couldn't tell if anyone was there. It smelled familiar—old barrels, cool stones, air from the cellar with wine on its breath—a savour of olives and salt-fish from the counter. She could just make out a scatter of tables looking like shadows against the burnished stone of the floor, and the long, curved bar with its occasional gleam of glass and polished taps. Then she noticed the solitary figure, a man, standing with his back to her, leaning on the bar. No-one else, as far as she could see. The tables were empty. Rosa, the bar owner, was nowhere to be seen—gone into the back, fetching him a plate of something, she supposed.

Annya had visited the Bodega with Simon a few times now, and she'd succumbed to Rosa's charms. The woman was a tonic in herself—sympathetic ear, good-natured volubility. Simon had laughed, 'Can't you *see*, little Anns? It's all chat-up.' But her effusive friendliness seemed genuine enough, and Annya had begun to think of her as The Rose with a Heart. Except, right now she didn't feel like conversation with anyone. She was still reeling from her dream.

67

Then she realised with dismay the man must have seen her when he pulled up alongside. Oh, God, she thought, he's bound to start up talking. Her hand went to her hair. He probably saw me with my mouth open. He doesn't look English—or Spanish even. If he turns out to be German, anything beyond please and thank you I just don't do, so that lets me out nicely. I can slink away and disappear into that dark corner at the back. But that's no good; it won't get me my drink, will it?

The man shifted his weight from the elbow he'd been leaning on, a manoeuvre which neatly brought his head round to face her. She had to look at him now. He smiled, a courteous incline of the head before turning back to his glass. His features had caught the light from the door, and for an instant a pair of sapphire eyes glinted from a bronzed face. She smiled back, and began crossing the room to the bar.

Without its usual crowd the bodega seemed cavernous. Her footsteps clipped and clopped. Aware of her heels on the flagstones, it seemed as if they were tapping out in code everything she was trying to hide. She forced a semblance of confidence into the last few strides and gave the bell knob on the counter a punch.

Rosa appeared like she'd been waiting in the wings.

'Cara!' Her warm contralto seemed to fill the room. 'Sola, Annya? Where's the handsome Simon? Non ha venido? Never mind, dar-r-ling, let me give you a hug. I'll have you *all* to myself.'

Rosa frowned at the lack of response. Normally Annya would have been more forthcoming. Yet there she stood, running her fingers through her hair, limply gesturing apologies. Puzzled, Rosa leaned across the counter to stroke Annya's cheek as if wiping away the strange pallor there. Concerned, she peered into her shadow-haunted eyes. The man, who'd been studiously contemplating his drink until now, looked up. He signalled at Rosa with his empty glass, and muttered something unintelligible to Annya

Rosa took his glass and began uncorking a bottle.

'Und das fraulein?' he said, gesturing plainly at Annya.

It was a soft voice, but deep and guttural. Annya, flustered and bereft of a language in which to reply, whispered to her friend. 'Tell him thanks, will you? But, Rosa, all I really want... I'm dying for a drink of water. Tell him, sorry, but if it's OK with you, I'll just sit down over there, quietly. Bring me my wine later. And sort out a few tappas. Can I leave it with you? You know the sort of thing I like.'

The shaft of light from the door was suddenly broken. A young couple came in, closely followed by a small group. The German's eyes remained on Annya, but she couldn't meet them, and kept her face towards Rosa who handed her a glass and jug.

Then a noisy family came in. The place was filling up. Abruptly Annya turned from the bar and began squeezing her way, jug of iced water in one hand, glass in the other, past occupied tables to the cor-ner she'd got her eye on; a stone alcove with a cascade of plants. It was still free, and she slumped down gratefully.

This had always been her favourite spot, even on good days. The seat gave her the advantage of a screen of leaves, and she loved the fact that the unmortared wall behind was covered in rare plants. Rooted naturally, according to Rosa. They'd sat here often, Simon and herself, sometimes intimate, sometimes with his friends. But today, alone, she could merge into the background.

She poured a glass, gulping at the water, then put it down and sank her head into her hands. Perspiration began trickling between her fingers. Despite the cool of the stones at her back her face and neck were on fire. She tried a deep breath, but the room was gently rotating. She held onto the table, but the floor started to ebb and flow, just like that time she'd once had a bad crossing and the ground hadn't stopped pitching for hours, long after they'd disembarked. Afraid to let her eyes close in case the dream returned, she sat miserably, waiting for it all to pass. The giddiness, her life, before her eyes—drowning.

That was it. That *was* the problem. It *had* all come back—in the car—clear and intense. Ground beneath her, heaving, water pitching and tossing. A tidal wave thrusting up, meters high out of the ocean floor, sweeping her in towards the shore, tumbling her, scouring her, polishing her. And other things had come back, too. That meteor, burning red, homing in from out of the sun. She was struggling now to remember, but the scene was already fading.

Noise levels in the room had risen. The place had obviously become popular of late. Most of the tables were full now. Laughter, children's shrieks, clinking glassware, scraping stools—she tried to ignore the commotion. At least the floor felt a bit more stable now. She jolted nervously as the chair opposite skreeled against the floor. But it was only when a faint cough, followed by the chink of a wine glass being placed on her table penetrated the muzz in her head, that she finally looked up.

But it wasn't Rosa.

'I hope I'm not intruding,' a soft voice whispered, 'but I thought you seemed troubled.' The accent was strong, it was male and it was deep. The way he pronounced 'troubled'—she almost smiled in spite of herself. 'Rosa asked me to bring you these,' he said, holding out a plate of tappas. 'I'll retreat, if you wish, but I thought you looked unwell. Could I help? Manfred Haandel, by the way,' he said, offering his hand.

It took an effort, but, ignoring the hand, she managed a weak smile. 'It's very kind, but I'm alright. I don't think anyone can help. It's all rather complicated.'

'Are you sure? I'm happy for complications.'

Her head slumped again. Happy for complications, she said to herself? I bet you are. What's he after? Well, I can guess. These men. Pick up any lone female looking vulnerable. Then immediately she started feeling guilty. Letting her imagination run riot like this—him an innocent stranger. Sure sign she wasn't herself. Well, she *wasn't* herself, not today. And anyway, could she really start pouring out all her stuff and dump it on someone she didn't know? 'I can't. It's too bizarre, and there's so much I don't understand myself.'

'Bizarre?' he echoed.

She pressed her fingers to her mouth. How on earth had she let that slip? 'I'm sorry. Herr Handle, is it? If I started on this you'd soon come to the conclusion I'd lost my marbles. You know, gone crazy. And I'd rather not let myself in for that. I've just got to sort it out myself. Thanks for your offer, but I have to say, sorry.'

'That is a pity. Well, if you're sure. But can I at least offer you a pilule. Take it with that water. It will help, I think.' He shook a couple of white tablets onto the table.

Again her mind leapt to conclusions. Now he was trying to drug her!

But if so it was quite a subtle act because he was already half way to the bar and taking a well-mannered leave of Rosa. Without a backward glance at her, he exited the door, and his footsteps began crunching over to the parked cars. Then his motor revved, and the wheels spat. Glumly, she listened to the sound of the engine meandering over the hills until it faded.

That's it. He's gone, and serves you right. She scolded herself for a suspicious fool. What were you asking for this morning, if it wasn't someone to talk this business over with? Your prayer gets answered, and you tell him to bugger off.

To appease her conscience she picked up his pills and swallowed them.

It was stifling again in the apartment next morning. The fans were threatening to helicopter off the ceiling, but still it sweltered. She went into the bathroom where it felt cooler, to splash some water on her face, and caught sight of herself in the mirror. Before her spectral visitor could peep over her shoulder again she retreated. This, she told herself, is paranoia. And you're not handling it very well.

She'd have to find someone to talk to. So, back to that again. There was no-one suitable. What was she doing out here anyway?

She slumped onto the sofa and slid her sweaty bare feet under the coffee table. The dead cactus flowers had oozed more sap onto the table. She dipped her finger into the syrupy pool and sucked it. Packing up would be defeat, and get to the bottom of this thing, she would. At least the fever felt better today. Those pills must have done the trick after all.

Anyhow, she told herself, she'd made a good start now with getting back to normal. She began with a tidy-up, and cleared away the crummy plate and things left around from the day of the drowning scare. But the pile of old magazines and journals were still strewn about. A recent local freebie complete with gaudy cover—tourist issue—lay on top. Its colours screamed for attention, but its contents didn't. She'd skimmed a few pages half-heartedly already. Mostly commercials. Beauty therapists, baby sitters, doggie counsellors, exotic gardeners, wanters-to-buy, wanters-to-sell. But nothing the least bit interesting. Well, maybe check out that exotic gardener...

She shuffled and straightened the pile. Read them all. She was bored.

Not this one though. She hadn't seen this. It had been hiding at the bottom. Simon must have left it. She remembered him buying it at Gatwick; an ecological, alternative lifestyle type of thing. This looked more promising. Loads of articles—volunteering in Africa, eco-architecture in India, black poetry and reggae down the Portobello Road. Even so, she wasn't in the mood right now.

'Simon. Oh God, Simon,' she whimpered. 'Where the hell are you? How's it going, wherever it is you are? I'm scared for you, out there. Bet you're not thinking about me, though. Bet you're not scared for me. You'd never guess the half of this, would you? Wouldn't believe me either, even if I could tell you.'

She skimmed the pages, flipping through to the end. He'd bought it. He'd held it. Like the ghost in the computer when you thought everything had been deleted, the paper might hold a trace of him. Her eyes glided over the print. Personal ads mostly. English communes, organic farms in Spain and Greece, a couple offering yogic meditation! She blinked. That phone number printed at the end. It was local. It not only had the Island's code, but they were English and lived here, in this very resort. It had got to be Simon sending her an answer—a contact number? People she could talk to. Far too much of a coincidence not to give it a try.

Then it all began to seem crazy. The ad must have been placed months ago, before they even thought of coming here. What on earth did *she* want with meditation, anyway? Long-haired nutters with beads. But she scribbled down the number. Hadn't she just been given a lesson about pre-judging people? Maybe they were perfectly normal too, like her German. She could at least phone. The office would still be open. Nothing to lose.

She sped down the hibiscus-lined path, blurring her way past flower-filled patios she would normally have lingered by. She skirted the swimming pool scattering assorted children gathered at its edge and reached the office out of breath. With a cursory nod and a wave of her bit of paper at Tom behind the desk, she slammed the coins in the slot and dialled. The number began to ring.

A woman answered. German voice. But certain she'd dialled the right number and the ad clearly said, *English couple in Puerto Azzuro offer blah de blah*, she ignored the stream of German, and slowly enunciated, 'I am telephoning in response to the advertisement you have placed in the New Lifestyles Journal. Could I possibly speak to the person who placed it—visit you, perhaps.' A halting reply ensued.

'The Herr Doktor? Lifestyles? Journalist? You desire visit with him? Interviews for your English paper?'

Oh Christ! She's got the wrong end of the stick all right. How the blazes did I say any of that, she thought. She tried again. 'This is the right number, I'm quite sure. 707 4598. You are advertising meditation. I just wondered... could I come and see you and have a talk. Just to meet you. Compatriots, English. I thought...'

'Ja, you have the correct number. Is ringing all day, this number with English. I don't speak. Just one moment please. I am calling for you the...'

The pips began to go. Her money had run out. Flummoxed, she replaced the phone. Saved by the pips, Annya. You're not handling this very well. That's odd, she thought. I've said that before.

Deflated now, she was sure she'd made a complete fool of herself. Tom looked up from the desk. He needed to see to something outside. 'You OK manning the office for a minute?' he asked. Mournfully gazing out of the office window she nodded. Across the pool attending his plants she could see the bent-over back of scrawny, dusty Miguel who did the gardening. Not in the most deluded of imaginations, she mused, could he be described as an exotic gardener. Yet what he managed to coax from the dry, black granules which passed for earth was pure magic. The azures and violets of his morning glories sang to the magenta, carmine, and improbable burnt apricots of his bougainvillea. Cool plumbago nodded beneath a scald of hibiscus.

With no further bright ideas about how to spend the rest of the day, she decided she could risk a dip in the pool. It would cool her off. Then the phone rang. Tom was nowhere, so she reached out her hand and lifted the receiver. 'Hello,' came a soft, deep voice the other end. 'Doctor Haandel here.' She almost let it drop.

'Hello. This is Doctor Haandel. To whom am I speaking? How can I help?'

'Oh God! *Christ!* Look, I'm *so* sorry to have bothered you,' Annya gulped, wanting to run, but with the receiver seemingly stuck to her ear.

Silence the other end.

He was still there, she could hear him breathing. Then his voice brightened as if some light had switched on, 'Surely, das fraulein. You are the young lady I spoke with yesterday, ja? At Bodega Papagayo? The troubled one. It is you, no? And now you call me. But I am, how to say... Where have you discovered this number? I am private, not listed.'

'Oh! But...' Annya spluttered, not wanting to lose him again, yet not daring to believe the impossible. She drew herself together and said, 'I am trying to contact an English couple. I saw this advert in a magazine. An English journal. I don't understand. This is the number given, yet I seem to be talking to you again.'

'What number are you given?'

Annya repeated the number, certain she'd got the right one.

'Ja, this is my number. I have from my wife that you were wanting to make some interviews with me... alternative lifestyles? Meditations? But I know nothing of this. I am somewhat... You say you are journalist? Perhaps you will make yourself clear.'

'This is awful! I've made a stupid mistake. I'm not a journalist.'

'You mean I'm not about to become famous at last? Ach! I am so disappointed,' said the voice down the line.

'Oh hell. I really didn't want to trouble you.'

'But I am not troubled. I think it is you who is troubled, my dear. Maybe the gods are joking with us. But let me ask you again, is there something in which I can help?'

Her brain whirled. Confusion. Embarrassment. Simon's magazine: it had got the number wrong. It was another of his jokes. Or was it in fact an uncanny response to her predicament? Disbelief vied with outrageous hope. In all these extraordinary events of the last few days, at no point had she come to any real harm. In fact, if she thought about it... But she hadn't yet. Rational thoughts had been crowded out by the irrational.

'I *am* in trouble, Doctor Handle.'

'Why don't you call me Manfred,' he said with a sound suspiciously like a chuckle. 'The name's *Haandel*, by the way. H - A - A - N—D—E—L.' It was definitely laughter she could hear on the other end.

MANFRED AND ALL THAT JAZZ

'Where are we? Where're we going?'

'You don't recognise it?'

They were climbing through featureless scrubland—hill after monochrome hill. Clouds of dust swirled round the car. Annya took out a cotton scarf and began folding it into a bandeau. Manfred, hands on the wheel, glanced at her.

'Getting blown about a bit—my hair,' she explained. But the wind snatched her voice and almost tugged the flapping scarf out of her fingers. He jabbed a button and the windows swished shut. He flicked another, and icy air streamed round her body.

'Gut, ja?'

Her original impression of him as the good-looking German with the luminous eyes still stood, but closeted together now inside the car she felt uncomfortable again. The suave slacks and linen jacket of that day in the bodega were gone: a designer Tee now graced his upper body, below which protruded a pair of hairy, muscled legs topped by the shortest of aqua shorts, and bottomed by a pair of large, health-besandaled feet. It was also clear he must be twenty, if not thirty years her senior. Why on earth had she agreed so impulsively to his suggestion? Sunday lunch. Up in the north.

She imagined, when he'd issued that invitation, they'd be heading for one of Simon's old haunts. But these desolate hills wound on and on without offering the hope of arrival anywhere at all, and all kinds of doubts were surfacing.

'Soon be here,' he said, as if divining her thoughts. 'Everything OK. You'll see.' And rounding a bend there were suddenly four or five smart villas nestling under an escarpment of rock, beyond which glints of sapphire fringed the rocky headland. They drew up alongside a group of parked cars and braked. 'Up there,' he said, indicating an imposing wrought-iron gateway, and was already running ahead, taking the steps two at a time. He gave her a moment to catch up, then discretely withdrew a silvered membership card from his pocket and flashed it in the direction of the flunky inside the entrance.

'Good to see you again, Señor,' the uniform whispered. 'Your table is ready, Doctor.' He indicated down to the left.

She stifled a gasp. Steep terraces with tables set among giant blooms she had only seen before in hot-houses at Kew, while luxuriant foliage cascaded down the face of what appeared to be an extinct volcano. They'd entered a natural amphitheatre. Such greenery after those dreary miles of wasteland was astonishing. Manfred shot out a finger-splayed hand with the air of having just produced the whole thing from a hat.

Simon had certainly never brought her *here*. Simon who knew all the secrets of the Island, or pretended to. Perhaps he'd kept quiet about it, reserving it to impress another of his women as a prelude to seduction. She grimaced, thinking, here we go! I'm even conjuring up doubts about him, now. Manfred gave her a curious glance, then pointed across to the far side where a five-piece jazz band were perched on a jutting-out ledge part way up the rock face above a deep pool of water.

'You like jazz?' He didn't wait for a response. 'What a place, hey! Also, you will soon discover, noted for our cuisine.' He grinned broadly. She wasn't sure if he was mocking himself—or her. 'We go look at the fish, later. Most unusual. And inspect these sculptures.'

'What? Those in the water?'

'Sculptures? In the water?' he said, a rumble of a laugh beginning in his chest.

'No, no, the fish,' she said quickly. 'You didn't mean inspect some fish for our meal, did you?' thinking of an ocean-side restaurant she had been to once. But she was embarrassing herself. 'You meant, look at the unusual fish in the water.'

He guided her to their table and drew out her chair, smiling but saying nothing. She sank down thankfully and looked around, trying not to seem naive. She could see the odd objet d'art placed at strategic intervals within the exotic planting scheme on the terraces.

'What do we think, Annya? These works of art—so-called? We'll take a look after we eat, OK?' A waiter appeared. Manfred glanced at the menu and ordered two beers. He hadn't asked her what she'd like. 'We shall inspect them, these sculptures, you know, and I'll show you some interesting signatures.'

'Oh, yes,' Annya said.

'Ja.' And, penning a flamboyant scrawl in the air, he whispered a name she didn't quite catch, though it sounded like some Hollywood heart-throb of the sixties.

'Mm,' she murmured brightly. She wasn't about to give him the satisfaction of asking if he was on shoulder-rubbing terms with the stars, but couldn't think what else to say. Here he was, making up her mind for her one minute, then curiously sensitive to her innermost thoughts the next. What was she to make of him?

The musicians began tuning up. Jazz wasn't exactly her scene, more her brother's sort of thing, but the activity on that ledge served her for the moment, and she was glad of an excuse to turn her attention elsewhere.

'What do we think, Annya?' He wasn't going to let up. 'Not so young, hey? Jazz players, these days—but not so bad either, don't you think? In the groove, on a good day, their performance rises in step with the refreshment we imbibe.' He took a huge gulp from his own glass and raised it. 'And now we soar towards brilliance.'

Well, she thought, you certainly seem to think so.

They'd swung enthusiastically into their first improvisation and his outsize feet were already tapping wildly. Embarrassingly so, as his knees had just collided with the lightweight table top, and she had to reach for their beer glasses to stop them sloshing over. The amphitheatre now resounded to trumpet and sax, bouncing off the walls—strident, bombastic, sinuous, haunting—its unfamiliarity and datedness assailing her simultaneously.

Let it just wash over, she decided. He's obviously chosen this place for a bit of life and colour where a girl my age can unwind. Though he seems to be doing most of the unwinding.

Yet the music must have been working its alchemy on her, because her mood was changing, and her tight shoulders were beginning to ease. She had to admit this *was* an extraordinary place. An animated meld of human artistry and organic elements. And the food, when it arrived, was pretty good too. She even started to relax about her decision to come along.

'Getting with it?' he suddenly asked. 'Feeling better now?'

He'd been glancing at her from time to time as though judging whether the moment was ripe to broach the big subject.

'So? This trouble. Want to tell me?'

She shook her head in dismay. She'd based her decision to accept Manfred's invitation on what was beginning to feel like a madly irrational hunch. That mysterious contact number she foolishly believed Simon had placed on that page was suddenly, in the clear light of day, looking decidedly ridiculous. No-one, especially a scientifically trained doctor such as Manfred, would assume anything other than— Annya is barking. So what then? Keep shtoom? Keep her dignity, and her nightmare? Or spit it out?

Yet, she had to speak out, and the only way is to jump in with both

feet. And before he could open his mouth with another verbal prod-
ding, she jumped.

'Oh God. Where do I begin?'

'Begin in the middle, I always say,' he suggested.

'OK. That day then, at the bodega. I fell asleep in the car, and you
woke me.'

'I woke you?' He sounded puzzled.

'Your car, drawing up. Alongside. Crunching. I was having a bad
dream... in my car, and you drew up.'

'Ah, I apologise.'

'No, don't apologise, please. I needed to wake up, but I also needed
to try to grasp what was happening... inside me... outside. But the
problem was, it disturbed me so much... The *dream* I mean. But you
don't want to hear all this.'

'I am listening.'

'I know, and I can't thank you enough for, well, trying to help, but...
You don't want to listen to me rambling on about a dream.'

'You haven't told me anything yet.'

The blue intelligent eyes were smiling, yet she was still uneasy with
him, as well as about the dubious confession she had just launched
herself into. But she needed someone to believe what she couldn't
believe herself, and maybe after all, fate had sent Manfred. She took
a deep breath.

'Well, I've begun in the middle, now I'll have to back-track. What
I *think* I was dreaming, what I *believe* it was all about, is a sort of
flashback. You see, it was a replay of something that happened the
day before. I'd swum too far out in the sea. Hadn't judged the conditions right, and the tide was against me. All of a sudden I panicked.
Thought I'd had it.' She looked at him, hoping he was following the
plot. He seemed to be, so she went on. 'I'd got myself a long way out,
and on top of that the wind had taken me down the coast. I'm trying
my damnedest to get back to shore, putting everything I've got into it.'

She began demonstrating for his benefit, miming wild breast strokes. 'But not making it, you see. Getting exhausted.'

Heads of a few fellow diners now began to turn in their direction. She giggled. 'God knows what they're thinking about us.' But he didn't seem to have noticed. He seemed away in the distance watching a buzzard which had alighted on the top of the escarpment.

'Replay, you say,' suddenly back with her. 'This is interesting. Flashback, you call it? You are thinking your last moment is come, ja? I have had this similar experience myself.'

'Really!'

'Most certainly. I think it is a common experience. Traumas of war. Soldiers—they live again the experience too awful at the time.'

'But you say, you too? Can I ask? Would that be impertinent?'

'No, of course. It was many years ago. I was younger, a teenager, climbing in Switzerland with a school friend. Daring each other. I was—what to say?—roped up, yes? But, oh, so very high up. Many hundreds of meters with a big drop below. Ice on the rock, and my feet go, whoosh! No fingers. All of a sudden I'm in the air. Can't get a hold.'

'My God, Manfred. But you *were* on a rope.'

'Yes, round and round, dangling. But, like a fly on a spider-thread. Desperate, clutching for the rock. Thinking, I am dead. Then the rope tugs. Tug, tug, little by little, inch by inch, and my chum is pulling me, red in the face, sweat running, while I myself am twisting and bouncing. At last I get a finger-hold on the ledge, this wide—' He indicated about half an inch. 'My friend is on the ledge pulling, hauling me up to him.'

'Wow!'

'But you see. He is not belayed. Neglected to tie himself on, and my weight is dragging him off.'

'Christ! But you're here today, thank God. You must have some-how...' Her fingers played the air, lifting him up. She could see him, the fair-haired boy with a taste of death in his mouth. She wanted to swoop in, grab the rope, and guide those young feet to safety.

'But you...?'

He smiled again. 'Survived, of course.'

'What about the replay though.'

'I woke during the night. In a flash this whole scene visited me again. And what returned was of such intensity. Every detail, every sound, texture of rock, sting of ice, tightening of rope. And my own self completely present in that moment experiencing the shock of fear like a bomb had gone off in my head. At the same time I was outside myself, seeing myself dangling, feeling the moment of panic, how my biology and instinct were behaving. All these things I seemed to be experiencing together, in a way I didn't notice as it happened, in real time.'

'That's it!' She was clutching her throat. 'The same super-intensity, only there was something more. Maybe a lot more. I think I may have seen it from outside myself too. Only it faded as I woke.'

'As *I* woke you. You see, I do have to apologise.'

She reached across the table and took his hand. Surprised herself. 'You mustn't apologise, Manfred.' He leaned closer, his eyes searching hers. But suddenly she'd withdrawn again.

'There is more, isn't there? We've only scratched the surface, yes?' he asked.

Her heart jolted. 'But I can't,' she said, panic flaring, her voice throttled.

'What is it, Annya? Mein Gott! *Why?* I feel your fear, but... is it of me?'

Those luminous eyes staring into hers—the face in the bathroom mirror had reared up again. 'I'm sorry,' she said. 'I just can't. Can't explain. Let's call it a touch of paranoia.'

Their waiter, who'd been stacking a tray with dirty plates from the next table, came over with his order pad. Manfred, subdued, asked her if she'd like a dessert.

'No, I'm not hungry, thanks. But *you* must have something,' she said, trying to inject some energy into her voice. Why spoil his day? But the sound was squeezed in her throat. He wasn't bothered about dessert either. Distractedly, he asked for the check and waived the man away.

'If you're sure, then,' he said. 'Why don't we go down—there by the water-edge. Sit where we can see the fishes. I so *wanted* you to *see*.'

'Yes, show me, Manfred. I *do* want to see.'

He sighed. 'I think you love this, their colourings, Annya. They're so remarkable as they surface, phosphorescent from the deeps. We can get coffee later, or have strudel—when the appetite returns.'

She'd do it for him. Even force herself to eat cake.

The landscape, driving back, was oppressive; mist clung to the hills. 'Wow! What a place, Manfred. Phenomenal, like you said. And those incredible fish!'

Taking his eyes from the road, he turned. 'It's OK, Annya. I understand. Leave it for now, ja? Just let me know when you want to talk more.'

Manfred was right, Annya decided. They hadn't even scratched the surface yet; but something important had changed. She was getting over her jitters about being alone in the apartment, even managing to look at herself in the mirror from time to time. And yesterday, when her hand reached across that table to touch him, it had pierced an invisible barrier—one she'd been carefully weaving about herself. What it let in disturbed her—a different Manfred. Perhaps a Manfred stripped of the false picture her mental state had been creating?

Speaking of images though, she couldn't stop thinking about that unearthly face peering from her bathroom mirror. It had been there a mere split-second, but she'd caught herself sneaking a sideways look recently, half expecting another glimpse. What would Manfred have made of that? There'd have been some clinical explanation, no doubt, some ridiculous pseudo psychology. But they hadn't got onto the subject of the invisible man yet. She'd call him in the morning. Get it off her chest once and for all.

Meanwhile... Meanwhile what?

There was a new magazine on the table. Maria must have left it there when she did the mid-week clean. Annya leafed though dismissively. But an article on the Middle-East war by some local scribbler caught her attention. Thinking it was bound to be the usual codswallop, she gave it a cursory look, but as she read on her anxiety flared up.

Simon! No news from Simon. Phone Peter quickly and see if he's heard anything, a voice in her head shrilled.

Bad thinking, Annya, it contradicted. No news is good news.

She hadn't exactly been expecting a 'wish you were here' card with minarets and camels. She wasn't expecting *anything* this soon, because he'd made it clear it would be a hush-hush mission with no leaks. Nothing to give away the team's location or identity. But *something*. Something concrete would have helped. Her agitated fingers flicked the pages. Do something, Annya. Take a dip. Go for a walk. Better still, treat yourself to the most fantastic ice-cream of your life under those palm trees on the beach.

But she didn't move. Pages of lines and squares, blocks of print, black and white blurs, held her. One stood out. Another ad. Since the night of the lightning flash in the mirror she'd begun to worry about her eyes, and now a postage-stamp sized rectangle of print was highlighted, glowing as if painted with phosphorescence. She'd have to get her eyes tested; they were definitely playing tricks. She blinked sharply, then blinked again. But it was still there.

The highlighted message read: *Come with us. Explore the Island waters in our glass-bottom boat. Watch incredible rainbow-coloured fish, or explore your own depths. English couple invite you...* The phone number at the end was horribly familiar. 707 4589. Same number! She looked closer. Same but different. One digit transposed. 89 instead of 98.

Christ! That's it! Bloody English couple, they got a misprint in that magazine of Simon's, and this time it's the right one. Simon, Simon, what are you telling me? *Annya, don't be a fool.* Is this what you're telling me?

Her hands were shaking as she scribbled down the number.

They were still shaking moments later as, breathless from her dash down the path, she slotted in her coins.

'Hello,' said a decidedly English voice.

FINN'S THING

He couldn't get her out of his mind. Wherever he had gone, journeying throughout the vast starfields of the universe, Li-Ona's image had been with him. Ever since that childhood day when a wave of intense feeling had overtaken him and tipped him out of the nest; that was how he saw it—launched before his feathers were dry from the egg. Before he'd had enough time with his mother, Cléa, to drink his fill, he'd been fledged. After that, something always drew him on, tempering, bending, testing, but always something calling him to the next adventure which never filled that void inside him.

Li-Ona.

She had cast her magic around him before she too was able to understand her power or recognise her strength. A few years of childhood together, running through the flower meadows, fashioning leaf boats, hiding, seeking; they'd grown up quickly. But ever since that day, playing ball in the campo, he'd known he must kiss her. Yet the realisation came upon him gradually that it was already too late. He would never kiss her now, not until... And this *until* had been the thing propelling and drawing him on.

Such beauty. Not a single being in this twenty-first century world he'd entered came anywhere near her. These primitives, flesh like skinned rabbits, who you didn't want to get too close to—didn't want to feel. Gaia, of course, she was different. Her body was magnificent— as befitted a goddess. He desired her, he decided, as a child desires the mother, and desires her also as a lover. But that which he yearned for in the depth of his soul was the sweet girl of his childhood.

The power of that thing he couldn't name at the time seemed greater than he knew how to handle. He'd tried to talk about it with Mandy, but in the end it had driven him further away. Yet although he'd travelled hundreds of earth-years since, her image went with him. She'd sleep-visited him many times, but he'd only seen her as if on the other side of glass. He'd reached out his hand, but not been able to touch. She'd whispered, yet he'd not caught the words.

Beautiful Li-Ona. Tall and graceful she'd grown with limbs like temple columns. The silk of her hair billowed. The translucency of her bronze skin with its scintillations of gold played upon his mind's heart. When she smiled through the transparency which separated them, symphonies came into being, seas of flowers bloomed.

Yet, here he was, returned to his home planet, obeying his summons, while Annya, who he'd been observing now for some days, mysteriously emanated that same vibration. It resonated at a lower octave, had a duller edge to it, yet it was beginning to spark feelings in him which went beyond simple benevolence. No-one now to discuss such things with, was there? Certainly his little talk with the Goddess this morning hadn't helped.

In a region noted for its daybreaks, today's had been just another sublime example. The sea, a deep midnight blue less than an hour ago, had mutated into the most ultra of ultramarines with a million sun-stars breaking on its surface. In the air above, a few wisps of cloud were beginning to cluster round the mountain peaks. But they would dissolve shortly.

Meanwhile, upon one of those feathery pillows, lounged Finn, musing to himself with the air of a prince viewing his domain.

He'd longed to do this ever since he was a child. Basking in the solar rays, free from gravity. Absolute indulgence, anyone would admit, but who'd be mean enough to complain. And it opened up such wonderful possibilities. Riding the winds, surfing the waves...

He knew he was tempting fate. He knew, although he neither heard nor saw anything definite, that he wasn't going to be allowed to indulge himself this morning. A voice was speaking to him. There were no words; the sound came at first like a gentle tap on the shoulder, but inside, in his heart—and repeated—insistent. Then it came again, soft and honeyed, this time resonating all around him from the sky, the sea, the mountain tops. And although quite unlike the volcanic reverberations which had greeted him on that first day, it was unmistakably Gaia.

'*Such* a morning Finn! How you must be enjoying the feel of sunrise on your belly! A word in your ear, perhaps.'

'Mother Gaia, what a surprise! Indeed, a dawn to rival the beauty of your own countenance.' Kreepin krittins, he thought. Whatever's coming next? Hope I said the right thing.

'How delightful,' she continued, 'to see a human cavorting like a bird. If you were to peer round my curvature and look into my dark face, you'd see thousands of your kin swooping through the midnight skies in their dreams. The longing to soar seems to be a common desire among humans. Yet to have one of you consciously, and in daylight, disporting himself in this way is quite a sight. I take it as a sign that you are ready to begin your work.'

'My work?'

'Your contract. Surely you haven't forgotten?'

'N-n-n no, of course not. Remind me.'

'Finn!'

The voice coming at him now, from nowhere and everywhere at once, had a tone which carried the unavoidable message: Gaze around if you will, but you'll soon discover there's no hiding-place, so, when Gaia speaks, you'd better listen.

'OK.' He sighed. 'I just thought...' But the ground began, ever so slightly, to shake and rumble. 'I haven't forgotten, Mother, it's just... surely there's no rush...'

'Are your ears so closed, Finn, that you have become insensitive to the urgency of the situation? In the silence of the night don't you catch the sound of Gabriel's trumpet? The whole Universe strains with me as I prepare to birth myself anew. Yet catastrophe stares into our face. Unless humanity transforms itself, instead of our long awaited renaissance your race will witness the death of its mother planet.'

Finn sat up sharply. 'Catastrophe, mother? That sounds like understatement! I may have skipped a few important bits of my education—been out of things for some time, interplanetary business and that—but one thing I *do* know: if one planet goes defunct, all the rest get knocked out of balance. Solar planets would collide, and that spells disaster for the whole system, not to mention any chain reaction.'

'To be frank, Finn, although it was ordained from the beginning that humanity and I take this step together, if I have to save myself, I can and *will* do so. But the consequences are stark. I have waited for my children to mature since the day we spewed forth from the cauldron of creation together, but instead of deepening the wisdom of their hearts, your race has grown arrogant. Where there was once stewardship, now they abuse my body, rape and plunder. They are close to reducing their mother to a shrivelled husk.'

He opened his mouth, but she wouldn't be interrupted.

'I am longsuffering, Finn, but my patience is not infinite.' Her voice was rising and the air wailed. 'I approach the point of no return. And this, as you know quite well, is why you have been summoned and why you have responded.'

'I was created in the dawn of time,' she went on, 'for one specific purpose, to nurture every life-form who has come to experience my uniqueness. My energies are abundant, available to all creatures on, in and above my substance. Gaia loves her children; loves, above all, her

90

prodigious son who comes to help at this critical time; this instant of shift in world consciousness; and, Finn, I implore you, let me share my energies with you. Allow me to draw you down, plant and root you so your feet may tread my soil again.'

What could he say? Of course this was why he'd responded, why he'd travelled at the speed of light to be here. But much as he longed to draw upon the Mother energy, he hesitated—hadn't really taken it all in—the implications of it—this mammoth task he was being asked to perform, *and he'd like more time to consider it, please.* What in the name of All and Everything was she asking of him? Tectonic plates! Hemispheric alignments! Pull together two sunken continents separated way before this homo-so-called-sapient race existed! Great balls of hellfire!

A considered decision then: he *would* make this touch-down. But it wasn't going to be the kind of homecoming party he'd had in mind.

The practicalities of his mission began to swirl about his head. The risks. His need for a body, and how far to go into the process of materialisation. He tossed a few half-baked ideas around. What if I just create a pseudo-body? Could I get away with that, he wondered? But even that might involve cooking up an identity—creating the necessary paperwork. What a waste when I don't intend staying longer than necessary. Long enough to gather what information I can to complete my contract. Form whatever relationships are proper, but detach and return to my own century when—OK, *if*—I manage to fulfil this darned assignment.

But supposing *they've* got other things in mind? Heaven help us! That could mean getting well and truly immersed in time and gravity. Irksome to say the least. It's all right for these Lords of Karma to summon me back to Earth like this. They can stay above it all. If I get drawn in, natural laws could mean a period of gestation in a womb, followed by all the stages of development normal for this era. There have to be better options. 'Come on, fellas, tell me what to do. My energy levels are dropping. This is urgent.'

But answer came there none.

OK then, he decided. But I'll wait for a moonless night to make my touchdown. It'll give me time to think.

The spot he chose wasn't one of those breast-shaped cones which had first delighted him, but a mountain peak which had been in existence long before that volcanic tantrum of two centuries ago, the Gaia Spectacular, as he thought of it. It had been a landing pad for ships and extra-terrestrials for millennia, and an ultraviolet beacon always burnt on top. Invisible to sophisticated eyes, its light seemed, to many of the indigenous Islanders who'd seen it glowing palely on dark nights, like an ancestral connection with the infinite. And they were right. Familiar himself with such inter-stellar guidance systems, Finn locked on to its frequency, and landed.

As his feet met the once familiar earth a shudder of excitement went through him.

'Oh Mother,' he whispered as he knelt to kiss her.

'My son,' came the answering voice.

Whether it was the shock of physical contact after so long, or the emotion of reunion, tears welled up and he began to weep. Like a dragonfly struggling to emerge from its watery pupation into the lighter element of air, his frame trembled. 'Mother Gaia, help me,' he sobbed.

Gaia's voice became gentle. Quietly she suggested he might sit in the age-old lotus asana with the base of his spine in contact with her ground. The sensation was immediate and familiar. His father, a master of meditation, had taught him how to link the divine wisdom in himself with the deepest energy of the earth. He could tell that important connections were being formed for whatever was to come.

He then spent the rest of the night curled up on the peak. But with the dawn, as the sun's rays touched his back, he felt his body lifting up again. He'd taken enough nourishment to sustain him, but he wasn't yet ready to commit fully to material reality. There was a lot to consider. He wanted to watch the girl some more, and even Gaia's cryptic clues had hinted that Annya could hold the secret to his mission. Locating her should be easier now that he'd made these ground connections.

Meantime he'd practice a few touchdowns, skim around these wonderful craters, do a few minor avalanches with this yellow ochre stuff, mix in a handful or two of the red, toss it around and see how it looked against the cobalt sky. Then, after his fun, he'd look in on her, see how things were progressing, later in the day.

Also he'd begun feeling less queasy about human flesh. That initial repulsion, after tearing off from a world of such rare frequency, and travelling at the speed of thought, then coming across all those bodies on the beach, his shock was subsiding. It was time to move on and see what Annya was up to. Even from this distance he could detect the scent of the lotion she was rubbing onto her legs. He had a strong line to her now. The sun would soon be down. She was getting ready to go out for the evening.

He moved closer.

As he watched her setting off, freshly showered and dressed, he was already seeing her in a different light. Her clothing had an aura which lent the energy-field around her body frequencies of shimmer. He was very close, within touching distance now, and his heart beat faster. Merging into the greens and pinks of some vegetation clinging to the metal grid surrounding her dwelling as she passed by, he blew gently, and petals fell at her feet.

With a select and gift-wrapped wine in her bag, Annya pulled the gate shut, and strode the few metres of magenta-strewn pavement to the end of the street. Bougainvillea, leaning over the ironwork fence, were blowing in the breeze. As she turned the corner, her floaty organza shift moved with her body. Whatever they chose to throw at her, be it a room full of candles and crystals, napkins and silver service, or sitting cross-legged on the floor with nuts and dips, she would be ready. She was about to meet the English Couple.

Since her outing with Manfred, in spite of a few lingering qualms, she had begun to feel things were in hand now. Simon was with her, helping her. Things were falling into place in some meaningful way, and since this meaningfulness, vague though it was, coloured her new mood of confidence, she wasn't about to question it. The presence which had invaded her flat and her life might still be a mystery, but she could live with it. And if the worst came, she had at least one person on the end of a line to call, and maybe she was about to discover two more.

Finn, who'd stopped to do some whirlpools with the petals, caught up with her in time to hear her thinking, *What if they're useless, or worse, these English? What'd be worse? Better not start down that one, Anns. Think positive. Where is this dratted house though?*

She'd found the street easily enough, but the houses were set every-which-way, numbers out of sequence. Although it was barely ten minutes from her apartment, neither she nor Simon had ever ventured into this neighbourhood round the corner. It had shacks with dirty children running in and out alongside smart, substantial villas, all to the accompaniment of cooking smells from pavement braziers.

Finn watched. Annya had stopped to peer through wrought-iron gates into a well-kept landscaped garden with sprinklers at full tilt. This time he decided to observe only. He'd learned his lesson about trying to intervene; done his best for her earlier, but look how *that* had backfired. He saw her walk to the end of the street, turn and come back. She did the trip again, and children, running after her, began calling 'Allo mees' and pestering her for money. And when she showed them paper she'd written a number on, and asked if they knew where it was, they laughed and ran away.

As her footsteps began to sound less certain, he was also noticing the luminosity, which had bounced and sparkled around her at the outset, starting to fade. The sky, too, had grown dark before she spotted a modest house set back from the street, between two large villas. No number, but I could enquire here, she was thinking, as she tiptoed up the path expecting challenging voices and savage dogs. But she'd gone only a few steps when a young man in a loose white tunic ran out of the door calling, 'Annya, are you Annya? Hi! Come on in.'

Curious to see what kind of place these people lived in, Finn peered through the rattan blinds and gave the room a swift check. Civilised, airy, comfortable; he could have happily joined them on the sofas, drinking and nibbling. Life in these times didn't seem bad at all, particularly with such tantalising smells drifting in from a side room. He must investigate. He sidled along the balcony, slipped in through the kitchen window and began lifting lids from cooking pots. A sensation he'd not felt for ages sprang to life in his mouth. He was salivating! Picking up a wooden spoon, he dipped it into a pan, then stirred a few of its saffron-coloured drops into another. Then he held the glistening spoon to his nose. Delicious! But this succulent-looking sauce from this spicy smelling dish, which he'd no means of processing in his present state, was starting to make him homesick.

You're here to gather information, not to indulge old fashioned senses, he reminded himself. He hung around a while, listening, but the chatter seemed altogether insubstantial, nothing the least vital to his mission. So, bored, he zoomed back to his mountain.

Around midnight, Annya returned to her stuffy room feeling she had made a significant contact. The evening had gone well. Not wanting to overstep her welcome by launching into tales of the inexplicable, she'd decided to keep her anxieties to herself until she knew these people better. But to say she'd set out with a fistful of prejudices about them, from the moment formalities were done, and drinks were being poured, they were like old friends. They were *her sort*. True, she reflected, as she drew the bolt, securing her own door for the night, Tammy and Lester were into this meditation thing in a big way, but all the trappings she'd feared—smoky candles, chinking chimes, Red Indians lurking in the shadows—had been thankfully absent.

She kicked off her sandals, sank onto the edge of the bed and yawned. 'If you're listening Simon, thanks, you're brilliant. That phone number really hit bull's eye.'

Somewhere in the small hours she jerked upright, fully clothed, with damp organza clinging to her breast. She must have passed out. Struggling to orient herself, her head rattled like a discarded beer can someone had kicked in. Items of furniture were twirling and swirling a macabre minuet in her field of vision. Ceiling fans whirred, manically twisting bed-sheets into dancing partners. Her bedroom had become a haunted ballroom. She fell back on the mattress with sweat trickling down her face and neck, while bizarre colours fractured and exploded inside her head. Was she having the worst nightmare yet? Was it the wine? The food? Or, dear God! was it this abominable apartment?

'Manfred. Gotta ring him,' she gasped, dry mouthed. 'Wha' time's it?'

But she daren't look. The room was spinning. Forcing her eyelids open a fraction she glimpsed the grey light of dawn sidling through a chink in the curtains. She lay still, holding down her nausea. After a while the spinning seemed to settle into a swell, then a gentle rocking motion, and the next moment she was lying on the floor of a glass-bottom boat gazing into fathoms of water with shoals of rainbow fish swimming past.

When she opened her eyes again, it was the late morning sun that streamed in.

'OK Annya. Let me have it.'

Manfred, adorned in jungle-print shorts, stretched his legs. Their bronzed form, dappled by swaying shadows and golden light, looked for a moment like a sculpture she had once seen in a garden in Rome. Some Greek god or athlete.

As soon as she'd managed to pull on some clean clothes, she rang him, and he'd said, 'Can you meet me? There's this place up near the Monument. Turn off the main road, watch for a sign for San Orlando, left and left again. A rough track. It will take you to Carlos' estate. I am here now. Do you know it? Can you find it? If it's urgent, come.'

'It *was* urgent,' she said, sipping the drink he'd poured for her. Lemony. Chunks of ice. And Annya grateful to find herself cooling down as willowy strands of pepper trees moved above their heads.

'Well?'

'Well, you know you said—last time—as we were leaving—you said, maybe we haven't scratched the surface yet?'

'Ja.'

'Well, this is it. I mean, we hadn't. But now there's more. And again, I don't know where to start. But I'm not going to play games; I'm going to trust you. There's nothing else I can do. Manfred? OK?'

He nodded. She took a breath.

'I'm being haunted. That's it.'

She waited. But he went on with his drink, looking at her, saying nothing. No expression.

'OK then. Beginning at the beginning. Remember me telling you I almost got myself drowned? Well, that was only for starters.'

He nodded again.

She went over the scene, trying to tell it how it was, remembering, filling in all the detail. Missing clothes and key; grinning youths; making her way back and then not being able to get in because the door was locked. She'd tried it. Given it a good shake and a kick. Tried everything. Office shut for the night. Neighbours out. She told him the lot. The key inside the locked safe along with her wallet. Lost clothes folded by the bath.

97

'Manfred? How'm I doing? Shall I go on? There's more.'

'Let's have another drink,' he said. 'I'll put a splash of something stronger in it this time, OK?' And he reached for a bottle on the tray, some local white spirit. It was her turn to nod.

'Why isn't your face telling me you think I'm crazy? Why're you not interrupting, interrogating me?' she asked, almost pleading.

'If there's more, I want to hear it. Right to the end. All of it.'

'But why? What I'm saying is *crazy*. You can't *possibly* believe me. I don't believe it myself.' For the first time she felt she was going to break down. As he passed her the refilled glass her hand was shaking.

'Annya, my friend, you are putting this much trust in me, yes? Let me return the compliment. I'll listen all the way along to the end. OK?'

'But I don't understand. Why would you do this for me? Give me your time like this?'

'You say there is more? I shall listen with interest, and if you question me 'why', I shall tell you, this is my hobby. That the word? Hobby? It's my interest. Now, I see you looking with suspicion again. But maybe there is good reason you have suspicions. So! I am beginning to understand. Correct?'

Not sure of the required response, she nevertheless continued. 'Yes, unfortunately, but there's more and more to come. Curiouser and curi...'

'Ach! Your esteemed Charles Dodgson. Did he too not make curious explorations with mind-states, changed realities, dreams, visions? That why you bring him in?'

'Visions, dreams? It's odd you say that, Manfred. I was coming to that.'

'This I remember. At our first meeting, wasn't it? You told me, I think, how I trod upon your dream...'

You and your big feet, she said to herself, smiling.

'...with my big feet, ja? So Annya, are you an Alice travelling through the looking glass?'

'Christ! Manfred. Now *you're* spooking me, for shit's sake!'

Annya had been on the point of telling Manfred about the face in the looking glass when he'd leapt in with his Yeti feet and that reference to Alice. All this time she was so certain he wasn't going to believe her, yet desperate for his acceptance, and now he'd gone too far. Not only did he seem to be taking her story seriously, but he was seeing into her mind again. It was creepy—intrusive. As bad as having someone break into your flat, she thought. It would have been more comfortable if he'd tut-tutted and suggested a visit to one of his colleagues; one of the couch and notebook variety. At least that would have confirmed her sense of reality—the world would be as it had always been where a few unfortunates every now and again go cuckoo. Now though, to have him accept her out-of-kilter version of reality as a possibility—that was worse than patronising smiles and pats on the head.

'You've gone quiet again, Annya. Looking pale. You OK?'

'I'd better go home,' she said, limply.

'You sure? Home? What is it you mean by "home"?'

'Oh no, of course. I can't go home. England's home.'

'Back to your apartment then? This you want?'

She grabbed her bag and stood up.

'I must go.'

'But where, Annya?'

'I don't *know*. Oh...'

Her legs refused to move in any direction, and she collapsed onto the chair again, sobs beginning to shake her. Hating herself for letting him see her tears, she struggled for control. And he was stretching out his hand to touch her arm, but changed his mind.

'We'll go for a walk—round the garden,' he said gently. 'I show you. Come. You want to take my arm?'

She shook her head, but meekly got to her feet again. Robbed of the power of choice since no better solution presented itself, her legs were taking charge and seemed intent on following him. Probably the sanest thing to be doing anyway, she thought—as long as they didn't bump into any Red Queens.

'Tell me about this home, Annya. How did you come here. Not travelling alone, I guess? But you're alone now. Is that so?'

She went through the motions of filling him in, wary, not wanting to give too much away. If she let on about Simon and how his sudden departure left her bereft and vulnerable, that might not be too clever. So she chatted aimlessly, dropping in a mention of 'my English friends, Tamzin and Lester,' without admitting she'd only met them the night before.

'We'll take the scenic route,' Manfred announced suddenly. 'I'll show you round first—many fascinating things. So, this Simon? The boyfriend, yeh?'

'Well, not quite. Well, sort of. I mean we...' and the sentence faded.

Manfred's eyebrows rose. 'Meaning I shouldn't probe, or meaning what?' She'd sunk into gloom again. But he wasn't to be put off. He'd remain as sunny as the day itself. 'You like windmills?' he asked, pointing to the tops of some white vanes circling behind a group of farm buildings. There had to be some response to that.

There was, and her face brightened for an instant. 'Really! Do they work?'

'Sure. They work great. Ancient cranking. If we go close, inside the mill, we shall hear. You come again and maybe we taste our famous bread. I'll show you the pressing vats too. Blood red... amber wines. You must see. Massive casks you'd never believe, like giants. We'll sample, OK? Another day though, and I'll also show you dromedaries. Carlos, he breeds here. I've known him many years, but he is flown away just now. We'll make our introductions later. Ah, here we are!'

They'd wandered across a courtyard, an intricate pattern of cobbles with two beamed farmhouses, tall on either side. Obviously centuries old, Annya would have been bursting with curiosity about them normally. Any day but this, she'd have bombarded her escort with questions on the whole estate, and certainly quizzed him about the absent Carlos. Today, her surroundings barely existed. Even a primitive scullery hung about with outlandish implements and strange smells failed to draw comment. But when a narrow passage they were cutting through on the way to the garden finally ejected them into a dazzle of light and aromatic air, he ventured the hope, 'This you like?' He was rewarded.

'Manfred! It's incredible.'

Her delight seemed spontaneous and real.

'Oh, the scent—and *colour!* I've never seen a garden like it. Not here, not on the Island, I mean. No-one gets lilies and roses to grow here. It's so dry and everything. You need real soil, humus. Miguel would give his right arm to get results like these.'

'Miguel?'

'He's the gardener at the apartment. He does wonders with the stuff there, but... look! Jasmine over the arch. Here!' She broke off a sprig and held it to her face, then was on her knees, pressing the leaves of some herb. 'They're sweet, sort of lavendery. Do you know what it is?'

He shook his head. 'Not one I know. We shall ask Carlos. He's the expert. But come now.'

Pleased with himself, he began ambling off down a path between tall, herbaceous plants. 'Here,' he said, patting the bench he was easing himself onto. 'Sit. Breathe it all in.' This time she and her legs were in accord. She came—and sat, and Manfred held his breath. The sun beat down; Annya sighed. But it was carefully chosen, this arbour seat, and he was counting on nature, as he often did, to work with him. Annya, leaning back, nestling into the cool leafy trellis behind her, gazed up at the dappled light. Clambering overhead, sprawling, spilling out across the cobbles, was a cacophony of bougainvillea, a fluorescence of hibiscus, an entwinement of morning glory.

'Dear old Miguel, wouldn't he just love this. He's got every one of these—all these colours on our patios, and... Oh God, Manfred. It's my dream. It's all coming back.'

'How do you mean?'

'When I rang you this morning, remember? You know, I was in such a state. I'd just had another awful, incredibly disturbing dream. Absolutely desperate. I wanted to tell you. I did try, but when I started I realised I'd have to tell you all the other stuff first, otherwise... but I didn't get the chance to finish. You know—about what happened before.'

'Annya, please to God, go slower. I'm not with you. Before? Which before are we talking about?'

'Before I met you up at the bodega. After all that stuff about the key in the safe and my clothes and that, all folded with my sunglasses at the foot of the bath. And then there was that face in the mirror. And you freaking me with that Alice and the Looking Glass thing.'

'Face in the mirror? Better tell me that.'

'I will, but now, all this—these colours, Miguel and everything— it's brought the dream back, the part I'd forgotten. And I'd better tell you that before I forget *that* again. So I'd better do that first. But I'm not sure how well I *can* remember. It's so... fractured, horribly unlike a dream. You're going to ask me what I mean by "unlike". Well, it was too vivid. More real than real, and yet impossibly unreal.' She paused. 'Like I was being visited.'

'A visitation.'

'Don't freak me again, please, Manfred. But I suppose, yes. A visitation. They came into my room. That's what made me think, is it this room that's haunted? Not the wine the night before?'

He couldn't help it. None of this was making sense, but he had to smile. Her gobbledygook had a crazy logic to it. Even so, maybe she was missing a trick or two. Not haunted wine, but how about spiked? What kind of people were these English, the 'my good friends, Tammy and Lester?' How well did she know them? But she was off again before he could get his thoughts out.

'God, you know, Manfred, I really think I just can't go back to that room. I have to get out of it soon anyway. You know, the next lot of visitors—meaning holidaymakers this time. They're due in a couple of weeks, and I have to be out of there. I should be getting ready to go back home, to England. But there's all this business with Simon. I haven't told you about that either.'

'Hold it, hold it, Annya. Give me a chance to catch up. Business about Simon, now. This is too much complications, even for me. I begin to understand how it is for you. You introduce multiple reasons for concern. I can't keep pace. But I see now why you are so stressed. And you leave all this telling to the last moment, so now it's getting late, and unfortunately I have another appointment to keep. I don't wish to see you in turmoil, with no place safe to return to. I really sympathise, but there is not much I can immediately suggest. I must think.'

'Manfred, please, you mustn't worry about me. I'll be all right. Really. I'm OK in daylight. I can go back. I'll be OK. It's just... sleeping there. But honestly, I'm fine.'

'Let me think, Annya. We have these five more minutes, and I wish you would finish just one item. Why don't you tell me about your visitation before we have to leave.'

'I think that might be a good idea, if you can bear to hear me out. I'll make it snappy.'

'But calm,' he insisted. 'No hurry. Make it clear.'

'Well. This incredible figure came into the room. Only there was a whole lot of vivid colours first. Flying round and round. The room, it seemed to be spinning out of control. Oh, I don't know, I thought... you see, I was soaked in sweat and thought, I'm having a bad trip.

Either that or it's a stroke—only aren't I too young? But I knew I hadn't done any stuff, not to my knowledge, but they might have, you know... spiked...'

'Who *they*? The Englander?'

'Yeh, but they seemed so straight. Never know though, do you? Anyhow he was dressed in all these colours, the youth. Magentas, pinks, morning glory blues, scarlets, greens. Glowing. But that's nothing like it. It wasn't a *glow*. Vivid isn't it, either. Radiant, possibly. It was more, electric, but so powerful you almost couldn't bear to look. Just like the face in the looking glass. That too. Blinding. Yet like no human being I'd ever seen. Indescribably strange, but beautiful beyond anything. Well, this boy dressed in all these colours whirling around... so fast, it was making me sea-sick. It was *him*.'

'*Which* him?' For God's sake, he added silently.

'The face in the looking glass. But like a tiny angel.'

'Annya, you've lost me again. Slow down. This is the face you saw when? You saw him before?'

'Yes. Before I met you. I'd seen him when I got back into my room, and found my key locked in the safe, and all my stuff folded in the bathroom. He was in the mirror.'

'This boy?'

'It *was him*. The same face.'

'Tell me, Annya. Was this a dream too—in the bathroom?'

'No. Absolutely not.'

'How? What was different?'

'Oh, everything. Everything real, solid. You could smell things, touch them. I even banged myself on the wash-basin. I could show you the bruise. And it *wasn't* my head I knocked. So you see... Everyday, solid, real, except the face in the mirror. But that was blindingly clear.'

'OK. But you say, *they*. Are we having more, or two of him now?'

'No. There was a man with him. He just stood there, but much more human-looking. He certainly wasn't an angel, but he didn't have a solid body either. I mean it wasn't a ghost or anything, but sort of... you know... flimsy-filmy. But he was real alright. Large as life, recognisable. Without the beard he could have been your brother.'

ROLLING CARPETS

Finn zoomed back to spend another night on the peak. Strange that this exposed place gave him such a sense of peace, he thought. It was as though Gaia, having coaxed him down, was now contriving to nestle him in her arms. Maternal conscience, maybe. But he wouldn't be rushed. He was in no hurry to take on a full physicality. The energy his etheric body was receiving from her would do him well enough for the moment. Yet in spite of her motherly concern a shadow of loneliness had begun to creep up on him.

There was the girl, of course, Annya. From the moment he'd seen her struggling in the ocean some instinct had alerted him to her plight. Yet look what happened there: his actions had only managed to cause fear. He was beginning to think his sensitivities might not be well enough attuned to this epoch, even though his intentions were of the best. He'd followed her into her home—only meant to keep a friendly eye on her—but she'd caught sight of him, and that had been enough to tip her into a state of emotional unbalance.

That in itself was curious—that she'd *seen* him. No-one else down here had noticed a thing. So Gaia's hints about her being a significant factor in helping him with this enigma might have hit the mark after all. Annya's instincts must be a great deal better honed to the needs of these times than his. 'Strange, mother Gaia,' he yawned, 'but these Earth rhythms of yours seem to be having a powerful effect on me all of a sudden. Feels like my balance must have gone askew. Did we have a sunset? I hardly noticed, but it's gone dark completely. It's making me want to fold up.'

An irresistible urge to curl himself into a foetal shape overtook him, but the instant his head touched the ground, everything seemed to dissolve into a well of blackness. Yet, only seconds later, it seemed, he was sitting up, stretching, yawning again, and rubbing his eyes. There, cross-legged by his side, watching him in the moonlight, sat a familiar figure. Like some Buddhist sage, his posture was so still, his expression so serene, he might have been sitting there for minutes, hours or weeks.

'Mandy?' Finn whispered, barely audible.

The face, which in the cool light of the moon had looked to be carved from stone, came alive. The eyes gleamed, the cheeks grew warm in tone.

'Mandy!'

His visitor cleared his throat with a little cough, then smiled. 'How's things, Finn my boy? Give us a hug.'

Overjoyed. No other word would do. Finn leapt to his feet, hugged and hugged his friend, his old mentor, and Mandelbrot hugged him back. Finn grabbed him by both hands and pulled him up, then round, until they were spinning and dancing like a couple of kids. As they came to a gradual halt, Finn released the older man's hands and stood back. This was a very human human-being, beard and all. Yet it wasn't difficult to see that both their bodies were of that peculiar, and to earth-eyes, insubstantial material, ether. And not only their bodies, but their clothing, too, shimmered as if lit from within by an unearthly brilliance. Mandelbrot, careless as always of his own image, was attired in the same cords and shirt he'd put on that morning, long ago, before he'd hurtled through the dimensions to make his bewildered appearance in front of a group of twenty-third century beings on a twenty-third century lawn. His concession to fashion, which had always been a source of amusement to the infant Finn, consisted of a few subtle changes of colour from day to day as the fancy took him. Simply by throwing a mental switch, his tutor had varied the tones of his shirt and pants to suit his mood. Whereas Finn's tastes often ran to extremes. Even with the simple tunic and leggings the kids had worn in class, he managed to display a bewildering array of hues and ever-changing patterns. The psychedelic parrot suit, Mandelbrot had called it, teasingly.

Mandelbrot eyed him. 'A lot of water under the bridge since we last met, eh, Finn? It may be the effect of this moonlight, but...' His pupil's exotic tastes, he was noticing, seemed to have matured somewhat. 'You've changed!' he said, pointedly fingering the pearly silkiness of Finn's sleeve. 'And for the better. Only to be expected, I suppose.'

'You like it?' Finn asked, pleasure colouring his voice. 'So Mandy! But you haven't changed a bit, I'm glad to see. We're both still in the same dimensional vibration we were before, which means I don't have to bother descending into a flesh and blood body like our brothers and sisters down here have to manage, just to give you a hug.'

'Is that the problem, Finn my boy? I heard on the grapevine that you're finding things down here in physical reality a bit tricky. They sent me in case you needed me, to give you a hand, you know.'

'And you'll never believe how glad I am to see you,' Finn whooped. 'Whether I need you holding my hand is another matter. I'm taking my time, Mandy, but I think I am working things out—slowly. Anyhow, who is this "they" you mention?'

'Surely you know who they are. The back-up. The Council. You've been intercepting our signals haven't you?'

'I tuned to the beaming-down signals the other night, but there's been nothing more communicative so far. In fact I'm still pretty well in the dark. Gaia, she's been making her presence felt, *and* in the most substantial way. But if this mission is as crucial for the Earth and mankind as she tells me, I have to admit I'm just a touch worried. Frankly it sounds way beyond my capabilities—at present, that is.

109

'A bit of a challenge, eh, my boy? Even for the strange and precious? Well, here's yours truly, at your service. You didn't think they'd leave you floundering about on your own, did you? Didn't she mention—?'

'I'm not exactly floundering, Mand. Just taking my time reconnoitring. But it's a real man-sized job, you know. Bigger than anything anyone has been presented with before. It's going to, well, initiate the most enormous transformation in the earth's consciousness. Save—'

'Save the world? You're going to save the world single-handed, is that it, S and P?'

'You don't need to call me by that silly name any more, you know, and of course I don't have illusions of that sort; it's just, well, overwhelming. Possibly the most crucial undertaking ever, if what Gaia hints at is to be trusted, and there are moments when I wonder if the Council might be playing with me. No-one gave me a clue beforehand what to expect. I just got this summons to report to Earth, and was told all would unfold. You know, like a carpet rolled out in front of me. But I didn't imagine things were going to turn out quite this way.'

'Rolled out? Expecting the red carpet treatment, were we?'

'I've no idea what you're talking about, Man,' he replied, vexation beginning to creep in. 'Is that one of your old twentieth-century concepts again? You were always coming up with anachronisms.'

'My word, Finn. Where did you learn that one? Anachronisms. That was one you never knew in the old days when you were a kid.'

'No idea, Mandy, where it came from. It just mm... popped into my head. But all sorts of words are doing that, sort of materialising for me now. Ones I never knew before. They arrive, er, as and when— when necessary, it seems.'

'Well, my boy, it...'

'And you don't have to call me that either, Mandy.'

'OK Finn, man to man then. As long as you don't go calling me Man, and me calling you man. That could get irritating. This anachronism, then. If you *do* know what it means, you'd know that you're right back where I was before I dropped in on your time-reality, back in the old days. Except they were future days. Complicated, isn't it? But we're here together now, in the Now. And you're grown up and light-years ahead of me, except you ain't. Oh, let's forget all this time-warp stuff and give ourselves a hug again. You'll never know how much I've missed you, Finn.'

'And I've missed you, Mandy.'

They hugged some more, and danced around, patting backs. And the more they danced, the more Finn began to feel exactly like that tiny child he'd been when both of them began to sense that special bond. And not only were tears forming in Finn's eyes, but the old man was wiping his too.

'Mandy, you don't suppose I'm dreaming you, do you?'

'What makes you think that?'

'Oh, I dunno, but this all feels rather strange—the way I fell into a dead sleep just now, as if someone had slipped me herb-drops, and then—there you were. Anyhow, here you *are*, and I'm touching you, so you must be here.'

'And I'm touching you, Finn my boy. Anyhow, I'm here, as far as I know, unless I'm dreaming you. But let's not get into that stuff. Dreams are mysterious things, as I'm sure you know. After all, you were off on dream-trips as I remember it, while you were still wet behind the ears. If you want me to give you the latest research on that and related matters, I'd be only too glad. Dreaming *was* my pet subject. But I don't think that's what you're after right now, so why don't you tell me where things stand with you and this challenge. You say it's overwhelming, but you haven't got a clue what it is. That right? Why don't we sit down?'

So they walked around the peak a while until they found a comfortable perch, a rock with a view of the early dawn-streaked sea, and Finn told him what he'd gathered so far. Hints gleaned from Gaia;

things he'd learned from observing the lie of the land. Various conversations he'd dropped in on, in particular certain intimations he'd picked up from Annya, plus a few of her recent contacts.

'I don't have any hard facts as yet, Mandy. Not much I can communicate in words. You understand what I mean, don't you? What I'm picking up from viewing individual energy-fields are mind-pictures, colours and occlusions. But these tell me a great deal.'

'Tell you about *what*, these occlusions?'

'You know, Mandy. At the simplest, level one, there's a whole lot of brain junk. The business that really interests me, though, is deeper in. Only this flotsam swarming about among the clearer colours is easier to describe. Inner monsters—I've seen some real horrors. Even got the features to go with it, some of 'em.'

'You mean faces?'

'Yes. Mean and ugly. But mainly they're just a lot of dark sticky lumps covered in suckers. Mental plane stuff.'

'But what do they tell you, Finn?'

'At a guess I'd say they're everything their owners refuse to own—squashed down.'

'Squashed down?'

'Repressed. Denied. What makes them so dangerous is they're packed with energy, ready to spring out, letting off a few emotional fireworks as they go. Then of course there's the stuff that can't get out, the rigi-frigids. Frozen desponds and cesspits, toxic suckers and that. Even more terrifying.'

'Good God, man! Fine picture you're painting of the human race. This what you're seeing with your Annya?'

'No, this is all general stuff—what I've been noticing in the crowd on the sand, down in the streets. And you did ask about occlusions.'

'OK. But when you say, *crowd*... Just checking, you understand.'

'Well, it's something else I'm getting a feel of. They're not all the same. There seem to be three races here on the Island—one set which clump together like they're desperate to cram something in. They jet in in these flying machines, then stuff indiscriminately, drug themselves with substances, swallow smoke, all the time subjecting themselves to a blare of sound, then fly out again. These are the ones I saw when I first came back, strung out along the beach like racks of self-basting fowl.

'Then there's a stable population, less slumpen, still managing to carry themselves with a touch of dignity. They seem to make a living off this first group while quietly despising them. But the really interesting set—and there are far too few of these—are the Indigenous. A rooted race I think, going back thousands of years. I want to know more about these. But they all have dark clouds to some extent. It's the sort of garbage most humans down here seem to collect. They're drowning in it. Annya's not all that different, mind you, but I'm looking further in with her. You get a history of mankind, when you really look deep into a person. It's quite an art, you know, this extra-physical viewing. All of human evolution is there.'

'"Holistic vision", they called it in my day.'

'Don't know about your day, Mandy. For me, when I scan I'm seeing multi-dimensionally, and that's where words run out, because words are train-track, one after another in a line, unlike telepathy which sees the whole multi-dimensional picture. And this is why people in your world were so limited. Track-minded. Linear.'

Mandelbrot nodded. He seemed to know exactly what Finn meant. What the boy could see deep down, he couldn't communicate, because the world they were now in hadn't yet found means to express the All and Everything, All-at-once-ness that he saw unfolding in this one person. He probably glimpsed the mystery of his own past and future in her too. But now that his feet were becoming rooted in Gaia's present consciousness, he was beginning to sense and share the fear of what he saw. Empathy, he called it. He was proud of his boy. Done some growing-up after all. He seemed to be attuning himself to the vocabulary people were using in these times, too. Either that, or the Council were feeding him suitable translations.

'Agreed. Three-D or even four-D info is a limited tool, Finn, taken by itself. But the guys in this era set a lot of store by it. Blinkered bastards. Something tells me, though, that things are about to change regarding this narrow-band perception, and maybe this is where we—that is *you*—are about to come in. Whad'ya think?'

'I think you may be right, Mandy. Great changes, that's what Gaia said. Though she didn't specify. So that allows us a lot of leeway, doesn't it? We could *really* go to town.'

'And what precisely had you in mind?' On second thoughts, Mandelbrot thought, Finn's growing up was still somewhat patchy judging by the way his shape kept shifting, adult to child and back again. 'Not sure *town* is where I'd want us to go, unless I know what leeway you're aiming for.'

'That's metaphorically speaking, Mand. OK?' The joy at having his old mentor around was in danger of diluting just a smidgen if it meant his style was going to be cramped. This was *his* show. His assignment. Impossible it might look at first sight, but they must have believed him capable of cracking it or they wouldn't have given it to him.

Mandelbrot studied him, and Finn started to feel uncomfortable. Undoubtedly his own energy field was being scrutinised, *and* beginning to change colour to boot. He was back in the schoolroom.

'Metaphorically speaking, hey Finn? Classrooms?'

'Jeez, Mandy. This is a bit too close for comfort. I'd forgotten how sharp your scanning could be with that mind-reading of yours. Well, if you want me to pick metaphysics with you, you'd know that outside of linearity, neither past nor future exist, so going *back* doesn't happen, any more than going forward. Everything that happens, happens now. And that's why several layers of my energy field are warming up right this minute. I'm being caught out like the naughty child. So *that* puts us in our place nicely, wouldn't you say? You professor, me kid.

Kid with grandiose ideas. Kid with infantile ego problems. Doesn't want to share his big deal with anyone.'

'Classrooms exist, Finn. We never get away from them. However far we go, we're never anywhere but Here, and Here's where classrooms bump into us. They just keep coming around. Classrooms, challenges, vacations—then classrooms again.'

'Do I take it that this "we" includes yourself, Mandy? School without Teacher doesn't make sense.'

'Of course it includes Yours Truly. We *all* come back to class, but who teaches whom, who sets the questions, who decides the answers, doesn't always go the way you'd expect. So, how about it? Hadn't we better get down to business and start chewing on this challenge of yours? Neither of us has any answers right now, but at least you've made a start.'

'You think so?' Finn looked pleased.

'You've been communicating with the Lady Gaia herself, you tell me. What did she have to say? Whatever it was it's put you into a tizzy. Consciousness changes, Earth transformation. Sounds to me like you're about to get involved in this Quantum Leap stroke Civilisation-Crunch Catastrophe. The Big Bang that's goin' to put the lights out for Good and All scenario. We're talking Armageddon, I take it?'

'Arm a—?' But Mandelbrot cut him short.

'Gaia's no fool. She's already made her contingency plans, no doubt. But she's giving us humans a last chance, and that's why she sent for you—along with a multitude of other lightwarriors from out there. So don't get ideas that you're some latter-day, end-times Saviour. Precious you may be, but you're nothing special, and you've been out of the picture, vacating, a long time. Nothing wrong with that. You've been gathering other kinds of experience that might come in handy.

'Let's look at what we've got so far, then, Finn. Have you picked up anything useful from these reconnoitrings and scannings?'

'Actually, since you ask, something interesting seems to be

happening right now. I'm getting whines and clicks in my ears. Earlier this evening, before I fell asleep up here, I'd been observing Annya.'

His tutor eyed him. The old, aye, aye. The 'my little eye' from his childhood, look. But Finn brushed it away.

'Anyhow, she's on a mission of her own—also following signals,' he said. 'But she's blind to their source or importance.'

'Is this what your scanning tells you?'

'The girl's confused and very scared. I can see this clearly. At war with herself. But along with all the freak-show monsters battling away inside her, there's a million-watt light-show trying to get out.'

Angel wrestling contest? Mandelbrot wondered, but didn't bother to say it.

'Nevertheless,' Finn streamed on, 'it's all led up to this meeting, this man and woman. My sense is that they have some vital knowledge, though I'm not sure *they* realise its significance either. So this is one piece of the puzzle. Anyhow, another vital clue...'

He looked about to draw breath and rush on, but Mandy slowed him down. 'Take your time, for Chris'sake, Finn.' But Finn seemed unable to stem his flow.

'Anyhow,' he continued, 'this healer guy, sort of shaman or doctor, he's already playing a major role. He has feelings of protectiveness—fondness for her.'

'Who her, Finn?'

'Annya, of course. While you and I were fooling about spinning and dancing a while ago, she picked up our energy.'

'You know that, Finn, do you?' Mandelbrot asked sarcastically. But Finn either didn't hear or ignored it.

'She's an interesting case, Annya. I see her awareness developing fast, so some parts of her mind are beginning to work at deep unconscious levels, and some at quite high levels of multidimensional intelligence. Yet her 3D linear consciousness is rebelling against what she's discovering. So much so that she's off balance in quite an extraordinary way. Fortunately, this healer guy—I'm getting him strongly now—Jeez, Mand, wait a minute, he looks like you! Take off your beard, dress you in decent clothes, and you could be brothers.'

'Steady on, Finn. You sure what you're seeing?'

'I know what I'm seeing alright, but as to what it means...'

PHANTOM POTATOES

Manfred fiddled with his pen and notepad, drummed the desktop and frowned. 'Don't worry,' Annya had told him, waving cheerily as he watched her get into her car yesterday up at Carlos' estate. 'I'll be fine,' she'd insisted again as the ignition fired.

Annya's case had him hooked. Her plight bothered him, her mental state troubled him. She shouldn't be left alone in that apartment, he felt sure. Not that she was in danger from your average flesh and blood sneak-thief—although such characters abounded these days—but, in his estimation, the real threat was that these paranormal visions she was having were tipping her into a mild psychosis. His professional opinion was—and he underlined one of his scribbled notes—that he should persuade her to return home to whatever family she possessed and seek treatment. Hopefully it was only a temporary condition. He could emphasise that when he next spoke to her. Away from the trigger locale and its attendant associations, in the right hands, with a sympathetic and intelligent doctor, she'd be—what was that phrase?—back to normal in no time. That would do.

But this clinical view existed in one compartment of his mind only: his true feelings spoke otherwise. This 'sympathetic, intelligent doctor' in England who'd put her back on her feet, was a load of hooey. The only such doctor he knew of, he told himself, lived here, on the Island. And his name was Manfred Haandel. Yet where was she to go in the meantime? He had to get her out of that room, and he was racking his brains.

He put his pen down and fell to gazing out of the window, chin cupped in hand.

Thanks to a bequest from a favourite aunt, Manfred, in the last few years, had found himself free to indulge an ever-active curiosity about the nature of the human being, body, mind, spirit, as well as a few other passions of his. These included experiments with alternative cures. This change of direction had really begun in Germany, much further back; soon after he'd qualified, in fact, though it didn't arise as a conscious decision until some years later.

The arching spray of the garden sprinkler was at work on a patch of grass under some palms just outside the window. Watching vacantly as it twirled from side to side, his mind began to wander to a conversation he'd once had with Carlos.

'It was a while back now,' he'd told him, 'in my early days as a medic. Eager young chap came to see me, Carlos, thinking about entering the profession, you know. Well, he wanted to discuss his future with me and during our chat he let it drop he'd been investigating alternative medicine. Told me he'd visited this acupuncturist. Been given some herbal concoction, he said, which had done wonders for him. I'm ashamed to admit it but I stupidly lost my temper. Climbed on my high-horse. Denounced the boy's beliefs—threw the book at him. Quackery. Mumbo-jumbo. Anything else that came to mind. There I stood, pompous and ridiculous in my shiny white coat, pockets stuffed with qualifications, standard-bearer of modern medicine—knowing it all. When actually all I was doing was spouting the traditional line of my contemporaries, and tub-thumping on about placebos and how gullible could the fellow be to fall for all that nonsense.'

'I'd like to have been a fly on that wall of yours!' Carlos had laughed. 'But actually I can see it perfectly.' He'd stood up. Pouring himself a Laphroiag, he handed another to Manfred. 'So, you old reprobate, did your barbs prick him?' he asked. 'Finish him off?'

Manfred knocked back the whisky, savouring it in his throat before replying. 'Far from it, I'm glad to say. The young rascal rounded on me. "Tell me Herr Doktor," he demanded, "which of us is the smarter? The one who analyses, diagnoses, consults list of drugs and scribbles prescriptions? Or the one who believes, and is cured?" I was the one deflated, Carlos—though, you can be sure I gave nothing away—not even to myself, for many years.'

Manfred had become silent. But after a pause he'd said, 'I know rather less today, my friend, but in the painful process of shedding useless knowledge, I think you'll agree, I've learnt much more.'

Certainly much had changed. Now, thanks to the cushioning of that will, and, at the age of fifty-six, fit as a flea, Manfred was semi-retired. His was the luxury of being able to take on a handful of the most interesting patients. He made his selection either from the well-off, who came to him as eager to unload liberal amounts of cash as they were to be relieved of inconvenient symptoms, or from the impecunious unwell. These deserving but unusual cases had little chance of getting the time-consuming attention they needed elsewhere.

His friendship with Carlos had strengthened over the years. Not long after Manfred settled in the Island in the late seventies, he came to realise that the Spaniard owned much of the land around the place. Breeder of horse and camel, collector of art, this suave and, by local standards, sophisticated Carlos was investing much of his fortune in grand schemes. His particular obsession, a complex of Eighteenth Century farm buildings where he now lived, gained him the reputation for being *public benefactor number one*.

Finding himself seated next to a local estate manager at a friend's dinner party, Manfred soon understood why. No-one, according to the manager, involved themselves in the welfare of his workers, nor in the care of his animals as much as this grandee. And the fact that he was also prepared to roll up his sleeves and get his hands dirty on occasions clinched his popularity among the Islanders. Unsurprisingly, Carlos was on most of the Island committees too, including the ones which regulated medical standards.

It wasn't long before Manfred had wangled himself an introduction to this, the Island's most celebrated son. Luckily, he and Carlos hit it off almost immediately, and the friendship had grown to a point where he felt it possible to confide in him some of his most troubling thoughts—problems he couldn't always share with his own wife, Matilda.

'Can I speak frankly,' Manfred had asked one day when he and Carlos had been walking through one of the walled gardens surrounding two of the old farm buildings. It was a few years back now. Carlos had only recently taken over the estate, and Manfred, at the time, was still feeling his way into his own plans to diverge from conventional medical practice.

'This must be something serious, amigo,' Carlos said with a smile. 'Surely you know me well enough by now. You have my ear at all times... As you have access to my cellar. Is this not so?'

Somewhat reassured, Manfred set about explaining his dilemma. He took out a handkerchief and wiped his face—it was a warm day. 'I guess you know that I've been experimenting with certain alternative practices.'

Carlos laughed. 'I know most of what you get up to, you old dog. Now! Is there something I've missed? Spit it out. Are you in trouble?'

'It's because I'm hoping to avoid trouble that I need to talk things over. You realise then, I've been testing out a few unorthodox remedies from time to time—for a while now, in fact. But I've always been careful to sound out my patients first.'

'And only treat those you can rely on to keep quiet, huh?' Carlos chuckled. 'Presumably you manage to justify this to yourself? Come! What is it you want to discuss? You realise Manfred, I have my spies!'

Manfred swallowed. These jokes of Carlos weren't so funny. The Spaniard knew him better than he knew himself. Always knows which buttons to press, anyhow, he thought, wiping his brow again.

'Come! We'll sit here in the shade.' With an expansive sweep of his arm, Carlos indicated a seat. 'Feeling more comfortable, now?' he asked mischievously as Manfred lowered himself onto the bench.

'OK, tell me frankly,' Manfred began. 'What's the talk among your friends on the bench—the Council? They're saying I'm overstepping the mark, are they?

Carlos took out his own handkerchief, but instead of wiping his face, he unfolded it, spread it out and appeared to be studying the folds like a map as he spoke. 'Maybe I can put your mind at rest,' he said quietly. 'It's unusual even for a quack such as yourself, Haandel, to veer into these areas—naturopathy—energy medicine—whatever it is you get up to. But it isn't actually against any law pertaining in the Island at present.'

'But, in these areas? Without recognised qualification?' Manfred inquired tentatively.

'I can't guarantee that is how things will be indefinitely, amigo, but for now, that's permitted. Of course we keep our eye on you and assure ourselves you stay well within ethical boundaries—according to our codes.' Carlos grinned. Not for the first time, Manfred noticed his teeth were unnaturally white. 'We both know our native Islanders have used such remedies, and to great effect, for hundreds of years. If we pass laws for one, we must pass for all. And at present what works well—we don't intend to fix.'

If Manfred's mind wasn't entirely at ease as their discussion had drawn to an end, at least he seemed to have Carlos' approval. Their deliberations had been robust, but amicable. He'd got things off his chest, and at the end of the day he had the knowledge that his carefully selected clients were as eager to keep his procedures to themselves as they were keen to have access to them.

He reflected on this as his hand trailed doodles on his notepad. It must have been fifteen years ago, that conversation with Carlos, and his practice had flourished in that time. Yet Annya knew nothing of his reputation, he was sure. Their meeting had been pure chance, and though he'd offered her help that day at the Bodega, she'd made it clear it was unwelcome. A young woman alone in a bar, she'd been suspicious of him right from the start, and he was never the person to press attention on anyone. Yet... Pure chance? Was it chance that she'd come across that dud phone number, and it had led her directly back to him? The whole thing could have been a cunning device to entrap him; her tale a pack of lies; but if so, her act was professional to a degree. No, her story was far too incoherent to have been rehearsed. Her physical presentation, the sweating, the pallor, the charming naivety, her embarrassed blushes, her... No. All this would have been impossible to contrive. And now that she was beginning to trust him he mustn't let her down.

He'd thought long and hard about how he was to get her out of that place, and had a word with his wife about putting her up in the nanny's room. But she wouldn't buy it.

'But look, Tilda,' he'd said as they had relaxed together in the lounge the previous evening, 'we're just a middle-aged couple, my dear, in danger of growing self-centred, don't you think? A bit of young blood about the place... A fresh face.' He'd smiled fondly into his wife's familiar features. She didn't smile back. He'd tried another tack.

'Our own children... Of course we were delighted for them, proud, then secretly relieved when all three of 'em left.' Now she was glaring. This wasn't going well. 'You surely don't deny you felt just a little bit pleased. No? Oh well! But it gave you opportunities, my love, freedom to travel.' Conscious of Matilda's frozen face and stiff shoulders as she suddenly sat upright in the armchair, but still convinced his powers of persuasion would melt her resistance, he pressed on. 'And you have to admit you were proud when Helmut got into that prestigious school you were so keen on. Then the twins at universities in Salamanca and

Heidelberg. But they're long ago gone now, and with my practice taking up more and more time, Annya might...' he twiddled his fingers. 'Well, you know how you're always complaining of being dogsbody here, running the house, acting secretary, tea-maker and handholder for my private patients. You'd like her, I'm sure. She could be... You know, a sort of home-help-cum-receptionist for a while. Give you back some of that freedom.'

But Matilda's face flushed with anger now as she pulled herself to her feet. 'Who is this Annya,' she demanded, 'that you're so keen to have her run my house? The girl knows no German, very little Spanish. In fact, Manfred, she's completely *clueless*, and *far* too pretty.'

'Oh ooh now. Come, darling, come! I'd thought better of you than this.' He was taken aback by the vehemence in her voice. 'If you only met her, spoke with her, understood how urgent her case is.'

'I have,' she snapped. 'Remember?'

'When did you meet her?' Manfred sounded nonplussed.

'I've spoken with her!' And his usually sweet-tempered wife strode out of the room, slamming the door.

'If that's how it's going to be with you! Annya's no femme fatale! The last thing she needs is your stupid suspicions!' Pretty? How did she know that? He was sure they hadn't met. 'And besides, you got telephone x-ray eyes now?' he shouted after her. But her brisk footsteps had reached the end of the corridor. Hell! Maybe he had pushed things a bit, he realised, sinking back into his chair. I let my mouth run away with my brains. Was I really stupid enough to think she'd welcome the idea? So, it's plan B then. Except I don't have any plan B.

There was Carlos, of course, but he'd been visiting his estates in Sri Lanka, and Manfred wasn't sure if he was back yet. He'd half a mind to contact Salvador, his farm manager, though. This was an emergency after all. Carlos trusts me, he told himself. Virtually grants me the run of the place when he's away, and old Salvador's wife might be a bit more accommodating than Matilda. They're a good natured couple.

They won't mind making up a bed—perhaps in the old mill. On second thoughts, that could set Annya's imagination off again. It might be a romantic place in daylight, but alone and late at night, with the wind creaking the wooden sails, it could seem even creepier than that apartment of hers. No. What she needs is a cosy little room; four walls, a window with a view over the garden, and a door she can lock.

But even as he let his thoughts run on he knew it was all fantasy. I shan't give up though, he told himself. Something's bound to occur to me.

In another part of the Island, a high place with an overview, another conversation had been taking place. Destinies were converging.

'I've had an idea, Finn,' Mandelbrot announced. 'You're keen to go to town. That right? Well then, how about this...'

After taking her leave of Manfred at the estate, Annya drove back to the apartment and the rest of the day had passed without event. She even managed a sleep free of dreams. Yet in spite of a better night than she'd had for some time, the room still felt claustrophobic, and Simon's absence was overpowering. While they'd been together the walls had never been this close, she thought, nor the furniture so intrusive. It felt airless now, as though Simon's presence itself had been enough to lighten and open up the space around them.

Even so, she decided, her visit with Manfred had made a huge difference. Things *were* improving. She felt differently about herself, better able to cope. She could even begin picking up her life once more. She could phone Tammy and Lester—maybe suggest meeting up again. Even give them a meal in return. Not here at the apartment though. Somewhere on neutral ground. Invite them down town. That nice restaurant down by the harbour, a table on the veranda, lights twinkling on the water, lots of people. She could manage that. Besides, she needed to get out and about. Do her good. If afterwards she still had her suspicions about them, at least she'd have done the hospitable thing, but wouldn't need to see them again.

The long balcony of Restaurante Oceana leant out over the harbour. The sea lapped, and shoals of tiny fish were playing hide among umber blotched pebbles in the shallows, while sea birds swooped, picking off an easy supper. Above the water a burble of laughter mingled with the sound of popping corks and clinking glasses. Toasts were being offered to the setting sun, while the luminous roses and violets streaking the sky melted into the incoming tide, and tinged the upheld goblets and upturned faces of the diners.

Annya, smiling as she and her two companions took their seats at the table overlooking the sea, glanced from one to the other approvingly. They'd really made an effort this evening, she thought. Lester, tieless in a cool and comfortably expensive Italian job, and Tamzin in subtle sands and greys; a hand-blocked silk number with tiny flecks of volcanic orange which Annya had drooled over when she'd seen one like it in an exclusive boutique in the old city.

'To friendship.' Lester, smiling, lifted his glass to Annya.

'No, we'll do it this way, Lester,' insisted his wife, her cheeks aglow, and she demonstrated a drinking ritual she'd learned from an Island couple recently. Pouring Annya and her husband an inch or so of aperitif, she recited a toast in the native dialect, then directed them to lean closer across the table, and toss back their tipple with arms entwined. 'It binds us together in fellowship,' she enthused. Annya managed the manoeuvre almost without a spill, then sat back gazing at the sea. With the kiss of sky on her face, and a warm breeze on her bare shoulders, she savoured a moment of perfection. The collective mood of gaiety was infectious. She'd already made up her mind to leave suspicion behind, to relax and enjoy, from the moment they'd arrived and Lester steered them to this balcony seat. 'What will you ladies have?' he'd asked, hailing a passing waiter.

'Oh! Lester, no. This evening's my treat,' Annya, clutching her hands, had urged.

He'd brushed the offer away. 'Won't hear of it. So, what are we having? Annya?'

This trifle of convention settled, and Island rituals observed, they were ensconced with their glasses when another waiter appeared for food orders. This one was so handsome, and his English so good, that Annya, after tossing a few light-hearted compliments in his direction, embarked on an intimate conversation with him before she noticed how her tongue had loosened. The waiter even forgot himself to the extent that he pulled up a chair beside her and busily regaled her with tales of his previous career on a Canadian cruise liner. Remembering her guests suddenly, Annya turned, putting her hand to her mouth in confusion. 'What am I thinking? How rude!' But apart from some amusement at this ex-sailor's chat-up lines, they seemed content with basking in the evening peace, thinking their own thoughts. Lester waived her apology away. 'Sundown casting its spell. It's the way of the Island, Annya. But islands all have a peculiar mystery, don't you think?'

'And magic,' Tamzin added, thoughtfully fingering her glass.

The waiter had begun a discrete withdrawal as Annya's attention focused on her guests.

'Of course! You two lived on an island the other side of the world before you came here,' she remarked.

Lester picked up the bottle, and nodded towards her. 'More refills? How about you, Tamz?' Both ladies shook their heads. He helped himself. 'Hawaii, yes. Did Tammy tell you?'

Annya nodded. 'I was asking her about this glass-bottom boat thing in your ad. The rainbow fish. We were chatting in the car coming down, and she said it all began in the South Pacific. But what took you there in the first place?'

'Long story. I'm sure you don't want to hear it.'

'I wouldn't ask if I didn't.'

'It's Tammy's story really. I only put my oar in... Well, yes, figuratively and literally.'

'He's the man of the sea, Annya. Been messing about in boats since he was a kid, and we bumped into one another—he was tarring his bottom—the boat's, of course—on the beach. You sure you want to hear this?'

Annya gave a weak smile. 'Not sure about the tar, but the rest sounds intriguing. How you met. Your rainbow fish even turned up in one of my dreams the other night, you know.'

'Oh!' Lester's eyes lit up. He sat forward, leaning towards her. 'We're interested in dreams—both of us. Do you dream a lot?'

'Well...' Annya wasn't ready to say. She needed to learn more about the two of them first. She still hadn't made up her mind where things stood. Except, since the beginning of the evening, coming down in the car together, she'd asked herself what possible motive they could have had for getting at her food that night. There was nothing in the least sinister about them as far as she could tell.

'We all dream, don't we? Nothing unusual,' she said, hoping to pass on and turn the conversation back to them.

'But there are dreams and dreams,' he insisted. 'Mental-clearing dreams at one end of the scale. The sort our psyche uses to rebalance and reorganise our brain before the morning—according to some narrow scientific theories, that is. At the other extreme, visions; messages from "up there". He gestured heavenwards. 'But they can be the voice of our personal unconscious too, warning us where the hidden rocks are, the tangled weeds, the wrecks—rotting sailors maybe. This is Tammy's subject though, and I'm letting myself get carried away.'

'Off with the fishes again, you see, Annya. He's incorrigible.'

'But you said something in your ad about meditation and exploring the depths, and I suppose that's what hooked me. God! Now I'm at it! But aren't you both exploring the same thing—in different ways? He's talking about—what is it? Consciousness?'

'Precisely!' Tamzin's expression was animated. 'Symbols. Metaphor. The language dreams use to communicate. Telling us about things we'd sooner let lie sometimes. Sunken things. Fears lurking in the shadows—and these could include *unacknowledged powers*, you know,' she said, emphasising the last point with a finger. 'But dreams show us what needs bringing to the surface, too.' She paused, and simultaneously all three of them became silent, gazing into the distance.

A silver moon hung in the sky, and the sea, black now like spilled ink on a sheet of crinkled foil, seemed to be dissolving into a mist-blurred horizon. Held by the silence as it flowed out and back again to its source, no one moved, until Tamzin's voice broke in. 'We're all sleepwalkers, Annya. We doze along in a few inches of consciousness, when there are fathoms of it, miles, and infinite miles for us to discover if only we were a bit more adventurous. It was exactly this which took me to Hawaii. I'd started a training in psychotherapy, but got bored half-way through.'

Annya's own consciousness had, she felt, for a moment, slipped from her grasp. She'd been away somewhere she couldn't account for. Had *she* sunk to some deep place, her mind dissolved in mist? Desperately holding on to the one thread she felt might draw her back to reality, she managed to rejoin their conversation. 'Why bored?' she asked.

'Oh, you know—I thought they were being too rigid, doctrinaire. I was disappointed it wasn't allowing me freedom to develop new pathways. Then I read something. A book about Huna.' She paused, uncharacteristically hesitant. 'You shouldn't have got me onto this. I told you— Look! Your waiter's coming with our orders, Annya.'

Thank God for food, thought Annya, her food suspicions now completely overridden. I'm sure I shouldn't be able to cope with Huna, whatever that might be. But abandoning Huna to explain itself, Tamzin was now riding off on another hobby-horse of hers, local specialities, and how historically the natives managed self-sufficiency in this arid land of wind and fire.

Sailor-boy winked at Annya as he set an array of dishes down. Red sauce, green sauce and creamy-white. Then a big silver bowl of walnut-sized, salt-bespeckled, fire-roasted spuds in their skins. Tamzin had suggested them as a starter, and Annya had pulled a face. But Lester persuaded her they'd be delicious like nothing she'd tasted before. Besides, she told herself, unless they'd bribed the waiter already, potatoes should be a safe bet.

They were absolutely delicious. And like nothing on earth, except that's what they *were* like, fruits of earth, flavoursome beyond expectation. They all dived into the one silver dish and dipped in and out of the paprika-red, herby-green and saffron-creamy bowls.

The conversation did then return to Huna, which, it transpired, was an extremely ancient psycho-religious system. Tamzin, taking a swig of house red, leaned towards Annya and hissed behind her hand. 'The name means "secret" in Hawaiian, you know,'

'What! You mean blood oaths and sacrifices, or something? Voodoo?'

'Stop trying to scare her, Tamz!' Lester chided. 'It's nothing like that, Annya. Far from it. Huna's one of the most civilised belief systems in the world. In line with some of the latest thinking on child rearing, progressive education, healing—even transpersonal psychology, would you believe! At the same time it goes back so far into the mists of time that its origins are lost. There are no written records. Its roots are buried in folk memory—long before the great flood.'

'But it means secret, all the same,' Tamzin insisted. 'And I wasn't trying to scare you Annya, just intrigue.'

Scared? Annya scared! Whatever gave them that idea! 'Yeh, it does sound fascinating,' she said aloud, hoping the sudden falsetto in her voice didn't show. 'The long-ago-in-the-mists, I mean. How long ago was that, do you think?'

'No-one knows. That's what intrigued me.' Tamzin leaned close again, eager, radiating enthusiasm. 'When you really go into it, it's like following a trail which takes you so far into the pre-historic that your head spins. We always think of human evolution as progressive, don't we? Our present selves at the top of the civilisation chain. But with Huna, you begin tracing back into more and more primitive eras— stone-age, bones and flints and all that. But then there's this sudden break, and you start thinking, well, we're coming to the end of the line now. But no. This pulls you up sharp. A previous civilisation, possibly more advanced than our twentieth-century one, suddenly looms up.'

'But surely! Where's the evidence?' Annya felt she'd suspended healthy scepticism long enough.

'There *is* no evidence,' Lester admitted. 'It's only fair to tell you straight. Nothing tangible. No artefacts, scrolls, tablets, masonry. Nothing of that sort. When Tamzin talks about following a trail it's more a trace in the ether. You know, a "pricking of the thumbs." He began demonstrating, delicately fingering the air. 'Clusters of potent signs appearing as if by chance; feathers in the breeze.'

'Like what people call being psychic?' Annya wondered aloud.

'Something like that. We wouldn't expect anyone to believe what we've come to believe ourselves. That's why it's so difficult trying to explain. Unless you're psychic yourself.' Then that searching look again. 'Are you, Annya?' he asked.

Annya shook her head emphatically.

'But when you return to the present and make a study of the practices and beliefs of the Ka'huna people, which is where all this began for me,' Tamzin said, peering at Annya, who, feeling herself scrutinised by them both, shuffled uncomfortably. 'Although these people lived centuries ago, there's no lack of hard evidence here. Yet the concepts by which they lived are bang up to date. A blend of modern psychology, psychosynthesis, a la Carl Rogers, Roberto Assagioli et al, and the ancient miracle-workings of shamanism, *plus* a social system to rival that of the most enlightened humanitarians alive today.'

'You're boring her, Tamz,' warned Lester.

It wasn't exactly true, and she shook her head again, this time she hoped more convincingly. She wasn't bored, it was just that she felt out of her depth for one thing. And for another, a button had been pressed and she was struggling with what its resonance was doing to her insides. But Tamzin rode on in spite of Lester's scowl.

'*I am responsible for my reality.* Did you know that Annya? At least that's what I discovered, and it woke me up, I can tell you. It took me on this fascinating journey of discovery. I began asking myself: Who am I? What, or indeed *who* is it that creates my identity? Good question, OK? And one of the answers which came was: Maybe I am not *only* myself, my present self that is.'

This was a step too far for Annya. What the hell did that mean? Tamzin's voice was taking on a note, a strange hypnotic tone. 'Do I exist elsewhere, in another time, another universe? Or is time itself an illusion?'

Was she asking or stating? Annya, discomforted but strangely riveted, didn't even notice her sailor-boy clearing away the starter dishes. Lester, however, drew her attention to him when he reappeared from the kitchen at the back of the restaurant bearing another tray.

'Looks like he's bringing our next course, folks.'

Thankful for her release, Annya glanced away. The room was still crowded. Three or four tables back from where they were sitting two men were in deep conversation, heads close together. One, the eldest, was a broad-chested bearded man she couldn't see clearly. He was in the shade of the awning. She watched them. The bearded one held what looked like a small potato in his fingers while the younger opened his mouth like a baby bird waiting to be fed. She could see *him* all too clearly. Loose ultramarine curls framed his astonishing, but familiar, moonlight-blue, translucent face. His tunic was a subdued blend of all the colours of the mountain peaks which she had seen silhouetted against the sky moments before the sun disappeared. Deep violet, dusky rose, and most mysterious of all, deepest indigo.

Annya's mouth dropped open, any colour she herself possessed draining from her face.

'You're shivering.' Lester reached for her wrap which was draped over the back of the chair. 'Put this round you and get some more food into you. It'll warm you up.'

Tamzin was tucking in now, and so intent on the contents of her dish she didn't notice the expression on her husband's face as he leant towards Annya and whispered, 'I hate to come out with such an obvious cliché, but... you look as though you've seen a ghost.'

Annya's mouth still gaped, but as no sound issued forth he followed her gaze hoping to glimpse the object of her consternation. Mouth dry, but with tongue freed slightly from its paralysis, she croaked, 'Over there. That table. Two strange men. Can you see?'

'Which table? Which men? Are they bothering you?'

'There! Four tables back from us, against the wall, under the awning. The one with the beard, and the... the... blue one.'

'Blue what? Where?' inquired Tamzin, distracted from the delights of her goat stew at last.

'No, no, don't all look,' pleaded Annya. But too late. Other heads began turning in the direction she had been looking.

'I can't see anything. Blue what? What's she mean, Lester?'

'I think she means that table,' he said, nodding towards the one in question.

'But it's empty!' pronounced Tamzin.

And so it was.

THAT FROM WHICH THINGS ARISE

'Pomme de Terre, Finn. Try one, it'll earth you.'

'You sure? I'm not. I don't think I can manage, Mandy. Not eat.'

'It's all right. I've dematerialised it so you get the essence and all the elements without the burps. Look, I'm having some.'

'Yes, but you seem to have the knack. You got that chap in the black pants and white wha'd'ya call it? Shift? Skirt?'

'Shirt.'

'Shirt then... to bring us that dish. You *appeared*, materialised yourself. You did *this* with your fingers,' Finn said, snapping his, 'and he came over to us, and when you talked to him, he scribbled on his block of paper.'

'He's called a waiter, Finn.'

'OK. Right. Why though? What's he waiting for?'

'Never mind, Finn. Aren't you enjoying yourself? We've come to town like you wanted, and here's your girl, Annya. And she's just seen you, so you must be catching the knack from me—only now she's looking pretty sick, and heads are beginning to turn this way, so perhaps we'd better fade out again. But, tell me, did you catch what they were saying—Annya and the couple with her? I thought that was really quite something, that stuff about Huna. I think we might be getting somewhere with that. Didn't you? Were you picking any of it up? That Tamzin creature's onto something, don't you think?'

'Oh, bells started ringing alright. I was getting several layers of images, but they were interfused, hard to make sense of.' He hoped Mandy appreciated how keenly he'd been observing. 'The older two, they seem to have done a lot of—what would you say—homework, groundwork? Gone into things multidimensionally.'

'Mmm. And did you notice how your Annya came over for a few seconds?'

'Over? Ah! You mean when she took a trip out of her 3D consciousness and merged with our dimension? But I thought she slipped her moorings quite a few times. She certainly registered us. Pity she goes to pieces whenever she sees me.'

'*That* I can understand, Finn, but she didn't exactly whoop with delight when she set eyes on me. I'd have thought my star quality appearance would have been much more to her taste. Anyway, how did that potato go down? You OK?'

'I'm very OK, thanks,' he said, eyes smiling with satisfaction while his mouth worked on the virtual texture, transferring the quick-burn carbs to his system.

'Good. I think you'll do, then. If I get called away, you'll be all right.'

'How do you mean, Mandy?' His eyes left their smiling for a second. 'You're not thinking of leaving, are you?'

'I may be needed somewhere in a hurry. There's no telling. But you'll manage. Just a bit rusty. Got out of the knack of how things work down here, Finn. You'll find it all comes back now, though.'

'But Mandy, you seem to be forgetting. I never knew how things worked here. This was your century. Things, as you call it, were rather different where I was born. I was already in the fifth dimension. How'm I going to make out in this antiquated, dimension-restricted era? I'm out of sync. It's all so... Don't Mand. Don't go.'

'I'm not planning to. But as you so rightly reminded me a while back, this is your show. Yours and hers. So keep tabs on her and you'll be OK. The clues are beginning to pile up now.'

'Mandy!' he cried, his eyes blank and dazed now as they stared into space.

Finn had gone to town all right, and now here he sat, alone, at a table, empty except for the remains of their potato meal. 'Mandy!' he called again. He even thought of snapping his fingers, but thought better of it in case he accidentally made himself appear. He wasn't sure what part of the gesture had summoned the waiting man to their table, and which part had manifested Mandelbrot's visibility. Neither did he know if Mandy had conjured his, Finn's own image, or if he'd done it himself. Whichever it was they'd caused a bit of consternation, particularly to Annya. On the other hand, perhaps it was those potatoes. They'd earthed him, Mandy said. In which case... kreepin krittins, this 'knack' thing was taking its time—him getting the hang of it. He secreted one or two of the left-over spuds in his holding pouch under his tunic. Maybe they'd come in useful.

Keep tabs on the girl. Well, he'd better do just that then, since Mandy'd buggered off.

The man at the table with Annya was wrapping some warm-looking amber cloth round her shoulders, and the woman seemed to be steadying her while she got to her feet. They'd done some deal with the waiting man, and now, one on either side, they began escorting the pale-faced girl down the long balcony, between tables, and towards some steps leading outside. Finn decided to follow as far as the steps.

'Everyone thinks I'm pissed,' Annya whispered behind her hand to Lester.

'Of course not. We explained to your waiter you were feeling unwell. It's all right. Everyone understands.'

'Oh God. I didn't pay!'

'It's OK. I gave him something. We'll settle up later, but let's get you home right now. Or better still, why not come back with us and we'll give you one of Tamzin's patent restoratives.'

'Oh, God! I don't know what to *do*.' She pressed her hand to her spinning head as she tried to assess the sequence of everything that had happened. They'd all drunk the same wine from the same bottles. Eaten from a communal dish, taking pieces of food at random. And she'd hardly touched her main dish when the apparition in blue caught her eye for that brief second. If anything was suspect, it was her sanity.

Finn didn't know what to do either. What was Mandy thinking of, coming and going like a Cheshire cat? He would try the finger trick after all. That must be what Mandy intended. But then again, how could he risk materialising himself. That'd set the cat among the pigeons alright. Strange, these phrases, dropping into his head like this. He was watching Annya and her friends take a short cut past a heap of nets and buoys and broken boxes, when a cat suddenly leapt out of the shadows. It snatched a fish from a group of large, white birds on the quayside, and set them circling and dive-bombing, squawking with anger. He didn't think these were pigeons, though.

Keep tabs, Finn. That's the thing.

They were crossing the cobbled quay now, heading for their vehicle. What now, he wondered? Should he follow? Get in the vehicle with them? He felt the need to act, but act responsibly, reassuringly. Put his arm around her like the other one had done, or a hand on her knee. But that would set her off squawking too. Couldn't risk that. Maybe he could sit beside her, yet do it so unobtrusively no-one would notice. But it seemed they'd decided differently. Lester was to drive, and Tamzin would get in the back with Annya so she could comfort her.

Right then. He'd get into the front seat.

Lester turned a key, and the engine fired. Smells, vibrations, hums and roars; then rattling and bumping they set off over the cobbles. He hadn't noticed his extra passenger! This was weird! This was fun. The car turned into a street thronged with humanity, and hung about with lights. This must be 'town' all right!

Lester glanced over his shoulder. 'You OK Annya?'

'She's fine.' Tamzin answered.

'Let's get out of this crowd, and I'll put my foot down. We'll be home in no time. You're coming back with us, aren't you?' He signalled left.

Annya was still thinking it over. But if she took too long, Tamzin would decide for her again. So, playing for time, she asked, 'Which way are we going? I don't recognise this.'

'I'm taking the scenic. It's a bit further, but quicker in the end.'

'But there are no lights on this track, and it's pitch black. I never drive up here at night. Too easy to come off, and no-one to get you back.'

'Don't worry, Annya.' Tamzin patted her hand. 'He's like a bat at night. Extra-sensory. Sees in the dark what no-one else can see. A bit like you, eh?'

None of this was making Annya feel any safer—or surer. Decisions, decisions. Back to her apartment, or trust herself to her new friends? There was no way any human agent had caused her to see what no-one else could *this* time. And, whether by intent or instinct, they'd encouraged her all evening to open up. Lester had already guessed a lot, she was sure, and both of them were more than willing to admit her to their club—Psychic's Anonymous. So why this resistance? Why was she squirming like a butterfly on a pin? If she'd hidden a stinking corpse under her bed, she couldn't have felt more terrified of being outed.

Finn didn't feel any more comfortable. If this Lester had psychic vision too, he was thinking, it wouldn't be long before his cover was blown. The next time he glanced round at Annya, Finn was sure Lester's eyes would get a fix on him. He had to do something—keep a flow of conversation going. Guide their thought, even.

'Won't be long now, love.' Tamzin gave Annya's shoulder a squeeze. 'So, what's it to be? Back with us for a little pick-me-up? You need something to settle you after that, doesn't she Lester?'

Lester's eyes were fixed on the road. They were moving through blackness. Deep in concentration he said, 'One of Tamzin's specials. Just what you need.'

'I *will*. I'll come back with you then. Thanks,' said Annya.

Finn surveyed the interior, glancing from one to the other, and smiled. It was too easy. And clues were piling up too, just as Mandy had said. I'd better see what we've got so far then, he thought. The main one is sea. Depths. Sunken things. Annya's confused and suspicious, and it's not just about seeing me, or Mandy for that matter. Though curiously both of us seem to scare her stiff. I'll stick with them, protect her if necessary, and see if anything else emerges. Important, though, that she doesn't get the idea again that these two are up to no good, influencing her mind, taking advantage of her in any way, or she's bound to clam up.

'Here we are!' Lester pulled on the hand brake. He hopped out and opened Annya's door, helping her onto the pavement. As they trooped up the path Finn slipped into the house by the balcony window ahead of them. He was trying out a lounging position on one of the sofas as they came into the room, but he beat a hasty retreat behind the kitchen door. Discretion still seemed called for at this stage in the game.

Lester crossed the floor in the dark to the coffee table inches from where Finn had been reclining and switched on a lamp. 'You're looking better already. Why don't you sit here Annya, and Tamzin'll get you a nip of something.'

Annya sank into the soft, warm cushions, and put her head back. The sofa felt seductively relaxing. She could hear Tamzin in the kitchen sorting through bottles. She saw them in her mind's eye; tiny phials, different colours. Potions, tinctures, essences, distillations, infusions. Convincing herself nothing worse could happen now than had already happened, she allowed herself to sink deeper into the enveloping comfort.

'Annya! You've nodded off.' Tamzin was standing over her holding out a glass. 'Well, that's a good sign. Here! A few drops in spring water. Here we are!' she said, giving the glass a swirl.

'Oh, thanks.' Annya struggled into a sitting position, blinking. 'What is it though?'

'A flower elixir.'

'Flowers!'

'Well, flowers, roots, barks, and a touch of...'

'But Tamzin, I...'

'Go on,' Tamzin crooned, smiling warmly, her voice solicitous. 'It's an old Island charm. It'll do you good. I selected it carefully.'

Bending over her in the soft light, now with a cardigan round her shoulders, Tamzin reminded Annya curiously of her mother. She put the glass to her lips, and sniffed. Hardly any smell. She tongued the surface and cautiously swallowed a drop. 'But tell me about it. You selected it? What from? How many are there? How did you know which to select?'

Tamzin laughed. 'Which one first? Well, there's a Greek woman here. Xena. She's been growing herbs and things all her life. She and the German, they have a magic kitchen—sort of laboratory with stills, retorts and mysterious vapours. No end of interesting stuff hanging from the ceiling. Shelves full of packets, boxes of roots and bark, all labelled. She picks a lot of them herself up in the mountains. You're not drinking! Don't you like it? It's quite innocuous. Go on. That's right. Lester gives her a hand too, don't you Les? When he goes on one of his hikes up in the hills, he's on the look-out for anything useful to bring back.'

Annya glanced at Lester slumped against the cushions. He screwed up his eyes and blinked them opened, then awkwardly sat up. 'Yeh,' he said, making it clear he'd been listening. 'They're hard to spot at first, but I'm learning. Xena's hot stuff when it comes to identifying virtuous species. You know, plants with medicinal properties. Fascinating. Even up in Devil's Country, the fire-fields where nothing apparently grows, there's an occasional spoor clinging to life in some crevice. Or do I mean spore? You'd better ask Xena. Rudimentary lichens and succulents can be the most potent, so they say. All depends on what effect you're after.'

'But when you say "they", who do you mean, the German?'

'Yes, Haandel.'

'The doctor?'

'Yes, the doctor. I've not met him yet, but he's well-known out here. He grows his own stuff too. A lot of it up at Carlos's estate with the help of his manager, Salvador. The old man got him interested.'

'So it *is* Doctor Haandel you're talking about!'

'Don't tell me *you* know him, Annya?'

'I've met him, yes.'

'Wow!' cut in Tamzin. 'We've been wanting to meet him too, haven't we, Les? Perhaps we can all get together? But Annya, how are you feeling? Any effect yet?'

'Surprisingly, yes,' Annya had to admit. Her head felt clearer, her tension gone.

'Calming, uplifting. Dispels anxiety. Diffuses shock. That's what I asked for,' Tamzin told her.

'You asked?'

'Well, I mean dowsed, of course. But I do ask. Invoke as I dowse.'

'What exactly... Who, who d'you ask?'

'You sure you want to know?' Annya nodded she did. 'This is going to sound silly, OK. Well I ask the devas, the plant spirits. But this time I'm not sure. It was as though...' She didn't finish.

Annya prompted, 'As though...?'

'I'd better leave it at that,' she said with a look that implied she'd already gone too far.

All very interesting, thought Finn, but when will they get back to Huna, or something equally important? He'd been monitoring the situation and slipped out of the room to see what Tamzin was up to. But the alchemy of kitchens was nothing new to him. Mandy had been right that far at least. *That* knack had definitely come back to him, and Tamzin had been all too ready to accept the suggestions he'd put into her head. She didn't seem to *see* the spirits when she consulted them, but her sensitivity to their guidance was good. It had been a simple matter for him to intervene, and the devas looked delighted to have him join them. He'd added a trace of one particular essence which he hoped would unbottle Annya's throat. He could see the constriction there. He was also beginning to see the reason for it, but not clearly enough yet.

'I wish you'd tell me, Tamzin,' Annya piped up suddenly. 'I really don't need the kid-glove treatment, you know, even though I must have given you cause to think so. I've behaved stupidly, but it's all been a shock one way or another this evening.'

Finn smiled. Her throat colours were clearing.

'Sorry? Tell you what?' Tamzin asked.

'Oh, it's all right. You just said, "it was as though." But I'm the one who's being unforthcoming. I should have told you I met this Doctor Haandel—Manfred. Why I'm making such heavy weather of this I don't know, but the reason I went to see him is connected with all this business tonight. What, or *who*, I saw. I already made my dread confession to him about seeing this... well, this ghost, and once I'd gone through all that I didn't expect any of it to come up again. It felt like absolution—exorcism even. I thought I'd got rid of my spook.'

'Until, there he was! Sitting behind you at the restaurant table!'

143

Lester filled in for her with a barely concealed air of triumph, his suspicions confirmed.

'How exciting! Oh, sorry Annya. It obviously wasn't for you. You looked ghastly. Sorry.' But Tamzin sounded just as triumphant, and not at all sorry.

'It may be exciting for you two; it's anything but for me!' Annya exploded. You don't know the whole story. You've no idea! It was utterly... It's completely... How could you know what it feels like... turning up in your dreams, peering at you from the sky, staring out of your mirror, over your shoulder, appearing, disappearing.' The whole saga poured out. 'Everything you lost on the beach carefully laid out for you in the bathroom. Rescuing you from drowning...' She came to a sudden stand-still.

On the sofa opposite, the other two sat open-mouthed.

'Your ghost did all this?' Tamzin squealed, flinging her arms out and hitting the cushions behind her, while her legs shot forward.

Lester, neatly avoiding an elbow in the face, was on the edge of his seat. 'Rescued you from drowning? Good God, Annya! Some ghost! I wish *I'd* seen him.'

They all burst into gales of hysterical laughter at the sight of Tamzin, limbs akimbo. Annya most of all.

'I don't know why I said that,' Annya managed to gasp out at last. '"Rescued from drowning". The whole thing's absurd. But honestly, it *did* all happen, and though there's no way of knowing if he actually rescued me from the sea, what happened out there *was* extraordinary. Supernatural. It's just that... I'm having a hard time accepting it.'

'I don't doubt it.' Lester leaned back again. 'Anyone would. But Annya, you're a star! What else can you tell us?' he asked, edging even further forward again in his eagerness.

'Isn't that enough?'

'I think we should all have a glass of something,' Tamzin suggested. 'Lester's got a nice liqueur. Or how about a tea? Annya will never get to sleep. Let's all calm down. I'll make us a pot of my "snoozythyme special".

But I don't want us to go to sleep yet, muttered Finn to himself.

'Good idea,' said Lester. 'Snoozythyme OK for you, Annya? I'll make it.'

No you won't, decided Finn.

'No, Les, you chat to our guest while I do it,' said Tamzin.

Finn smiled. He could see the devas foregathering again in the kitchen.

'But you *do* really believe he rescued you...?' Lester's voice was just audible.

Finn was back in the kitchen with Tamzin. Humming to herself, she was busy communing with the devas while she stirred her teapot. It should be an interesting brew, he thought. He could safely leave them to it now.

Annya glanced at Lester. His legs were up on the sofa now, and hands folded behind his head, he was giving every sign of indifference to what his wife was doing. 'Well,' Annya said, 'I wouldn't have thought that at the time. When your life's in imminent danger, self-preservation kicks in. It's instinct. Nature's survival strategy. But I talked to Manfred about it a lot, and we both came to similar conclusions. I had a sort of replay where maybe another part of myself was seeing... I really don't have the words to explain it.'

Tamzin, about to emerge from the kitchen, called, 'Another part of your consciousness, an out of body experience?'

Annya, continuing to address Lester, went on, 'And then you forget it immediately, like it never happened. So you see, if you tried to explain it, no-one would believe you, like if you said, "it was in a dream," they'd think, "Oh yes, but she only dreamed it." And of course that's what I believed, except Manfred confirmed it... Sort of...' She looked worriedly from one to the other. 'I'm not making sense, am I?'

'Not altogether, but isn't it interesting, Annya?' Lester agreed, grinning at her perplexity. 'But I guess there's a lot more to it than you're letting on.'

'Probably, but it's late and I don't think my brain is up to it right now. Why don't you tell me something more about this ancient sect or whatever, and why it fascinated you.'

Tamzin, with her tray of oriental china, began handing round cups of fragrant, yellow-green tea. 'You mean Huna?' she inquired, happily.

'Let's not get onto that again,' Lester sighed. 'Annya's right. It's late, and look, we're all yawning.'

Sinking down next to him, Tamzin stretched. 'We're all ready for bed,' she admitted, reaching for a golden dragon cup and taking a sip. The other two followed suit. The tea was good, and soon they were asking her to pour a second.

Calm descended. No-one spoke for several minutes.

'But why it so fascinates me...' Tamzin piped up again.

Lester yawned noisily, and Annya's eyelids drooped.

'... is that when you start going into it, the more it leads you to the bottom of the ocean—into the territory of the lost continent of Lemuria.'

GETTING THINGS TOGETHER

A night on the sofa, a shower and breakfast, and Annya felt more ready to face the day than she'd been since Simon left. In spite of her anxieties about him, she'd slept deeply and well, unaware that another had been stretched out on the sofa opposite for most of the night.

Finn, too, felt ready for the day ahead. Now he had a major clue: Lemuria. He was well pleased. And although he hadn't entirely involved himself in all the complications of physical existence, he was sampling it and enjoying it. Though discomforts of the kind that *flesh was heir to* weren't his problem because he was still occupying an etheric body, a sofa for the night had been a welcome change from that mountain top. There were dangers, of course. Annya's eyes, he knew, already saw him from time to time, and Lester—though his were only hunches so far—*he* would be the next. Yet with care he could manage to keep out of Lester's psychic range.

It had been quite an experience, being so close to Annya last night, and his qualms about physical bodies were changing fast. Of course, if she'd woken suddenly and spotted him lying there, that would have been a challenge—for *both* of them. But he'd got it just about right, he felt. That pot of tea. It had called for subtlety in its mixing and brewing, but the balance had been perfect; soporific enough to bring about a sense of well-being and peace, yet stimulating enough to call forth just the right degree of information. Then the final touch: deep sleep.

Finn was aware of the consequences of interfering with human free will, yet he knew an intervention that tuned in with the underlying intent of all parties concerned was permitted. You had to read the signs on all levels, of course, but he believed his expertise was developing fast. And now, thanks to Tamzin and the devas brew working in concord, he had the clue he'd been waiting for. Yet, from what he seemed to be picking up during the night, Annya had further revelations for him. Someone else had visited her in her sleep.

'How are you now, Annya, this morning? Any plans?' Lester emerged from the bathroom tucking a flap of shirt into his pants. He did a shimmy with his hips while frowning at his reflection in the mirror. 'Have to look the part today, you know. Got a guided tour scheduled for nine-thirty.'

'I'm feeling great, thanks to you two. I have to get a move on though. Make some calls, and all that. *And* I haven't forgotten I owe you for our meal. So don't argue. Tamzin told me what the bill came to. I've left enough to cover it on the coffee table.'

'Well, have a good day then,' he called on his way to the open door, 'and we'll meet up again soon.' He paused on the step. 'Why don't I walk you down to the gate? That's if you're ready.'

'I'm ready. I've said my goodbyes to Tamzin. She's busy getting her meditation room ready for a client.'

'You don't need a lift, do you? You're only round the corner. Patting his pockets, each in turn, and muttering, he walked her down the path. 'Hell's bells! Must have left 'em in the house. I'm going to be late! *Ah*!' With a jingle he drew a ring of keys from inside his jacket, and got into the car. The window swished down. 'Oh, Annya, if you talk to our doctor friend anytime soon... You know... See how he feels.'

'About getting together, you mean? I'll see,' she told him blandly.

He waved a salute.

Calling Manfred was one of the things she'd had in mind, but it wasn't the uppermost. Simon. That really bothered her. She needed to phone Amsterdam, but the longer it had been without news, the more concerned, and frankly, the more frightened she was becoming of hearing it. Must be done though, she thought. Rounding the corner, her pace quickened, and moments later as she arrived at the security gate she was so agitated she could hardly manage to press the buttons. Inside the complex all seemed normal. She strode anxiously up the path to her apartment, and inside, everything seemed normal too. She changed out of her clothes and hastily did her face and hair while the reassuring reflection of her own eyes stared back. Gathering a few things in her bag, she set off briskly towards the office. The morning air was warm and clear, the pool sparkled, and dear old Miguel, disbudding hibiscus, grinned good-naturedly as she ran past him to the phone.

Her call connected.

'Peter!'

Her voice was shrill. She could hear her own quick breaths as well as the familiar background sounds of his office down the line before he answered.

'Oh, hi, Annya. How's things?'

'Peter! You know why I'm phoning. Peter, I'm worried. Any news?'

His reply didn't come fast enough, and she 'Petered' him again.

'Annya, look. I know this is hard, but I don't have anything as yet.'

'Aren't you *doing* something? Where is he? Why is no-one...'

'Look Annya, there's no cause for concern. We expected something like this. It was always going to be this difficult. Simon did explain, didn't he?'

'But aren't *you* worried? Can't you give me *anything*?'

'Not over the phone, love. If there *was* anything I would, but the less we all say, the safer he's going to be. That's really all I can offer right now. Can you hold onto that? I've got your present number, and your home. Keep me posted, and as soon as there's anything this end, I'll contact you. Promise.'

'But when you say "anything", you mean one way or the other, don't you?'

'There's no reason to start going down that route. None of us are thinking the worst.'

'Not yet, you mean. Not thinking the worst *yet*.'

'I mean...' The voice was intoning, separating words, speaking as if to a foreigner, a child. 'We expected silence. That was part of the deal. We expected it.'

A stone wall, and she was banging her head on it. Through the window she could see children leaping into the pool, screaming. Their's were screams of delight. She was letting her crazy imagination get the better of her again. She'd better phone Manfred.

It had taken half an hour or so, the drive to Carlos's estate. Time enough to calm down. Thank God she hadn't flung herself at Manfred as he rose to greet her. Cool and in charge she crossed to the table under the tree where they'd sat before and formally extended her hand. But he ignored it and held out both his arms to give her a warm bear-hug. Her pleasure, as they embraced, was as real as his.

'Annya! How well you're looking. What's the news? Carlos is wanting to meet you, but we'll do this, these introductions, later, ja! Meantime, some citron? See, I've got a jug and glasses waiting.'

'Oh, is Carlos here? I didn't realise,' she said, and seated herself thankfully. It was already warm, standing in the sun.

'Some problem—him being here?'

'No, of course not. It's just...'

'OK, tell me. It's good to see you again, but you don't ring me for my pretty face. That it?'

'Manfred. Really! I'm very glad to see you. Very. And I'm looking forward to meeting Carlos, but as a matter of fact...'

'You *do* have a problem.'

'You know me. I guess they're like flies. You swat one and another buzzes along.'

'Until you learn to repel the little devils, ja? I teach you the trick sometime. But for now, better tell me what's biting you, huh!' He laughed his rumbling laugh. It was a sound she was beginning to find reassuring.

'Let me tell you my news then,' she said, 'and it's by no means all bad.'

She gave him an up-beat account of the last few days, leaving out the histrionics of the latest sighting. 'I was fine. Top of the world when I woke this morning, but it wore off. A vague feeling at first, a twinge of apprehension I couldn't put a name to. Couldn't connect it with anything, so I just assumed it was the usual morning-after blues. Only it got worse, and I began thinking... I seem to default to that... You know, the old paranoia, the 'someone's been getting at me, drops in my drink,' sort of thing. But I'd made this resolution to trust them early in the evening, and I stuck to it. Manfred, I honestly can't see any reason not to, now. But this awful feeling was mushrooming, and by the time I got back to the apartment it was full-blown panic again. I was desperate for news of Simon. It felt like some premonition. He'd been calling me.'

'Calling? You mean left you messages? Phoning?'

'No. I mean he sounded terrified. Calling for me in the night, and I couldn't reach him. I knew it must have been a nightmare, it was so disturbing. It felt so real. I had to have news, so I called his office— Peter. But it was no good. He stonewalled. I know there's bad things happening, but they won't tell me, Manfred.'

'Yet you say it was a dream. A nightmare.'

'I'd no inkling when I woke up, only this feeling of something wrong. A premonition. But I began to remember it, bit by bit. It must have been buried deep, you know, in my unconscious.'

He smiled to himself.

'I'm scared, Manfred. I'm in the dark. They won't tell me anything, so that means I can't tell you anything useful either. I know I'm not being fair. You can't help me with this. But I've come anyway,' she said finally with a gesture of helplessness.

'So why do you think you've come?'

'I'm sorry. I shouldn't have.'

'I didn't say that. I asked why you think to yourself, "Oh, it's Manfred I must go to"?'

She gave him a puzzled look.

'We know it's not my good looks.'

She took a moment or two. 'I think I trust you... That is, if I trust anyone.'

'OK,' he said, shrugging off the compliment. 'But, one, I don't have answers. And two, you give me nothing to go on. So what do I have? Why Manfred?'

'I can't answer. I don't know. But something happens when I'm with you. There *is* something. You *do* have something,' she said flapping her hands but smiling to show how much she meant it. 'Oh, I really don't know.'

He looked pleased. 'As a matter of fact, I do have something for you. Listen! Will you go back to England, or decide to stay put, out here? I may have an idea if you decide to remain for a while. It's up to you.'

The puzzlement surfaced again and mutated, her expression travelling through stages of interest to blank surprise.

'You *have* something?'

'Maybe. But let's move from here. Carlos will probably be disappointed, but things come to us better, I think, as we move. Ja? We shall flow. 'I'll take you for a drive and you will talk to me.'

'If you say so, Manfred, but I don't really understand. I don't have much. What do you want me to say?'

'Don't think about what you have or don't have. Let's move!'

They got to their feet and he led the way to where he'd parked his car. As they crunched across a shingle path at the side of the big house, a door at the far end opened. From it emerged a tall, dark, and presumably, Annya was thinking, handsome Carlos—if that coiffed, cravatted sort of thing turned you on. Manfred slowed. Carlos hailed him and strode towards them.

'Manfred, my friend! Surely you're not spiriting this delightful lady away before I have chance to greet her?'

'This is Annya,' Manfred announced, somewhat guardedly.

'So I assumed. Who else? Or are you thinking of two-timing Annya as well as giving me the slip? Come! We shall go into the house and take something cool and refreshing.'

'Carlos... Oh, Annya, *this*, by the way, is the distinguished and discerning Carlos. Please, amigo, no offence, but something has come up. Some emergency. Private business.'

The two men launched into a fire-cracker Spanish which she couldn't follow. Their exchange became increasingly heated, while Annya, shuffling gravel with her feet, embarrassed to be the cause of disagreement, looked on. But soon they were clasping each other by the shoulder and shaking hands like businessmen clinching a deal. Carlos held out his hand for Annya's, and she thought he was about to shake it too. But he took it in his, turned it, and ceremoniously kissed the back.

In contrast to Manfred's strong, broad hand, this one, though equally firm, was slender, and the nails were long manicured ovals. The smooth skin made her think of Simon—but the feel of it was so different. He'd barely let her arm drop when Manfred said, 'Let's go, Annya. We don't have much time now,' and put his hand on her shoulder.

'Oh! Well then. Glad to have met you, Carlos,' she told him with a limp politeness. 'I hope it won't be long before...' She was beginning to feel like a pawn—hands moving her across a board—not party herself to their game. She'd been curious to meet him, but now she was asking herself why? First impressions were not encouraging. Pretentious, smooth, macho. What did Manfred see in him? Or, for that matter, how sound was her judgement of Manfred after all?

'What was all that about?' she asked him when they were out of earshot of Carlos and about to get into the car.

'Don't worry. He's angry with me. Probably has every right. I take advantage of his good nature. Sorry if we embarrassed you. It's nothing to do with you really, it's other matters, things stemming from the past, and now... Tcha!' He rubbed a fist across his face. 'It was rude of me. Let's forget it.'

Nothing to do with her. Sulkily she climbed into the passenger seat. She could have refused and gone back to her own car, but there goes that fatal curiosity of mine, she thought. At least I should find out what this idea of Manfred's amounts to before I make up my mind.

They'd left the main road behind and were heading into that same desolate scrubland they'd driven through on the way to the jazz outing. All this time Annya gazed out of the window, sullenly not saying a word. Manfred spoke first. 'What's going on—in your head?' he asked.

'Déjà vu, I suppose,' she muttered. 'I was about to ask where are we? Where the hell are you taking me? Like I did last time. Except, I didn't say "hell" last time. But surely you're not taking me there again. So why this awful dreary desert. Except... Shit, Manfred!'

Manfred had suddenly clenched the driving wheel. He spun it, and screeching off the road turned a violent left onto a dirt-track which doubled back in the direction they'd come. Clouds of dust flew up. She grabbed the strap, barely managing to keep herself from being flung over onto Manfred's side. 'Christ! What the hell, Manfred?'

'"*Except*," you were saying? It's OK Annya, relax! We're having a bit of fun. Except *what*?'

'Except, last time we didn't break our effing necks! That was *so* stu—*mind that crater!* Where the fuck are you taking me? I want to get out.'

He took another vicious tyre-burning swerve and veered right. It was no longer even a track now. Apart from a few shrivelled thorns there was nothing in sight. They were racing over dun coloured ruts and stones in an inferno of dust, grit, and spikes. A boulder loomed up. He braked and backed, shooting the car into reverse in a staccato of pebbles.

'Did you hear me? I want to get out!' she screamed.

'And did you tell me you trusted me?' he yelled back.

He drove his foot down and the car roared, climbing rapidly, steeply, through choking heat-haze, until ten or fifteen minutes later they were streaking across a plateau. The engine began to splutter, ejecting billows of steam. The dust-cloud, which had surrounded them all the way, turned into a soup of brown fog. He switched off and coasted along the top. As the fog started to clear she was astonished to see that they were entering another cloud—cool, white and misty.

'Like to get out now?' he asked suddenly. 'Box of tissues to clean up.' He dived into the glove compartment, took one out and demonstrated.

She glared at him, searching his face for indications of demonic possession and imminent rape. Ignoring the look, he removed his sunglasses and dabbed at his brow. Then scrubbing ineffectually at his cheeks, she saw he was only managing to make smears with the sweaty dust. Where the dark glasses had been, two white panda-eyes stared beseechingly out. Instead of the devil she expected to find lurking beneath the mud-mask, she saw a ridiculous clown. She flipped down the passenger mirror and studied her own face, and was mortified to find another clown glowering back.

'Let's get out,' he said again. 'Got something to show you.'

'Is *this* your big idea, for God's sake?' She was yelling, but more for show now. 'Just look at me. Look at the car. We're wrecks. How the blazes are we going to get back?'

'You look great,' he said.

'I look a freak. My clothes are ruined.'

'I buy you some more. Anyhow, no-one out here to see us, and I think you look fabulous.'

'Bloody kink!' she spat at him.

Still, at the back of her mind she was appalled at her predicament. Well, she'd asked for it, hadn't she? Let herself in for it good and proper. Back there, when she yelled about wanting to get out of the car, she'd known it was fatuous with all those godforsaken miles of nowhere and no-one. If this maniac did have evil intent it would have been much more comfortable having your throat slit inside the car than out here.

But he was out there already. Not waiting for her, he'd set off, his figure blurred by the mist.

He'd disappeared.

Oh, what the hell, she told herself, and got out too. She followed him into the mist.

ON THE EDGE

'Manfred!'

After all that heat, her skin now was goose-pimpled with drop-lets of vapour. She could see only yards ahead. 'Manfred,' she called again.

'Over here!' A faint resonance issued from the thick of the cloud. 'Careful. Watch your feet. Come! See, I'm waving. No *here*. Look! I'm waving.'

At last she spotted him, but sounds and outlines were blurred. Was it him even? His distinctive shape, but she couldn't be sure. The cloud swirled, blanketing her more tightly and isolating her once more. Shivering, she inched forward. Then a sensation of warmth transfused with light and a smell of fresher air met her. In a patch of thinning mist there he was again, standing on a shelf of rock. From this distance it seemed to be floating.

'Take care,' he called, and his hand was up, waving. 'There are steps. Can you see them? You're right on top now.'

As the mist began to burn off, atoms of moisture sparkled in a halo around her. Gingerly she placed her foot on the first step. He must have trusted himself enough to go down them, she told herself. But they were steep, cut into rock, and she could see nothing to hold on to. Loose sandy soil covered the treads in places, making descent even more precarious. But as the visibility increased she noticed clumps of juniper and marjoram edging them. At least it was something to grab if she slipped. She paused to look round. The whole picture was beginning to come into focus, and she could see Manfred clearly now standing on a ledge overhanging what appeared to be a sheer drop.

A shaft of sun filtering through the mist fell on the ground before her, making it suddenly golden. Her feet had turned to gold too. She gazed at them, entranced, for a moment unable to go on. Yet some quality in the light must have inspired her, as invested with new confidence, and eyeing a tough-looking tuft of juniper, she ventured down several more steps. Only then did she notice the short wall and safety rail behind him.

At that moment a draft of warm air gusted up from the ravine beneath where he stood, carrying with it a medley of tangy scents. She just had to look over that edge.

A few steps more and her feet were on the level.

'So how do you like being in a cloud?' he called. 'Come Annya. Come see the view.'

She ran to grasp his outstretched hand. Almost vertically, far below them, cobalt and white waves swelled onto a strip of beach. To their left a dry gully dropped sharply, carving its way down a gorge, its sides thick with wild flowers and trees. She stared, unbelieving, absorbing every detail of the scene before slowly turning her eyes towards him. 'It's beyond beautiful, Manfred,' she whispered.

For a long time they stood in silence. She didn't want to break into it—shatter the magic. A turmoil of questions might be hammering on the door of her mind, demanding to be let in, but she refused to open it. Closing her eyes she breathed and felt the astringent air, cool in her nostrils, filling her skull, making a clear empty space. Was this what Tamzin meant by meditation, she wondered, because her head seemed to be expanding, a cave filled with light, and it wasn't the least bit scary. When she opened her eyes at last it was to find Manfred smiling into them.

'But how *are* we to get back?' she asked him gently. 'The car's kaput.'

'Don't worry.'

'But... Look, I love your big surprise, love it to bits, Manfred. I don't want to spoil it, but we have to get back to civilisation somehow, and I can't see how without a long, exhausting trek. Just to put my mind at ease?' she pleaded.

He shook his head and laughed. '*This*, Annya, is not the big surprise as you call it. We're not half way yet. You want to know my idea, then we have to walk some more. But we don't go back. We go forward.' And he pointed below into the dizzying space.

'That? That ravine?'

'What's the problem?'

'It looks impossible.'

'No. Not impossible. I've done it many times. Not so bad as you think. And besides, Manfred's here—Manfred of the Alps, remember? We'll do it together.'

'Surely though, you didn't bring me here on a rock-climbing expedition. I'm not in the right clothes and we don't have any gear. I wouldn't have agreed to come anyway. You really are a bloody maniac!' she accused, starting to get heated again.

'I haven't planned this, Annya, believe me. I didn't mean it this way.'

'Then what *was* the plan? How did you mean it? You careered us off the road, didn't you, and got us into this mess, remember?'

He shrugged.

'"Just a bit of fun," you said.' She was getting into her stride, anger taking hold. She spun away from him, about to march back to the car. 'I can't make any sense of you. Fun at my expense, is that it?' she shouted, turning and glaring at him. 'Why the big secret, anyway? What *is* the plan, Manfred? Come on.'

Instead of answering he took a deep breath, expanding his chest as an opera singer might, and extended his arms. But he said nothing. Still on the ledge, he hadn't moved. Evidently the outspread arms were speaking for him. Witness! they seemed to say. This, Annya—all of this is our kingdom. Would you have missed a moment of it?

Below them blue ocean and the long ribbon of sand fringing it stretched in both directions, so far that they faded into the distant haze. And not a single trace of humanity; no footprint to pollute its virginity.

'Perhaps I was brought here just as much as you,' he said at last. 'Don't you think, sometimes Annya, we are watched over? Guided? Look, enough of mysteries,' he said, changing tack. 'I take you to see my friend. This was my plan. She lives down there, hidden in the trees. This is her kingdom really, but she invites us.'

'Good God! Manfred. But how does she get in and out. And that's another thing. The trees. There *are* no trees on the island, everyone knows that. So what have you done? Spirited me into some fantastic neverland?'

'She gets out in her boneshaker of a truck, that's how.' he said prosaically. 'And that's how we get help. She'll rescue us, but we'd better get a move on. She's expecting us, but not this way. We were to come by road. It's a long route, many kilometres, half way round the island and in at the back door. Not that many go that road, and those who do miss the track to her house. Unless of course they know her already. But we *can* get down this way, and I'll give you a hand. Sorry, but it's the only option now.'

'The only option? *Well, if you say so, Manfred!*' This was becoming a habit, and she repeated the phrase, mocking and wagging her head at him. Two options really, she thought. She could go back alone the way she'd come. Up those steps again, into the cloud. But then what? Christ! The car! Jesus! OK. With him then; the only option. 'Lead on MacDuff.'

'Excuse me?'

'Nothing,' she said stubbornly. 'Lets go. And what about the trees?'

'We shall talk of many trees as we make our descent, and if you're good I'll explain. But I still wait for you. You have much to tell me yet, I think. Your Simon, your ghosts? You been seeing any lately?'

'What makes you think that?' Her tone was challenging.

'You hear any birds lately?' he said by way of answer. 'Little birds?'

'Well, yes, and that's another thing. I thought I heard—up there in the clouds—song birds. I told myself it was just imagination, but I can see all sorts now. Not only little ones but there—isn't that an eagle? Some bird of prey, anyhow. But song birds must be rare. I can't say I've ever heard one on the island. Gulls I've seen, and black chattery squawky things maybe.

'The reason being—well, you must know, Annya. You don't need me to tell you how everything changed after the volcanoes. Many hundred hectares of cultivation gone forever. Once we had more rainfall, a few springs and perhaps native species for nesting. But all gone! And now this one small enclave remains, unknown by tourists and inaccessible to anyone but your eagles.'

'And, presumably, your friend and her familiars?' she reminded him.

He looked bemused. 'Ach, we joke of course. You think she is a witch. Mm, I like that. But no, there are ways in, though long and over rough territory. The local mafia they sit in their chambers and calculate development costs, better roads, but they make all they want and more besides round the other side of the island. They already have their yachts and marinas, miles of profitable sand, their sewers and desalination systems. Here are massive cliffs, fierce rocks, dangerous tides and rough seas. So why bother? One day all beauty and peace will be gone, but for now... Enjoy, and praise the gods that be... And those that protect us.'

They'd been walking along the cliff top talking all this while, and Annya didn't notice the path petering out until it abruptly ceased along with the safety rail accompanying it. The ironwork was cemented into a wall of rock which decisively barred any way forward. She stared at him with an obvious 'now what?' on her face. On the other side of the rail a couple of hand's span of loose, spiky grass and herbage formed a platform before the ground fell away to the ravine. Unperturbed, Manfred grasped the rail and gave it a few tugs as though testing its strength. While she was still puzzling out why, he'd vaulted over it.

'Not bad for fifty-six, hey?' he said, planting his feet apart on the narrow sward and pummelling his chest. 'Tick-box still ticking OK, you see.'

'Christ, Manfred! I wish you'd stop these antics! I thought you'd gone for good that time. *I'm* not doing that. That turf will give way, and the rail's too high to get my leg over, anyway.'

'You just put your foot where I tell you, and trust,' he told her, his eyes glinting. 'Now! Ready?'

'I'm in your hands, Manfred,' she said with mock resignation, and pointedly held up her foot as proof-offering. Grasping it, he placed it firmly in a crevice in the rock about knee high, while she, accepting that *fait* was about to be *accompli*, attempted to swing the other over the rail. Squirming to avoid a painful crutch-straddling encounter with the metal bar, she slithered onto the grass beside him with a series of undignified grunts. Keeping herself as close to horizontal as possible she shuffled to the edge and peered over. Even looking made her head spin. But after a moment's pause for cooler assessment she decided that with assistance, the first eight or nine feet of rock-face might just be manageable.

'This is the worst part,' he told her encouragingly, 'and once we have our feet on that flat shelf,' he pointed below, 'we only need make a bit of scramble to the head of the gully. Water once poured down here, you know, and there are these—bed-stones. In no time we shall be in the trees. From here it becomes easier.'

He led the way; she followed. She was, after all, in the professional hands of the King of the Alps.

They'd been clambering down the gorge for some time, and the going was steep. They'd both tripped and sprawled on the ground a few times, and their already dishevelled appearance was not improved by further scrapes and bumps. But as one shred of her dignity after another dropped away, so did Annya's trust of the situation grow. She'd even begun to suspect that in spite of his protestations to the contrary, Manfred had planned it this way after all.

His assertion about it being 'a bit of a scramble' was a fair description—but only in part. She hadn't found it all that difficult in those places where the long-ago-stream had meandered through trees, but in others, where it had poured over vertical falls, Manfred's help had been essential. She'd trusted his hands to guide and place her feet. Even so, the climb was strenuous and her calf muscles had begun to feel shaky.

By this point they were having a break sitting under a group of pines in the shade of a few bay trees. The shrubs were in flower, dropping pollen and minute white petals which were sticking to Annya's sweaty, mud-streaked face—though of that she was unaware. A violent sneeze shook her, dislodging clouds of pollen from her hair. Dusting her front and shoulders with her hand, she glanced up to see a strange expression flitting across Manfred's face. His eyes gleamed with amusement, while his awkwardly twisted mouth looked as though he'd been about to say something and was struggling to bite it back.

'Something wrong?' she asked. But he shook his head, grinning broadly.

During their ungainly descent the atmosphere between them had grown warmer. He'd kept his word and addressed her curiosity about how the gorge had managed to become green when the rest of the island remained dry. This cleft in the towering cliff, he'd told her, acted as a funnel for cooler air and moisture, drawing it up from the sea to form clouds on the high ground. These then gave rain which fell, soaking the ground and collecting into rivulets which ran down the gully, more so in times past, but occasionally now in winter, so that a continually circulating micro-climate pertained. Trees rooted, migrating birds were attracted to abundant insects and seeds, which again were recycled, ground fertilised.

Noticeably, in turn, something about the unique nature of the terrain seemed to be affecting Annya's tongue. Her speech began to flow, as Manfred had hoped, and indeed anticipated. She chatted freely about the incidents of the night before—the whole story, ghosts and all. Then, casually, he dropped the question, 'So, what exactly is your relationship with this Simon?'

'Relationship?' Then, after a long pause, she said, 'That's a big subject,' and abruptly stood up.

'Want to go on a bit?' he asked. 'Down there, I mean,' he said, and steering her in the direction of the dried-up path of the stream, they set off again.

'Down there' issues, he instantly realised, was the hot topic, and hoped his verbal slippage, this prompt from his subconscious self, wouldn't freak her again. He'd followed a powerful impulse when he'd spun off the road. It had felt like nature herself, the gorge, had summoned him, and he'd learned through years of experience to obey the call of something he regarded, for want of a better phrase, as *higher instinct*. It had been a smart move, and Annya was beginning to open up. He'd trusted to nature's efficaciousness before and not been let down, but what he hadn't anticipated was that the gorge might have something in store for him. His own speech might be loosened too. He took out his crumpled tissue, and dabbing his face more than once they continued clambering down in silence for some minutes, panting heavily.

But Annya's thoughts were elsewhere. Although younger by a couple of decades, she was acutely aware that, not only would she be lost by now without Manfred, but exhausted and lying somewhere with her ankle broken. The water course was far from easy to keep track of, and now it suddenly seemed to have disappeared underground leaving a steep traverse of rock to negotiate.

'A bit tricky, ja?' he panted. 'Need a hand?'

When they were safely across he looked at her, concerned. 'Want another breather? That pine! We can sit there.'

Annya nodded. She didn't want to admit it, but she badly needed a breather. That last bit had shaken her. Her legs were like jelly. She crouched down gingerly on a patch of dry earth between the gnarled roots of the pine and leaned her back on its twisty trunk. Manfred joined her.

Her conversation flow seemed to have dried up, and thinking he'd have to prime the pump a little to get her moving on the subject of Simon again, he stared at the ground. An old cone, partly eaten by some creature, lay in the dust. He picked it up and began to prise little nuts out from between the scales. 'I'm thinking,' he said slowly, offering her one. 'Simon. Your feelings for him.' He cautiously glanced at her.

'Well?' she said.

Monosyllabic, but she didn't seem too put out. 'OK then. I am thinking of your dream and how maybe I can help. For you to have woken with such a piercing anxiety must indicate something to you.'

She gave a long sigh, and he had the awkward feeling now that he was about to hear rather more than he needed to know.

'It's difficult, complicated, Manfred,' she said. 'I've known him so long—ever since I was a child, and so in some ways I look on him as a brother. A brother, but not a brother.'

Having launched herself she wasn't to be stopped. Even the intimacies of their last days together poured out. As the story wandered more and more into erotic territory, describing how Simon's mouth felt *here,* and how her fingers had strayed *there,* both seemed equally surprised at her sudden lack of inhibition.

Manfred blurted out, 'But did you or didn't you?' before he could stop himself.

'You mean, did we make love that last day? No. I desperately wanted it, but just as certainly wanted the relationship to stay as it had been. Now I'm not sure.'

'So... What are you getting at, "stay the same"? What did that mean? And how did he react?'

'I didn't want to be just one of his women,' she said, her eyes down on the ground.

'Is he a Don Juan, then? Promiscuous?'

'He's divorced. I knew that, but he started talking about other marriages, other relationships, and suddenly he wasn't the Simon I knew. It threw me. Then he backtracked, but it was like he'd pulled the rug from under me. He's always been something special to me. I suppose I'd hero-worshiped him, and that was stupid, and all at once I realised it. I *felt* stupid. Naive. At the same time I wasn't going to be just another bead on his string. Yet there he was, offering the one thing I'd always dreamed of. And now, it wasn't a teenage fantasy any more. It was grown-up passion, and I wanted him, fully grown up. But I wouldn't let him.

'I want him now, Manfred, his body, more than ever now he's not present. In fact it's almost as if he is. I feel him touching me at night, and in such a wonderful way. Better, I think, than if he were flesh and blood. Isn't that strange? It's so powerful I cry out with pleasure. But what can it mean? That's why when he called for me in terror, in the depths of my sleep, it was *real*. I know him so intimately now, that I am one hundred per cent certain it was him. What is happening Manfred? What does it mean?'

'You're in love with him.'

But she was shaking her head. 'I'd know *that* without all this add-on nightmare,' she said. 'So what's all that about?'

'I don't know, but let me guess,' he said slowly. 'I'm thinking aloud, you understand. There's a natural taboo here, isn't there? But sometimes, say if all social prohibitions are suddenly lifted, the energy of attraction to one who is so close as to be—how to say—of the same family, then zam bang! Lightning strikes. Knocks you off your feet? But there are certain other ties.'

He closed his eyes, struggling with his thoughts. But she'd got to her feet, impatient to move on again. 'You mean like bonding?' she called, already yards ahead. 'That's what I feel, but that's what makes it so complicated.'

Manfred caught up with her. The ground, although steep, was more of a path now. Quite unconsciously he took her hand, and she, just as automatically, accepted it. They were both steadying each other.

'You know,' she said, 'Simon actually brought this up. He called it "propinquity". A bit of one-upmanship to unsettle me, I guess. But I think it was him, embarrassed.'

'How do you mean?' Manfred let go her hand, and fished for another tissue to wipe his face. 'I'd be unsettled by that,' he said. 'But this is one thing, family bonds, blood ties. Let us say not bonds, but rather something other than genetic. How about soul-family or spiritual family? You may not like my theory, but let's suppose these ties are from many lifetimes ago. These attractions can be extremely powerful, fateful. Contracted before birth. Destiny.'

'Predestination?' she exploded aghast, stopping in her tracks. 'But I don't believe in it.'

'Of course, and neither do I,' he said hastily. 'I believe we have free will. But in these cases, from the fullness of our free will we choose to fulfil our spiritual contracts. So in this sense, destiny is taken on willingly if it comes along with sufficient consciousness.'

'You've lost me,' she said, making for the shade of some shrubs. 'God, it's hot today! I'm not sure I'm up for all this. Let's have another breather.'

Manfred followed thankfully, and slumped beside her. That last speech! How uncanny, it occurred to him, that their means of communication, that English tongue which he'd also struggled with such difficulty to untie, was suddenly coming free. They sat getting their breath for some minutes before he picked up his theme and his courage once more. 'Well, let's say we fulfil our karma. Does that make more sense?'

'You're beginning to sound like Tamzin now, and *no*, Manfred, I don't believe in any of that rubbish either,' she told him, irritably.

'I'm only trying to provide explanation to both of your unsettling experiences. Your ghosts and your Simon dream.'

'Why? Do you think they're linked?'

'Possibly.'

'I can't see how.'

'All right, but hear me out. I'm thinking on my feet.'

'We're sitting down, Manfred. But OK, I know what you mean, or rather I don't. But I'll hear you out. Hadn't we better get off our butts though and start walking again? She brushed her hand down her no longer crisp, cream pants, dusting off leaf litter and insects. 'You know Manfred,' she said, 'it's beginning to dawn on me who it is you're taking me to meet.'

But he only grinned roguishly and told her she'd better wait and wonder as it wasn't far now.

'Well, I hope your mysterious friend offers us something when we finally arrive,' she said edgily. 'I'm famished, not to mention parched. Anyhow, what's she going to think when two wild creatures loom out of the woods? Or is she weirder than us? Come on. Give me some idea what I'm in for.'

He gave her another strange look. Whatever the amusement, he was keeping it to himself. But as he offered her his hand he burst into one of his laughs.

'Sooner we go, sooner you'll find out,' he said.

XENA THE GREEK

'By all that's wondrous, what has the wind blown in? Ye gods! It's Pan and Flora!'

A handsome olive-skinned woman with flowing silver hair stood outside the ancient farmhouse, crossing herself and grinning. Tall, fiftyish—possibly more, possibly less—her jet-glittery eyes stared out from a face slowly creasing into a grimace. Having crossed herself as many times as seemed appropriate, she threw up her hands, shook them in the air with a gesture of horror, and laughed uproariously.

'Well Manfred, let's have you inside and introduce me... This is your Annya, isn't it? What have you done to yourself this time? And whatever's he done to *you*?' She turned to Annya.

Annya felt her cheeks redden. But the woman, still laughing, strode up, gave her a hug, and putting an arm round her shoulder, led her inside. 'Find you some water, huh? Pan there can sit with a beer while you tidy up. Then we'll see to his majesty. When you're both scrubbed up, we'll all have something to eat. The food's been waiting for *hours*. Where the hell have you been?'

It had occurred to Annya more than once to ask how the woman knew they were on their way. It was obvious they were expected, but at no time had she seen Manfred make a phone call. When she'd set out, and it seemed an age ago now, the arrangement had been to meet him up at Carlos' estate. There had been no plan to go on elsewhere. Even the brief and uncomfortable meeting with Carlos had taken her by surprise. But they'd simply, on the spur of the moment, jumped into Manfred's car and set off. So how had she been informed? The woman *was* a witch. No other explanation.

The farmhouse was dark inside. She knew most of these old *finca* were. Walls were often a meter thick with tiny windows, for air more than protection, and built for maximum coolness. Coming in from the outside, Annya's eyes hadn't yet adjusted, and if the Greek—she was sure that's who it was, though Manfred had failed to do the introductions—if Xena hadn't been leading her by the hand, she would have collided with rickety tables and precarious stacks of boxes as they made their way to the washroom through one cluttered room after another.

Exiting the kitchen, Xena unlatched a peeling door which led into a dark lobby. A single sunbeam filtering through a small round hole in the roof provided the only light. As they crossed the uneven tiles into a scullery, a strange, roughly cylindrical stone object in the corner caught Annya's eye. In the gloom it stood out, as it too was lit from above. She'd seen one before, she suddenly remembered, that time Manfred had led her through the old timber-framed farmhouse at Carlos' estate. It had intrigued her then, but she'd been so eaten up with anxiety she'd forgotten. It must have registered though, and seeing one again almost stopped her in her tracks. God! she thought, what on earth is she doing with one of *those*?

Xena noticed the hesitation, but her raised eyebrows seemed to be questioning the reason. 'The washroom's here,' she said, indicating a wooden door sagging on its hinges. 'You'll see I've put a bowl of water, and soap, OK? And a mirror.' At this mention of a mirror her eyebrows went up some more and she smiled mischievously. 'I'll leave you to it, Flora. Sorry my dear, we don't have all mod cons. Water is short and we have to be eco-friendly. So when you've finished throw it onto my garden out there, if you would. Helps feed the salads.'

A dusty shaft of sun was streaming through a cracked window

pane; enough light to wash by. Candle and matches in a dish had been placed next to a blue and white striped bowl which held a couple of inches of water. On the other side, in a saucer, sat a fresh, but unevenly shaped slab of soap. Annya sniffed it. Home made, she guessed, but it smelled nicely of lavender and some other herb she couldn't identify. She swished it in the water and rubbed it on her hands. It lathered up well, and she lifted her soapy hands to her face. Only then did she inspect her reflection. The same panda eyes she'd seen in the passenger seat mirror stared out from a mud-pack, but stuck into the cracked, dry mask were scores of minute white flowers, while a coronet of leaves, moss and pollen-dusted curls encircled her face. If she'd been mortified before, she was mad again now. He'd been laughing all the time. She hoped he'd enjoyed himself. But after a moment of staring at herself, the corners of the mouth in the mirror began to twitch, widening into a grin.

Her toilet completed as far as the short water situation allowed, and running repairs made thanks to a sample tube of moisturiser and stub of lipstick in her shoulder bag, she retraced her steps to where she'd left Manfred with his beer. Xena was waiting for her, but Manfred had gone. 'Welcome Annya. Good to *see* you at last,' Xena said, still chuckling. 'His majesty's in the process of transmutation. He's cleaning up too.'

'What is this, 'His majesty' thing?'

'The divine majesty Pan, yes. He's in the process of transforming himself back to the Manfred once more.'

'OK. I see the joke about my face. I get Flora I suppose. But what's that got to do with Pan? You seemed to link us together—Pan and Flora.'

'You don't know your classics, your Greek deities?'

'Only slightly, I'm afraid.'

'So! Well, Flora. Perhaps we borrow her name from the Romans,

171

but she's consort to Pan, he of the pan-pipes, king of the forest, god of nature. And she—flower of Springtime, fruit of Autumn. That's for starters. But we'll discuss myth and magic as much as you like over our food. You must be starving. I know I am. Come!'

And she ushered Annya outside again, this time round the back to a paved terrace upon which, in the shade of overhead vines, stood a long table. It was beautifully set out, covered with a multiplicity of small bowls and dishes, so many it was impossible to take in the dozens of different offerings they contained. There were coulis and sauces; there were salads of leaves and petals; salads of fruits and roots. Baby artichoke nestled together in a bed with wild mushrooms, while marble-sized beets glistened in a basil sauce.

Annya stood transfixed.

'Goddess of fecundity and abundance, you see,' Xena remarked, grinning proudly.

Annya was still taking it all in. Each dish decorated with its individual herb or floret. Folded napkins, gleaming cutlery and polished glass complimenting hand-painted dinner plates. 'Flora, you mean?' she murmured.

Down the centre of the table were earthenware jugs of blowsy flowers out of which poked the violet-tinged heads of artichoke, while little posies lay demurely by each plate. On a wooden platter a crisply roasted chicken sat enthroned on crusted potatoes. Stuffed aubergine smelling deliciously of wine and garlic oozed red sauce across the bottom of a deep green dish, while breads and cheeses completed the picture.

Annya's 'eye-of-newt' preconceptions were knocked sideways. 'Oh!' she gasped. 'But it's a banquet! And fit for a king, if not a *god!*'

'Sit down. Sit! We won't wait for him,' Xena commanded.

Annya briefly ran considerations of etiquette past her conscience, but her appetite won. Ravenously she began piling her plate. Shortly, a spruced up Manfred joined them. He squeezed past Annya, and before drawing out his chair, stopped to pick a few fragments of leaf still caught in her hair. 'You've missed a bit,' he said.

Annya looked him over. Mud swilled off, and hair at least finger-combed. Eyes, human again. He seemed to have made a fair job of tidying himself up.

Sitting down heavily he gave a long appreciative sigh and slowly inspected the spread. 'Xena, you've excelled yourself this time. It looks and smells magnificent.' Then he too began to help himself, filling his plate from dish after dish. 'You wish me to carve?' he asked.

'Why not?' Xena handed him the knife and, smiling with pleasure, reached for a spotted jug and poured a liberal portion of wine into their glasses. 'Let's have a toast!'

'But what have we done to deserve this feast?'

'Nothing at all. In fact you don't deserve, Manfred. Have you any idea how late in the day it is? I go into my garden and pick. I return to my kitchen and compose a dish or two. Time passes, and I go pick some more, make more dishes. No-one arrives. So I make the feast for myself, and to honour the gods.' She rapped the table with her hand, and with the other raised her glass. 'To the gods!'

'Speaking of gods,' Annya said suddenly. 'What is that Indian deity thing you have in the corner of that room?'

Xena and Manfred stared at each other with wide eyes. Annya felt her cheeks colouring again. She'd blurted out the very question she'd been suppressing for fear of seeming to impute something improper to Xena, or more embarrassingly still, disclosing suspicions which she'd hardly managed to articulate to herself.

'Indian deity thing?' inquired Manfred. 'You'd better enlighten us.'

'Well, you know. That sort of Lingam thing,' she explained nervously.

'Thing? Lingam? We're still in the dark. At least I am. You know what she means, Xena?'

Xena shook her head, but her eyes shone. 'I've got to hear about it though. Another drop of wine, Annya? I knew the gods were with us this evening. I feel Bacchus isn't far away.' And she glanced up into the leaves, searching the hanging clusters of green, immature grapes.

'No, no. Wine always flushes my face, thanks,' Annya lied, trying to deflect the cause of her embarrassment. 'Mustn't drink too much.' They were still looking at her expectantly, and having come this far it now seemed impossible to go back. 'That object in the corner, I mean. That... Well, it's this shape.' She demonstrated holding her hands about fifteen inches apart and modelling a standing column in the air. 'About so high, but ending in a sort of cone.'

She finished it off, her hands sensually rounding the end as if it were malleable clay. Then self-conscious again, she went on hastily. 'You must have seen one like it Manfred. That farmhouse on Carlos' estate. They both have a shallow bowl-shaped object—under the shelf. It's so like an icon on an altar with that shaft of sun lighting it from above.' She clasped her hands, pressing them down into her stomach as if keeping further incriminating words like obscene, pagan, fetish, from leaping out, yet at the same time feeling foolish because she knew what the image was called. They must be thinking her utterly, stupidly prudish... which she wasn't. So she said it. 'It's a phallus. The Hindus call it Lingam and Yoni, I think.'

With this she clammed up.

'Go on,' Xena urged, her eyes twinkling.

'I don't know much more,' she admitted, shaking her head as if disowning what she'd already said.

'But you say it's a phallus—the Lingam thing.' Manfred wasn't going to let her off the hook. 'But what about the Yoni? What's that?'

'I suppose it's the female part. Represents the masculine and feminine together.'

'What did I tell you, Manfred!' Xena clapped her hands. 'The gods *are* with us. First comes Pan and Flora, now comes Lingam and Yoni. The divine procreative powers. Dark and light united. Bless you

Annya for giving us that. But as to my stone in the corner, I'm sorry to say it is a rather more prosaic item. Tell her, Manfred.'

'I wouldn't say prosaic,' he said. 'It's called a Weeping Stone. These things interest me greatly; the incredible ingenuity of the human race. But Annya, what is this "thing" doing, here in Xena's kitchen?' He leaned towards her, his face challenging. 'How came it here, this highly charged icon?'

'Will you please stop trying to bamboozle the girl with your amateur psychoanalysis, Manfred.'

'But I want to see what pictures she has in her mind—if she has visions of you dancing naked in front of the thing every morning, making your obeisance to the gods of fertility. Or even astride...'

'That's enough, Manfred!' Xena gave him a sharp look. 'Bacchus has you in his power. No more wine for you tonight. Take no notice, Annya. I know his humour all too well, but you may not. This clever old stone in the corner supplied the water in which you washed your face, that's all. It manifests precious drops of water.'

'Does what? Makes water? That's even weirder.' Annya's eyes grew round. 'I don't believe you!'

Manfred drained his glass and looked pleadingly at his hostess for a refill. She ignored him. 'But true all the same,' he said, turning back to Annya and surreptitiously pouring himself another. 'Just like the gorge we came down. Remember? Vapour from the mists? It condenses on the stone, comes in through the roof opening, and it drips, drip by drop through the night into your bowl beneath. Been that way since the earliest days. And did you notice the bowl? Stone too. You see, they had no pottery on the island either, because no adequate supplies of wood for firing.'

'No wood?'

'No trees, no wood.'

'No metal either,' Xena added. 'They had obsidian knives. They carved out their bowls, or simply rubbed them from soft stone.'

'But,' Annya said, 'I'm not thinking that far back. We know Stone Age people didn't have metal knives.'

'Sure,' Xena agreed. 'But you have to remember we're an island. Isolated. Isn't that what an island is? Anyhow, this one was. Miles from anywhere in the middle of the Atlantic. Completely off the beaten track, that is until the Spanish arrived. For the Islanders the Stone Age went on and on, and wood, like water, was a precious commodity. They waited for it. Went to the sea shore and prayed for it to come to them. So even thousands of years later every implement, every piece of furniture, was fashioned from drift-wood collected on the beaches. But doesn't that give you a thrill, Annya, if you try to get inside them, their minds, in your imagination? How do you think they regarded the sea? It must have seemed the most magical, precious gift from the goddess herself. These wonderful people surviving by their peaceful ingenuity—out here on their own. No cloth, no weaving, no metal, no wood, yet they developed their own civilisation in their own way... Don't get me on the subject of matriarchy and the priestess, or we'll be here all night.'

It had been growing steadily darker, the red sun bleeding its pink and orange juice into the evening mist. Xena suddenly reached for a box of matches and rattled it. 'I need to light our candles. Or maybe we should go inside for coffee. What do you think?'

Back to the here and now, and noticing the sun was about to touch the sea's horizon, Annya turned to Manfred. 'How *are* we going to get back?' she asked, genuinely worried.

He looked at the tablecloth and shrugged. 'Ah. Well. I'm not sure.'

'OK!' Xena gathered a few plates and stood up. 'I make us some coffee then, and why don't you two go inside and I join you later. We'll talk more.'

Aromas of coffee-making drifted in from the kitchen. In contrast to the parts of the house Annya had stumbled through earlier, this sitting room was orderly and comfortable. Although its one electric light bulb in the centre of the ceiling was a dim and poor affair, a clever placement of candles—even, one might say, were circumstances different, a romantic arrangement—gave the room a cosy glow.

'I think she's being very discrete, don't you?' Annya whispered. 'Leaving us alone to sort ourselves out. But honestly, what *are* we to do? It just wouldn't be on to ask her to turn out in the dark and rescue our car, or even get her to run us back. We've put her to too much trouble already. Any chance we could get a taxi? I don't even know if she's got a phone out here.'

'Ah. Well,' he said again.

"Ah, well!" she repeated irritably. 'I don't have to remind you, do I, that *you* got us into this? Stranded.'

'Annya, you didn't ask me yet what is my big surprise.' Her brow furrowed. 'OK, I'm not changing subjects,' he said. 'And I take full responsibility for this... inconvenience.'

'Don't you mean mess? Cock-up?'

'If you say so.'

'That's the first time I've heard *you* say that,' she glared.

'It's your copyright, sure—but I mean it. But you don't want to ask me?' He made a questioning gesture with his hand.

'Your surprise? Isn't this it? All this? Xena, her house, the garden, her food, her... Well, *her!* She's quite a woman.'

'Glad you like her, but I told you I have something for you. I tell you this morning, I think long and hard how I can take you away from that place, that apartment that so spooks you. I worry about you being alone, you know. So I ask Xena. I know this place is off the beaten tracks, and she may be a bit unconventional, a little... exotic, unusual. You provide me the word. But...'

'What are you getting at? Stop prevaricating, Manfred.'

He drew a breath. 'She offers you a nice little room.'

Annya stared at him not seeming to take it in for some minutes. 'You mean...?'

'We... You can stay here... At least tonight. Get the feel of it, *then* we make some decisions tomorrow... When you see the lie of the land, ja? Ah! Xena.' He turned.

A rattle of cups had preceded Xena's entry with her tray of coffee.

'I was telling Annya of your very generous offer.'

The clear message of Xena's darkly arched eyebrows was directed at Manfred as she handed a cup to Annya.

'Your offer for her to stay in your nice spare room,' he explained, sheepishly.

'He springs this on you now, Annya? Manfred! You haven't said anything of this to her before?' Her tone was sharp. 'The whole day, and you turn up looking like... Well, I won't ask, but I guess it's an interesting story. And what tales did you spin her of me?'

'Very little,' he admitted. 'I keep you as my surprise.'

'Manfred, I am growing impatient. Give me the whole story. You tell me you met a young lady that is in some sort of trouble. You hint at hauntings.' Annya stared at her. 'Forgive me Annya, I talk over your head like this, but I don't know how much is true. He tells me you are experiencing phenomena, maybe poltergeists, and he asks me if I can keep the mother's eye on you, you can't be left alone. And I tell him, I must see her for myself, and we must speak, both get to know one another before we mutually decide. Then mid-morning I get this call from Carlos that you are on your way. So, I prepare nicely for maybe a late lunch, and I watch for your car. I hear nothing, I see nothing. Then, four-thirty you spring out of the trees like you've been rolling in the hay with Dionysus at your back. So where did you leave the car? You came down the gorge, huh? Are you climbing back up there in the dark? No. Does Matilda know you're here, Manfred? No. I guess not.'

'Xena,' he said, his eyes blinking panda-wise, hands gesturing *what can I say*, quite forgetting he was still holding a glass of cognac.

'Manfred!' the two women chorused in unison as the contents sloshed over his knees.

He stood up awkwardly, apologised, felt for his tissues. Apparently, the women were ganging up on him, conspiring. Spontaneously, in that infuriating way women have, they were deciding not to throw him a life-line. He sat down again and tried to change the subject. But the Solomonic silence continued.

'OK, I telephone Matilda. But Xena, it will have to wait till morning now, when I can get over to Pacco's. It's late now,' he pleaded. 'Too late for that damn radio contraption of yours. There's no-one manning the office this time of night. OK?'

Xena shrugged. 'So, I'll make us some more coffee then,' she said coldly.

Since she'd no means herself of getting transport, and Manfred was making not even a polite show of shifting from the armchair, Annya felt she'd no say in the matter. Questioning him on Xena's telephone situation after she'd gone to make coffee, she discovered that Xena had some walky-talky contraption linked to Carlos' farm, and thence to other vital organs of civilisation—community clinic, mayor's office or the Island Council Chamber.

'It's too late now, you see,' Manfred insisted, 'to set alarm bells ringing out there. There's no direct line to my house, and it would be too discourteous to old Salvador and his wife to have them stumble out of bed just to phone Matilda. She's used to me stopping off here at Xena's. She won't worry—too much.'

Annya gave him a look, but by now she was beginning to feel that as long as he behaved himself towards her then he and the long-suffering Matilda weren't her responsibility, and with the arrival of the second brew of coffee Xena seemed to have called off her protest.

Annya longed for bed, but the two old friends seemed ready to go on all night. Downing two more slugs of caffeine and another of cognac they were well into their pet subject again, the Island's ancient history. She settled back into the cushions. Something moved in the shadows on the other side of the room, and her face took on an enigmatic, almost smiling expression. Seems we've got company again, it seemed to be saying.

'Lemuria.'

Annya rubbed her eyes. Burned out candles were smoking. She struggled to the surface from the enveloping depths of a sofa—not her own. Voices; a man and a woman were speaking in low tones. Still in Tamzin's lounge, she tried to make sense of it, where she was. It must be the middle of the night and she'd better get back to her apartment? No, that wasn't right.

'It's on record,' the man was saying. 'Your ancient Greek historians believed it existed.'

'What?'

'Xena, you're not listening. I'm talking about Atlantis.'

So, she wasn't with Lester and Tamzin, but she must have nodded off all the same. All these lost continents, far too confusing, sounding just like the conversation they'd had last night. She'd found it hard to believe then, with Lester and Tamzin, and now, apparently, here was Manfred talking about yet another. Not that lost civilisations were impossible in themselves—though not sunk overnight, as Tamzin had said. Divers came up with things; film of structural evidence. They'd discovered those peculiar causeways, foundations for columns and all that in the Indian Ocean for instance. You had to believe that. But this Lemuria business was a bit too far out for her. Way too far, actually.

'All right, Manfred,' Xena was saying. 'So let's hear your evidence for this Atlantis theory then. Ah! There you are,' she said, suddenly noticing Annya. 'We thought you'd drifted off. Are you going to give us your thoughts on this?' she asked, seemingly pleased to have her back in the conversation.

'Well,' Annya said, rousing herself, 'it's a strange coincidence but we were talking about another lost civilisation last night. Lemuria.

It's hard to believe two vast continents simply disappeared when no evidence exists. As far as I know, anyway. Well that's my opinion, for what it's worth.'

'OK, evidence then.' In spite of the hour and his body moulded into his comfortable chair, Manfred's eyes sparked. 'If you want it, I show you,' he snapped, though his belligerence seemed aimed more at Xena. 'Not now—I don't come prepared with evidence in my pocket—but I have cuttings, recent archaeological discoveries on the Turkish coast. And then there's our old friend Plato. He tells how he visited Egypt and was given a detailed story of how nine thousand years before, a great war between the Atlanteans and Athenians was fought. This results in a massive tidal wave which swallowed them all. For him it is fact. Not only that, but he places part of it here, right here in the middle of the Atlantic, right where our Island sits.'

Annya, scornful as ever, was far from convinced. 'So how can it be in Turkey and in the middle of the Atlantic at the same time? You see what I mean, it's all nuts, and I don't see how anyone, especially you, Manfred, can begin to believe it.'

'I didn't say I believe it.'

'But you did,' she argued. 'You said you had evidence in your pocket. No, well then, cuttings back in your office. I heard you say that.' She turned to Xena in search of support, but was met with a cryptic smile. 'Come on Xena, tell us what you think.' But Xena's mouth stayed shut.

Manfred cleared his throat and glanced from one to the other. 'OK. Xena, for whatever reason, keeps her opinions to herself, but maybe I look at it this way. Atlantis is a myth, and myth is where realities meet, many layers of reality co-existing. Factual, stones-and-mortar, pots-and-bones kind of reality, so! Then we have metaphor, our storybook, tales telling round the fire. Tribal histories and humanity's records. Big Dreams of the Elders merging magic with memory. Religious and mystical experience with shifting of shapes and times. All ways of transmitting profound truth. All of these coming together one on top of another. Understand?' He demonstrated, his hands building blocks in the air. 'Yet of course, it's never that simple. Sometimes beginning at the beginning—point A—then a leap to point C or D, then back to B, so realities are so mixed up that, come the Age of Reason, we start to cat-call and poo-pooh.'

Annya stifled a giggle, avoiding Xena's eyes in case she was giggling too. But her face, like Manfred's, was serious.

'So far as I understand your inebriated gobbledygook, Manfred, I'm with you,' Xena said, coming off the fence. 'Our scientists tell us we must have certain attributes, physical, like your building blocks, to be real. You must touch it, smell it, hear, calibrate. A myth lacks such properties, ergo it doesn't "exist", it's your Father Christmas down the chimney. Today you must bring him into a court of law and try him. Produce me an angel and I'll measure him, they say, and maybe then I believe. But even today, they tell me, some physicists are beginning to discover that reality isn't what they thought it was.'

'But where does that take us with this Atlantis thing?' Annya persisted. 'It's either got to be real or—well...'

'Call it the Quantum effect,' Manfred suggested. 'New Physics, then. It doesn't have to be material to be real. Or maybe some of it is and some of it isn't. Or it's one kind of real here, objective, and another kind of real, subjective, relative...'

'You've lost me again,' Annya began muttering.

But Xena put an end. 'Come, Annya,' she said suddenly. 'Time for bed.' Annya noticed the slight rawness in her voice; she looked weary.

'So, try this then, Annya,' Manfred persisted, deaf and blind to Xena. 'Our Atlantis exists part in concrete reality, part in invisible reality.'

'Sofa OK for you Manfred? I'll find you a blanket then,' Xena said pointedly, 'and make up that bed for Annya.'

'Let me help.' Annya jumped up, eager not to put her to more trouble.

Manfred, getting it at last, struggled out of his armchair. 'Xena. No, let me. Tell me where you keep the bedding. Annya and I, we do this together. Come, show me and then you shall go to your reward, the long-deserved Olympian rest.'

'I don't contemplate departing this mortal world yet a while, Manfred,' said Xena stonily.

'But Xena, you know I didn't mean that. It's because you look...'

'Look knackered? You know how to present bouquets, don't you Manfred.' But she was smiling, and Manfred, moving close, placed his hands on her shoulders and gave her cheek a tender kiss. It was becoming ever more obvious to Annya that these were very old friends.

'But you'll allow me to tuck you in for the night, yes?' he whispered into her ear.

'I'll manage, thank you Manfred,' she said, pushing him away. 'And I'll manage to make this bed for Annya. She can give me a hand. OK Annya?'

'Sure,' agreed Annya. 'I'm ready to drop.'

Her dirty clothes dumped on the floor, and one of Xena's fresh tee shirts slipped on, Annya collapsed onto the bed. Blowing out the candle, she watched the wick trail its smoky grey tresses against the surrounding darkness.

Barely twenty-four hours since the night on Tamzin and Lester's sofa, and now, here she lay on another strange bed. Simon's distress-call piercing the depths of sleep last night had been overtaken by events of the day. Would her exhaustion blot him out tonight?

THE PASSENGER

Manfred, struggling with the gears of Xena's truck, whistled happily if tunelessly as the rutted coast-road unwound before him. The sea seemed almost black in contrast to the brilliant white spume which came flicking and flying off the tops of the waves less than a yard from his off-side wheels. If he turned to look it would dazzled his eyes, the morning light was so intense. He jammed the brim of Xena's straw gardening hat tighter down on his forehead. Glad to be outside with the road to himself and something practical to get his teeth into, he was only minutes from Pacco's place and from the nearest phone.

No-one this side of the Island was connected to the main system as yet, but Pacco was the proud owner of a cell phone. About time Xena got herself one too. Perhaps he'd better stump up and buy her one. First thing as soon as he got to Pacco's, he'd ring Tilda and get that off his chest. Then Carlos. Get him to send Annya's car around with one of the chaps from the estate, then arrange with the garage to send a couple of men out to his stalled vehicle—hopefully still rescueable.

The stone gateposts of the Finca Feliz hove into view. He glanced in the rear mirror for a last glimpse of the ocean as he changed down, ready to turn in at the entrance.

'Dreams *are* mysterious things,' said a voice from the passenger seat. He spun round. The voice was so familiar that he fully expected the owner of the comment to be there. It was the fact that the seat appeared empty which startled him. So much so that he stepped violently on the brake. Sweat broke, trickling into his eyes and down his face as the truck juddered to a standstill, between the posts, in a cloud of dust. 'Gott in Himmel, not again!' he groaned, reaching for his box of tissues.

He wiped his brow, drove down the clutch, shoved the recalcitrant gear-stick into first, and revved. The vehicle shuddered, but deciding it wasn't done for yet, started forward in a series of jerks. His heart gave a few irregular thumps. Heat getting to him, he told himself. The best part of a kilometre up a winding track still to go. He'd take it gently.

'It was my pet subject, you know,' the voice continued.

Manfred forced himself not to look towards the passenger seat. Even without doing so, he knew that he would find himself sitting alone. The image that Annya had conjured up that day they'd sat under the arbour in Carlos' garden, that spirit visitor, "Little angel," she'd call it. She'd been struggling with it all—confused and scared. But she'd spoken of another—an older man accompanying the spooky boy. And for some reason it had been *that* one which had got to him. "Large as life," she'd said. "Without that beard he'd be your brother." Ever since that remark he'd been waiting for this alternate self, this variant from some parallel universe, to make itself known.

'This is a new one,' he muttered. 'Talking to yourself is one thing, but when your self starts talking to you, that's quite a stumper. Wouldn't you say?' But his passenger declined an opinion on that.

The truck's engine purred, and seeming to know where it was heading, began to take the incline sweet as you like. 'Consider yourself an expert then, on dreams?' Manfred asked.

'In my day,' replied his companion.

Manfred strained to decipher an accent. Germanic, he felt, but with an overlay of Dutch—and was there a hint of American? 'Your day?' he queried. 'And *when*, may one ask, was that? Oh, please. Second thoughts. I've decided. I'd rather not know.'

'In my day,' his companion repeated, ignoring the comment '... but theories come and go. For instance, there are those among you today who would tell you that a vivid dream, one in which you spend a couple of hours like a viewer in front of the box in your drawing room, but also occupying scene after scene as actor and scriptwriter, plus all the other subordinate parts, is actually played out in a nanosecond of time.'

'Well, my friend,' Manfred said, becoming animated, 'it might interest you to know that I am familiar with that theory, and though modesty would forbid me to say this to anyone but yourself, I too am considered to be something of an authority on the subject.'

'Authorities also come and go, you'll find,' said the other.

'I think I *am* discovering that, thank you,' snapped Manfred. 'Even so, speaking as a representative of today, I admit this theory of the microsecond is intriguing.'

'Nano. Nanosecond,' corrected his passenger.

'Ah! I haven't quite... Well, there you may have me—ahead of me even... OK, but I think we're onto roughly the same thing. New Physics, yes? Thinking outside the box?'

'Just so, my friend,' said his passenger. 'And as one authority to another, I expect you're also thinking all this splitting of hairs is perhaps irrelevant, especially since they also tell us that Time is an illusion. Not the same 'they', admittedly, but nevertheless those authorities who take it upon themselves to hand down authoritative pronouncements.'

This man's a bore, Manfred decided. 'By the way,' he said as a thought struck him, 'what exactly do you call yourself? Your name. Or would you say this is splitting hairs, too?'

His passenger obviously thought so, as, ignoring the invitation to divulge that piece of information, he continued, 'It is also said, and no doubt you are aware of this theory too, that another form of dreaming exists, an advanced state where the dreamer, conscious that he is dreaming, can direct the course of the dream at will. Annya, you might be interested to know, is occupying such a state at present. *If* she remembers it she will believe it took place over a period of time she will assess as maybe a couple of hours, and that the drama she took part in was real, yet inconsistent with reality. At least, not reality as she presently understands it.'

Manfred tried to form a response, at least ask his passenger how he knew all this, but his consciousness—that consciousness in which he still knew himself—was slipping away.

It's night. The sky is black with grey clouds and she is flying over a landscape, flat and lit only by a fitful moon. She peers intensely, hoping for that clue which will tell her where she is. But the ground is uniformly drab and featureless. Gradually she becomes aware that she is travelling over a long straight road. They continue on, she and the road, and it now seems that she herself is lighting it up, as if the body she is travelling in is a vehicle with a powerful spotlight in its belly which is pointed down, illuminating the tarmac. Ahead, at the horizon, a faint cluster of lights appear. She speeds up. It is a town, maybe a city. Her velocity is so great now that she loses control of the vehicle. Of its own volition it heads straight for the centre where the lights are closest and brightest. Suddenly she is a guided missile; her head is a warhead, and it's on target.

A spasm of intense fear sweeps through her—fear that's going to explode in her brain, and she no longer has charge of her will. No time to think, but think she must. Wrest control or become party to their game—and their game is war. Her vehicle swerves, rushes through streets, swerving, banking. She curves in through an open window and out through another. Exhilaration surges, and with the frisson of power it brings, she gains control. She's searching. Alleyways now, narrowing, still searching. No light now. Dark, darker. Passageways, cellars, urinals, spaces between walls, under floors and hatches, searching. And there he is! Trussed like an oven-ready bird, head smashed, torso twisted in a mass of filthy garbage, dark blood and excrement... She cannot look. The mouth is screaming!

Xena sits at the foot of the bed holding a steaming cup which she is stirring.

Xena put the cup down. 'Annya, are you OK?' she said softly.

'Where...?' Sunlight was bursting in noisily, hurting her head. She could see flecks of gold dancing in the searchlights criss-crossing the room.

'Annya?'

'Where is he? Where am I? What have they *done* to him?' Annya cried, distraught.

'Here, have a sip of this.' The voice was calm.

'What? What is it?' Annya took the cup, holding it, and sniffing suspiciously.

'Tea. A nice one. Sip.'

'No!' Annya's round and horrified eyes stared at the woman at the foot of the bed. Her throat, seared with the scream which had ripped through it, felt hollow like a desert-dry tomb.

'It is green tea, love. Take a sip. Or some water?'

Slowly she understood it was Xena, and that they were in the spare bedroom.

'Thanks. Tea sounds lovely. Thanks,' she whispered hoarsely.

'Is it the face again?' Xena asked, her voice soft with concern. 'Your haunting? Was it *him*?'

But the girl's eyes gazed back, vague and unfocused. 'What time is it? Where's Manfred?' she asked.

'He's gone to sort out transport and make phone calls. Matilda, Pacco, Carlos. It's past midday. We left you to sleep.'

Xena paused, and Annya, after a tentative sip or two, finished off the tea in gulps.

'More?' Xena asked. 'I've got the pot here.'

Annya nodded.

The second cup disappeared in seconds, and Xena handed her a glass of water. 'Well? Was it him—the face?'

Annya shook her head. Faintly, she said, 'No, not him. It *was* him, but not *that* him.'

'OK. No rush. We've got all day—what's left of it. Shall I leave you?'

The girl shook her head again. 'Please don't. Stay, please stay—a while—if you can.'

Xena meant she'd stay if she was going to let her in, but if not, she'd got things to do. She wasn't unsympathetic, but one had to be rational, and so she rationed her patience. If the girl was serious, in danger, she would keep guard, lend an ear, but otherwise it was over to Manfred if her problems were such as needed coaxing. 'I'll come back if you need me,' she told her. 'I shan't be far away. There's no-one around to harm you, but I heard you cry out in your sleep. Whatever made you yell like that was inside, and I can't help unless you really want me to know.'

'I *want* you to know—*someone* to know, but I don't know *how*, Xena. Inside. Yes, it's inside, but how can I make you understand that what I saw was real?'

'Try.'

Try! She throws 'try' at me; one word, and expects me to deliver an incommunicable experience, Annya thought. She *had* tried with Manfred, told him how it was a dream, but much more real. More than any dream was supposed to be.

Annya took a breath. 'If I told you what I saw you'd only offer tea and sympathy like I'd had a nightmare,' she gasped. 'I don't want that. I can't risk you seeing it that way.'

She drew another breath, holding on to it this time like a diver with water closing over her head.

Leaning towards her, Xena seemed to be restraining an impulse to slap her on the back as if she were a choking baby. But her knee-jerk reaction must have done the trick as Annya's words spluttered into life again.

'I saw Simon. Dead, horribly dead. Killed and very dead, but he was still screaming, Xena,' she said, a lost look on her face. 'Calling for me. And you can say it was a bad dream all you like, but I know different. He's dead, and he wants me, wants me to go to him, find him. I did. I went and I found him, but what now?'

'Where is he?' Xena's response threw her. She looked up into Xena's eyes. Xena looked back. They were talking. Woman to woman they were talking. Xena's eyes were no-nonsense. They spoke, and what you saw in them, you saw.

'I don't know, but I flew over a lot of desert, hard to see because it was night, but in daylight you could tell there's nothing much to see anyway. We flew over a long straight road and headed right for the lights of a city. None of it I recognised, but I heard—someone—like speaking over an intercom. 'Between two rivers,' it said. That's all.'

'And what did you understand by that?'

'Only something I half took in at school, and I sort of put it together. Mesopotamia. Between two rivers. Just guessing, Xena.'

'Baghdad then. You were heading for Baghdad. Do you know why?'

'Well, Middle East. That's what he told me. Simon, I mean. Even that I had to drag out of him. But I thought it was Syria he'd gone to. Baghdad's in Iraq.'

'U-huh!' Xena nodded. 'Anything else?'

'No. Not really.'

'Have you seen the news, watched TV lately?'

'Oh, there's a set back at the apartment, but I never watch. It's complete garbage. A couple of ear-grabbing headlines from an eye-catching senorita, all teeth and up-front disclosure. It's not your BBC out here, you know. I turn the radio on sometimes, but it's only when you tune to North Africa that there's anything.'

'You mean you listen to Arabic news?' Xena's voice was full of amazement. 'Then you've probably heard something.'

'No. What have I heard? I can't understand a word. I don't listen to news, but you get some terrific music late at night. Sensuous stuff too. And poetry. I love Rumi. You know, one of the Sufi poets, I can just about make it out then. But political stuff, news, you catch the odd word, but only if it's Western, one you know already. So, no, I haven't, in short. What rumours? What have you heard?'

'Look, I don't want to upset you unnecessarily. Let's wait till Manfred comes back. He won't be long now. We mustn't jump to conclusions.'

'For God's sake! Xena. Tell me. What have you heard?'

Xena had fallen into the trap she'd dug for herself, and began back-pedalling unconvincingly, until she was saved by the sound of footsteps crossing the patio.

'Manfred! Is that you?' she called.

They both looked relieved when his familiar voice answered.

Xena got to her feet and ran to the door to meet him. But moments later, as they both came into the bedroom, Manfred sank with a heavy sigh onto the chair Xena had just vacated.

'Any more of that tea?' he asked wanly.

'I'll make us another pot,' she said, her eyes drawing together, puzzled. Far from the gallant 'white knight on charger' entry she'd expected, this hero's return seemed more of a shell-shocked retreat.

She let him drain two whole cups before broaching the subject of Annya's latest dream. His face became drawn as he listened in silence. Attentive as usual, professional, yet with part of his mind elsewhere, she thought. As she herself had nothing more to offer, she decided to leave them both to rest, and busy herself with something sustaining and tempting in the kitchen. Her culinary skills might be the best answer for them all.

* * * *

As Annya told Manfred later, sitting outside watching the sun go down, the three of them once again finishing off the remains of a very late lunch, what she couldn't get her head around was the battle going on inside her over which was worse, *not* being believed, or *being* believed. Xena had taken her account at face value, which was what she'd wanted—until—until the implications registered. If her dream of Simon's death was real... She was convinced it was. She'd been given graphic evidence by whatever means. Yet what sort of evidence?

Xena, inspiration striking her, raised her fingers to the sky. 'Astral travel!' she cried. 'How about that for a possibility!'

'And what are your thoughts on *that*, Annya?' Manfred asked.

An image of Xena's cluttered back room filled with every kind of dried root and fungus flashed into Annya's mind. Fleetingly she saw herself holding that cup of green tea. Then just as suddenly she realised she'd drunk the tea *after* her Simon dream, and ruled that bit of paranoia out. Congratulations, she was learning to stay in charge of her imagination at last. Half smiling, she looked at Xena. 'The state I'm in right now, I'm willing to consider anything. But all that astral stuff belongs in La-La Land, you know. As theories go, it's make-believe. No kind of reality that *I* can accept, anyway.'

Xena's hands did a 'take it or leave it' gesture.

'And yet,' Manfred came back, 'you're convinced what you saw was real. Are you wanting it both ways?'

He was shuffling uncomfortably in his seat, she noticed.

'I don't want it *at all*,' Annya said loudly, struggling with her contradictions.

She looked at him, her eyes challenging, despairing, searching for answers. But before he could open his mouth, 'OK, you win,' she said.

He blinked. 'Haven't said a word.'

'You don't need to, it's written all over your face. Part physical, concrete reality. Part invisible reality. Isn't that what you said last night? Only now I'm even more confused.'

'*You're* confused. Join me in the lifeboat, then,' he said wearily.

'Sorry? In the *what*?' she frowned, and turned to Xena for explanation. 'What *does* he mean?'

'I think he means he's confused.' Xena seemed to be spelling it out for her. Annya tossed her head and with an exasperated 'Uh', looked away into the distance, then noisily began collecting plates and started marching with them towards the house.

'Sit down,' Xena said with her speaking-to-a-petulant-child voice.

'Yes, sit down,' Manfred echoed. 'We'll do that later.'

'Annya,' she said more gently. 'We both understand what this is doing to you, but have you noticed how Manfred isn't quite himself either just now. I'm sure he will tell us what's been going on in his own good time—given half a chance. Just because I haven't probed it doesn't mean I haven't noticed. We've heard from you, Manfred, how you've managed to sort out transport, and I believe you've had a word with Tilda. How is she by the way?'

'She's OK,' he muttered, looking at the table.

'Well, apart from the transport,' she went on, 'you've been pretty quiet since you came back. So, how's she taken your latest escapade? Did she throw you out at last?' He shook his head, but continued to gaze downwards.

At last, Annya said quietly, 'Sorry Manfred. I *am* being stupidly self-obsessed.'

Yet although he smiled up at her, he still seemed absorbed in a silence he couldn't shake off. Minutes ticked before he spoke. 'Last night,' he said slowly. 'That was all theory, last night.' With that he came to a stop again. The two women looked at one another, Annya mouthing, 'What does he mean now?' But Xena widened her eyes and shrugged.

Almost inaudibly, still scrutinising the table, he said, 'I think I had a taste of the reality behind the theory.' Then he lifted his head. 'Between the gateposts and the doorstep of Finca Feliz,' he said, 'the best part of a kilometre and a slice of my life disappeared. One moment that damn truck stalls between the posts; next I am outside the finca. Nothing in between. Yet when I return here, I know before you tell me, everything that Annya has experienced in her dream. I am in shock—still trying to make sense of it.'

Xena put a hand on his arm. 'You *did* look done in, I thought, Manfred,' she said quietly, lifting her fingers to stroke his cheek. But Annya, feeling she could ignore this show of intimacy in the face of her own mounting perplexity, demanded, 'You mean none of my dream was a surprise?'

'My surprise, dear Annya, was hearing all your story pouring from your mouth, and I say to myself your famous déjà vu. I arrive in a time-warp, then wanting to put my hand over your mouth and gag you. Stop it all from coming out, because what you are telling me I already have seen.'

His statement finally sinking in, even Xena sounded incredulous now. 'I'm shivering, Manfred. Look, goose pimples,' she said, holding up her bare arms. 'Bad enough Annya with *her* ghosts, but you *too!*'

'Oh, Manfred,' Annya cried, guilt ridden now. 'I thought you were being impatient, insensitive. Brushing me off. I got angry.'

'Of course you did. Of course,' Manfred said, with his hand poised to give her arm a pat, but mindful, in some vague way, of how she'd freaked out the last time he'd done something similar.

He was taken aback when she flung her arms around his neck now and burst into sobs. 'But, Manfred, is it *real*?' Her voice was hysterical, tears pouring down her face.

'Real? How should *I* know what's real,' he admitted gloomily. 'But let's all calm down and have a think-about.'

'But not out here,' Xena ordered, calmly enough, but it was definitely a command. 'Inside, both of you, and we'll take a cognac. It's growing dark, and I don't believe in ghost bumps. That's mist blowing in from the sea. Can't you smell it?'

The think-about was still in progress a couple of hours later, yet in spite of the cockle-warming effect of the spirits swirling in their glasses, no satisfactory explanation for the dream was arrived at. At least, not one they could agree on. In spite of Annya's hostility to the astral travel theory, Manfred felt it might be the best idea they'd come up with. It held out the hope that, since the astral is beyond linear time, what they'd both seen was a glimpse into a potential future, rather than an event which had already happened. Though, because it had impacted so forcibly on their senses, that fact added greater urgency to the need to do something. Perhaps another phone call to the Amsterdam office, however unwelcome the news might be.

As Annya climbed into Xena's spare bed for a second night, the faces of unseen guests stirred uncomfortably in her thoughts.

CLOUD OF DREAMING AND REMEMBERING

Educational though it had been, Finn decided he'd had enough of infernal combustion engines for the moment and would take a ride back to his mountain in his usual fashion, on board one of the thermals.

After watching Lester get into his car and Annya taking her leave outside the villa that morning, and keeping well out of sight, Finn had shadowed her as far as the apartment block. She'd be anxious to make contact with that Peter fellow in Amsterdam, he supposed, via that other clumsy contraption people use these days to speak across distances.

Annya's night-visitor, Simon, had visited her as she slept on Lester's sofa, and done so by a means far more familiar to Finn. In some oblique way he knew that, closed off from his everyday consciousness, Simon had glimpsed the shape of this thing to come; of something lying in wait. He'd seen it coming, and alerted Annya. Stripped bare of his sophisticated defences, in his sleep, Simon had called out, and in her slumbers she'd heard it. Though neither she nor her lover had any clear recollection of what had taken place when they woke.

In the same way, Finn knew that the place where all this happened was a world of spirit. In this space his mother Cléa came to him, and his own sweetheart Li-Ona visited him. It was through this astral highway, too, that Mandy came and went. This was also a domain of potentials and dreamings where realities were born to flourish—or sometimes die.

From the increasingly agitated pattern of Annya's thoughts as she'd neared the apartment, he guessed Simon's nocturnal visit must be breaking through into her consciousness. He hung around long enough to satisfy himself that all was well inside the complex, then, as she headed for the office phone, he trusted things to unfold for her, and that he could safely leave her to have this conversation over the ethers in her own way. He could now go back to base, be alone a while and think about his next step.

Not that he was relishing his solitary state *all* that much. Mandy's disappearance at the restaurant seemed a tad abrupt—not to say churlish. Even so he nurtured a sneaking hope that he'd find him sitting there on the peak, waiting for him.

One thing he didn't want was another visit from Gaia.

Spending the night on the sofa opposite Annya had been enjoyable, and the fun and games in the kitchen, quite like old times. Reminded him of all the exciting dishes he'd cooked up with Li-Ona when they were children, long ago yet as fresh as yesterday. He felt tears welling up, and he wiped them away before his heart began that thing it did whenever he thought about her. He would have to put such thoughts away or this task of his would never get done. Yet it wasn't proving all that difficult, he told himself. Clues *were* piling up. That comment of Tamzin's about a civilisation lost beneath the sea, Lemuria she'd called it, right away rang a bell in his head, and sent shivers through his body.

Body. Body. That too; the sound and shape of the word *Body* was resonating. The problems he'd encountered after his arrival from Zurillion, a planet which vibrates at so high a rate that it is invisible to even the most powerful instruments on Earth, were understandable. But, as with the lower colour vibrations here, he was getting to feel more at home with human flesh, seeing its attractions. Seems it's beginning to grow on me, he joked. Yet, seeing how Mandy had mastered the art of appearing and not appearing, he thought his own knack still needed a bit of fine tuning. Possibly, at the back of his mind, his initial reservations about taking on a body were acting as inhibitors. Mandy's trick of switching from etheric to corporeal and back again was cool. You had to take your hat off to him there. Yet hadn't he, Finn, in his *going to town*, sat in the front of that motor vehicle, then lain on a sofa enjoying every minute of it? I'm obviously starting to get into the feel of it, my body in touch with the matter of touch. Could this be the process of embodiment beginning, and I'm actually liking it? he asked himself. But this brings up so many questions.

And all were going through his mind as he rose with the air currents. This matter of descent; descent into matter, this body matter, this mass, this weight, this density.

Heading for his mountain peak he took another route this time. Just for the hell of it he'd wafted round the back of the island where the seas were crashing onto rocks. Once there, attracted by the vigour of their swelling energy, he was reminded of that moment when he'd first pierced Earth's atmosphere. The burn of entry as he'd met her gravitational field and her slower vibrations hit him again. Vividly he saw Annya just as she had been when, tossing and struggling for air in the water, he'd felt her plight in his bones. He'd homed right in on her like an arrow to the gold. But what part of his consciousness, he wondered, called up that boat with its wake which had carried her to shore?

Lost in thought, he didn't notice that the currents of air he'd hitched his lift on were drawing him towards land. Close to shore a drift of mist was rising off the sea. Collecting into a cloud, it was being funnelled up, Finn along with it, between high cliffs. They stood on either side of an inlet which had once carried a stream of water from the top of a steep gorge, the same gorge which Manfred and Annya would pass down later that day. As the saturated air became denser it dawned on him that he could no longer see the crashing waves. In fact he could see very little as a choking vapour blanked out vision and sound.

His limbs kicked and struggled. His hands clawed at the stifling substance filling his eyes and mouth. He'd never encountered such a thing before. As soon as he pulled one fistful of the stuff away it was immediately replaced by more of the same. He was still being drawn upwards, but the higher he rose the more the blanket closed in. Suddenly a weird sensation, a vibration of jangle and fire, shot up his spinal column. It had begun in the peritoneum—he could locate it with precision, a spot at the base of the spine, between his legs. But as the sensation reached, then flooded, his brain, it seemed to be knocking out his senses. The very tool he took so for granted, his glittering mental facility, seemed to have reverted to basic instinct. His body had begun operating from a program of primal instructions.

If ever a knack was needed—he needed it now.

Something was going badly wrong. Another sensation shot through him, a wave of ice-cold. Kicking and clutching wildly, he struggled for breath as it burst through his solar plexus and crashed into his heart. It was the same sensation, he guessed, the same helpless panic he'd observed in Annya that day in the sea. Only now it was him, and *really* hitting home.

There must be some reason behind what was happening.

Hardly had he formed the thought, when a voice in his mind whispered, 'Remember, Finnegal, you are now an emissary of the Galaxies. If you find yourself trapped in the limitations of lower vibrations, or up to your neck in dangerous waters, do not lose heart. Say to yourself: "I'm watching myself go through this."' It was a piece of advice he'd been given by one of the Anointed Elders before he left Zurillion. 'This statement is priceless,' she'd said. 'It is a statement to your conscious mind which signals the installation and initiation of your Watcher-Knower Self.'

But he'd been given so much advice before he left, and had not always listened properly. He'd maybe just stored it away, like those three cold potatoes sitting in his pouch right now, in case they came in useful later.

Well, this was later. So, what should he do? Stay calm and observe?

OK, let's see then. Shouldn't be too difficult! I'm watching myself go through this, he repeated. But what is the *this* I'm going through? Is it this substance? These sensations? This panic? 'Hell, Mandy, this isn't getting me anywhere,' he shouted into the cloud.

The hope that yelling his old friend's name might do the trick and make him reappear, faded when no-one answered. Only the grey mist wrapped closer around.

What else was in that piece of advice dropping into his head then? Something about initiation. 'A statement to your conscious mind.' 'Installation of your...' What was it? 'Your Watcher-Knower Self.' Well, maybe this is what it's all about then, he thought. Initiation. And anyhow, if that panic had swamped him completely he wouldn't be having this kind of conversation with himself. So at least he must be *watching*, if not exactly *knowing* himself.

Knowing himself; wasn't that what initiation meant after all? Wasn't it all about some damn awful test where you had to come up with solutions on your own? Well, since that was all he had to go on, he'd better do a spot more observing, he thought. All right then, nothing he couldn't handle.

Some of his faculties, he noticed, were in working order, some weren't. Although visibility inside this cloud was virtually nil, his senses told him he'd risen as high as he would for now. He could feel the pressure of its canopy on his head. He knew it was composed of nothing more than moisture molecules, yet it seemed to have acquired the consistency of an impenetrable membrane. Normally he'd only need to think 'move', and he'd have popped out through the top. But that didn't seem to be working now.

So much for his Watcher Self. But what about that Knower Self, what did *He* know? Perhaps he'd better do a little experimenting, and find out, he thought.

He discovered next that by directing his arms and legs to work as paddles he could move forward, back, up and down within the cloud. He played with this novelty for a while. So far, so good! The sense of ground beneath him felt flat here, but then, steering himself forward, he felt it suddenly dropping away. Alarmed, he backed off. In an instant, sucked again towards the edge of what he assumed to be a ravine, a ferocious uprush of air thrust him into a series of dizzying somersaults. This unfamiliar body of primitive instinct—which had somehow grown on him—began its automatic struggle to right itself once more.

No-one to turn to now. No Mandy to enlighten him on the extraordinary changes taking place in his body. But he *damn sure wasn't going to let that panic get to him again.*

'I'll get you that blanket then,' Xena had said. Manfred took it gratefully.

Lying in the dark now, images swam through his head. He pictured Matilda's accusing face, only to be succeeded—before he could say, 'But, my love, if only you understood'—by that of the tear-stained, frightened Annya. Tired though he was, his over-stimulated mind refused to allow him that slide into sleep which his body craved. The instant he'd dowsed his candle, darkness flooded the room, but the events of the last days had crowded, confusingly, in with it.

Maybe I *am* growing senile. That blackout in Xena's truck—'A bit of a funny turn, Doctor,' he mocked himself. Perhaps I'm not as fit as I like to think. Should I admit I've crossed over into Annya's territory, that land of movable realities they commonly call delusion, and diagnose myself 'a suitable case for treatment'? And why this dig at Annya, anyway?

He could no longer trust himself. His reality, the ground beneath his feet, had shifted. Hoping the familiarity of the external world would bring him back to his old self, he opened his eyes and stared into the darkness searching for landmarks, tables, chairs. Instead, lurid images of continents sinking beneath tidal waves rose out of the black ground, countless terrified humans shrieking silently as the inundation overtook them. He covered his eyes with his hand, but the images persisted, threatening to overtake his thoughts and drag him into further speculation on the nature of reality.

He groaned. Enough's enough, he told himself sternly. If sleep refuses to come, at least *I'll* decide what thoughts I'll think. But then... Annya and her damn problems! I'm sure it was a genuine desire to help, although in all honesty I have to ask myself... Fact is, for whatever reason, *something* brought us together. I've always known I was on dangerous ground ever since I took the alternative path all those years ago—selecting those I wanted to help, the most interesting patients, God help me! And she's not even a patient. There have to be rules and boundaries, I agree, yet I'm arrogant enough to think I can make my own. And now we're into this new ball game, and it's about time we took stock before I'm into it up to my neck, he chided himself, not noticing the serious lack of boundaries in the field of his metaphor.

Although questioning the concept of Fate, he nevertheless believed a series of circumstances which went beyond everyday coincidence had brought them together. And however one termed it, such a 'drawing together' had a greater purpose than simple chance. To have ignored such a call would have been more of a dereliction of duty than to follow the rules of convention.

Having set off in pursuit of his thoughts, thankfully the tidal waves now seemed to have subsided. He stretched and bounced a bit, testing the sofa for comfort, then turned on his side. Wrapping the blanket round him, he was asleep and snoring in seconds.

The transition from conscious to dream state came swiftly, from one grey blanket to that other grey blanket, a mere blink of the eye. He was back in the cloud, the grey-brown fog-soup, the white mist floating atop the ravine. There he was, watching himself, seeing himself yesterday about to enter the cloud, spinning off the road, making a violent about-turn.

A reverberant snore ripped through the room and he knee-jerked awake again.

Ah! That was it. Annya had been stuck, locked within herself, and he'd wanted to shake loose that stone stuck in her throat. He knew he had to do something, but didn't know what. Her anguish around the missing Simon was tangible, more so the fear. Yet she bottled it all up, mistrusting his motives. The situation had demanded action, and it was no good playing this one by the book. He never played much by rules anyway—it never got you anywhere—but he didn't have a clue right now—right then. They could have gone on, taken the long road, the orthodox route, ninety minutes drive or so, but that would have got them nowhere. He'd needed inspiration. And there it was—Inspiration! It had happened to him like this before. You run out of road, you're heading for the abyss, no bridge in sight, and suddenly... someone takes over the wheel. You know it's you, but you don't know the *you* who comes forward at that moment, he's a complete stranger. It's simply trusting the universe to come up with the goods. You make that leap into the abyss and you're there, beside yourself, coming to meet yourself. It's no good trying to explain this to anyone. You only recognise it when it happens. But this was different. This time he'd taken someone with him: Annya. Yet the same law of trust had been in operation. But it's one thing taking your own life into your hands... Though Matilda would have something to say about that of course. There are always lessons to be learned. Is this why I'm back in the cloud, he wondered?

It was wrapping him more closely, becoming softer, greyer. He turned on the sofa, drew up his knees and pulled the blanket tighter around him. His clenched fist, thumb protruding, crept to his mouth. Back in the nursery a dribbly smile spread across his face. 'Rocked in the cradle of the deep,' some far off memory crooned.

The cloud swirled, formed patches, grew thinner then thicker.

Finn had no idea how long he'd now been in this grey, stifling mist—days maybe. Though for all he knew it might as well have been eons. He was still wrestling with his predicament. There was his body; this new and unwelcome acquisition which behaved quite unlike any body he'd found himself in before. Then there was the cloud in which he seemed unwittingly to have got himself trapped. He felt like a blind man—or a creature, one of those grubs Mandy had once shown him on their woodland walks, swimming sightlessly, aimlessly around in a murky pool. "Awaiting Mother Nature's call to begin its mysterious transformation into some winged splendour," his old tutor, eyes atwinkle, had told him all those years ago. 'Only *I'm* not hanging around aimlessly waiting, Mandy. That call might never come. I'd be here till Doomsday.' Without realising it, Finn was having this out-loud conversation again. 'I *have* an aim,' he told him with some force, 'and that's to escape.'

But if his old friend Mandelbrot was listening, he was giving no sign of it. The only voice Finn had heard in this endlessly miserable boredom had been that piece of advice from the Zurillion Elder. And that had only been a voice in his head. Anyhow, much good it had done him. He'd Watched. Oh boy! had he watched! And, well—as far as Knowing, he admitted he'd drawn a bit of a blank there. But he'd persisted, gone through his repertoire, tried out a whole gamut of creative possibilities. He'd observed till his eyes, as well as his ears, were popping, and still he was stuck.

An age ago, though it may have only been yesterday, he'd felt he was on the edge of a breakthrough. A shrill, yelping 'mwee-o' had suddenly pierced the cloud, and he'd felt a beat of wings passing his face. The sensation was of something warm-blooded, soft feathered, powerful, like an eagle. His hands stretched out with the eagerness of a child whose birthday had come. Convinced it was a sign, that it would bring a message, he'd waited for it to return.

He'd waited, and he'd watched.

The draft of air which the creature's passage had created spiralled through the cloud, carving a tunnel of thinner, lighter mist. Then, curling back on itself, spinning and twisting, the substance began to form a shape. His heart leapt. The mist was morphing into a figure, human and familiar. That form was unmistakable. Indistinct though it was, there could be no doubt. 'Mandy,' he'd called excitedly. But, with an inevitability he was now coming to expect, the cloud had closed in again, wrapping itself about him, thick and choking.

He'd peered into the swirl of damp particles, staring at the spot the figure had occupied until tears filled his eyes, and a chill began to seep into him. It was difficult to believe that only days ago he'd lounged atop a similar cloud, viewing his domain like a prince. Yet now he was inside this inhospitable monster. Such nonchalance! How confident he'd been. As he remembered, he felt his power drain from him. Every attempt now to find a way out had been met with resistance. It was inexplicable to his mind that anything so vaporous should imprison him. Yet softly but firmly the moisture atoms had closed together and thrust him back. It was as if the cloud had some sinister purpose. A personality even, he thought with horror. 'God help us!' he moaned, 'I do believe it's observing me!'

Overwhelmed by this sudden sense of fallibility, it didn't occur to him to ask himself, *what* purpose. All thoughts of his sacred mission, of Annya, and even of his dear, sweet Li-Ona had been swept from his mind. Plunged into despondency, a darkness descended on his spirit, and a sensation so new, so terrifying there was no name he could put to it, pressed in from all sides. The cloud was beating him hands down.

Suddenly the atmosphere around him changed. It started to vibrate. As he listened, it seemed to him as though the cloud itself was transmuting. He shivered and clasped himself tightly. The vibrations increased and it seemed that all the billions of particles forming it had begun to resonate. Singing back and forth to each other, an unearthly humming set up. Its effect was unpleasant in the extreme. It felt like every cell in his new body was gyrating. Then the sound changed again to a beating, pulsing, roaring. His body shook, and he held himself even tighter in an attempt to clamp down the awful sensations that threatened to shatter it to pieces. The conviction grew now that he was inside some gigantic, living thing. An organism which, like a monstrous lung, had begun to breathe him in and out. Each breath squeezing and shaping, contracting and stretching, until he couldn't tell if he was being swallowed or expelled.

Desperate, he tried to summon his Watcher-Knower self again. But the magic words were lost almost as they fell from his lips, drowned by the dreadful sounds echoing round his head. He could only surrender to whatever experience this organism chose to subject him to.

The contractions stepped up, forcing and squeezing him. He was being passed along some canal, whether a throat, an anus, or what, he couldn't tell, but the sensations were more and more visceral.

At last it came to him that he might be undergoing a bizarre birthing procedure. He held his breath. If he'd dared to unclasp himself, he would have stuck his fingers into his ears. He knew without a shadow of doubt that he was about to hear that which he didn't want to know.

'Finn!'

Oh! That voice! Involuntarily his hands let go and he clapped them to his ears.

'Finn,' she called again.

'Gaia. In the name of Kristiamus! Leave me alone, Mother!' he cried.

'You know why I'm here, Finn. You know where you are, and you know why.'

'I'm in a shit-hole of a cloud,' he screeched. 'I'm in it and can't get out.'

'And you know that you put yourself right where you are and created your predicament.'

'Of course I didn't! That would be stupid. That *is* stupid, Mother.'

'I will say no more,' was her only comment.

'What do you mean, *I* put myself here? *I* created it?'

Cryptic as ever, 'That is for you to find out, dear child,' the Goddess replied, sweetly.

'What is it with you mothers and goddesses? Not to mention disappearing tutors?'

'We are here, all of us,' the sweet voice sang.

'But I just can't see you, is that it? What kind of joke are you playing? Just get me out of here! *Please.*'

'Would you like me to sing you a lullaby, Finn?'

'No! For shit's sake, *no,*' he wailed.

'Let me see, how does it go... Mmm... mmmm... mmmmm... mm... Rocked in the cradle of the deep... Sleep... Dee-eep... Slee-ee-eep...'

The cloud wrapped its arms about him, swaying to and fro, shuttling weft through warp, weaving a rock-a-bye cocoon.

In his own cradle of the deep Manfred rocked from side to side. He was in the middle of a conversation with his Other Self.

'I'm coming apart, brother,' Manfred wailed. 'I thought I had it all sewn up; tied up with ribbons, done and dusted. Thought I knew it all; who I was, what it all meant. But it seems I don't any more.'

'Shades of déjà vu, huh? Feeling we've been here before, are we?' said the now familiar voice.

'I'm in this fog, brother mine. Can't see a hand before my face,' Manfred moaned.

'Haven't you understood yet, that every time we think we know, what we've actually done is stopped growing—ceased living. This fog, as you call it, is the Cloud of Unknowing, my friend. Mystery and Dissolution. We all come here eventually—one way or the other—but the lucky ones, the wise ones, come many times throughout their lives. Each of us needs to let go his certainties, dissolve into the mists, scatter his parts, before he can remember, reassemble, and ready himself for the next step on his journey of expansion.'

Finn felt the blanket of cloud creeping around him like a silken mesh. The sound in his ears now was gentle and hypnotic.

But it's so dark, I can't see, Mother, a thought inside him whispered. And it's sticky.

'Mmmm,' the sound replied.

It's so dark, I don't like it, Mother, his little inner voice said.

Sh-sh-shush, hshhh, came the sound, repeating over and over, incessant like a tide, lulling him back to dreamland.

Then very indistinct and far away he heard another voice. In a quite different way from the swishing and humming, this too was familiar. And not only the voice, but the words. 'You mean sh-*she's* teaching *us*,' it said.

He struggled to remember. Which 'she' could it be referring to? The voice was male, but sounded wavery and cracked, and seemed to be travelling toward him down some hollow tube. He strained to catch the next wave as it came along. He thought it was saying something like, 'See-ee what I mean about classrooms, my boy?' His body gave a violent twitch, but before he could form a response, he heard his own wavering, tinny voice say, 'I'm beginning to see, Mandy.'

His body jerked again. In the recesses of his consciousness, whether awake or asleep he couldn't tell, he only knew that he had enough lucidity to understand that what he was hearing were snatches of a conversation he'd had many days ago. Mandelbrot's words and his own were echoing back, as if they were being played on some antiquated, stuck recording.

'Don't have any facts as yet, Mandy,' echoed his own frail voice. 'Not much I can communicate... Understand what I mean though, don't you? I'm scanning their energy-fields... occlusions...'

'Tell you about *what?* These occlusions, Finn?' the insistent record demanded. 'You mean she's teaching us... See what I mean about classrooms, my boy. They just keep coming around, around, around,' the voice echoed.

Occlusions. What had he meant? His mind, Finn remembered, had been so clear; clear and focused when he'd brought the subject of human brain-junk up with Mandy. But now, cocooned and immobilised by this sinister cloud, his brains were scrambling. 'You mean we're in one of them right now, Mandy?' he cried out. 'This cloud? You think all this is what we were talking about the other day? But this can't be *my* junk I'm stuck in, dammit. A real junk monster, this one. Not me. No way Mandy, not me!'

'We never get away, Finn... However far we go,' the broken record went on. 'We're never anywhere but Here, and Here's where they bump into us... Classrooms... They just keep coming around... I hear you've been talking to Lady Gaia.'

'Mmmmmm,' said the lady herself, evidently not part of any recording.

'But she told me I dropped *myself* in all this shit, Mandy. Why the blazes did I do that, for Chrisake?' the bewildered Finn wailed.

'Classrooms, Finn, classrooms. Round and round...'

'Rolling carpets, remember?' Gaia said.

His body gave another violent heave, while his arms and legs tried vainly to free themselves. But the more he struggled, the tighter the cloud rolled him up. The molecules were weaving a fabric, yet although it felt as dense and stifling as before, it was no longer sticky and moist. Something else seemed to be happening. But *what?* his

210

desperate mind demanded. What new horror is she planning now? Virtually blind, with arms pinned to his sides, he was choking and gasping for air. The fabric binding him felt rough. In fact, for all the world it was as if he was inside a filthy carpet, only now it was dust rather than fog filling his nose.

THE SHORES OF TIME AND BACK

Images flooded Finn's head, but rolled up tight, with no control over what was appearing on the screen of his mind, he could only watch. The only part of him which had any autonomy now was this new body of his.

A swarm of glutinous grubs, the sort which he knew feasted on corpses, slithered and wriggled in front of his eyes. Just as he felt he must scream, the picture changed and the screen was invaded by an army of bugs. He could feel them too; thousands of pairs of legs crawling over his skin. He shuddered as the insects stabbed into his flesh with their jaws. Working their way over him they paused to pick debris from hair follicles, ear whorls and eye corners. Even into his nose. His guts convulsed, but with a desperate effort he managed to fight off the desire to retch.

It was growing unbearably hot now inside the carpet, and his skin began to burn and itch. In his mind he saw the landscape of his body with its surface like a map, some piece of old parchment cracked and crumbling. Incapable of turning his eyes away he watched as a rash of colourful volcanoes began erupting from beneath the surface. He was breaking out in a mass of pustules! Nauseated by the sight as they began to boil and weep, his fingers clawed uselessly at his bindings as they instinctively strove to relieve the intolerable itching.

Helpless in his misery, he was plunged into a new nightmare of indignity when, unable to subdue his reactions any longer, his mouth drooled vomit and his bowels emptied. He was rolled up, skewered, and face to face with his own darkest monster. Everything he'd ever feared about the taking on of flesh had come to roost in the branches of his veins.

He thought he heard Gaia whisper in his ear. 'Human flesh! Now there's an interesting subject.'

Thousands of miles away in some other hot and dusty place, another pair of eyes was watching the glistening writhe of grubs.

Little Jamil could hear the dogs barking. They'd found something. His mother had screamed at him yesterday—forbidding him to go outside again. He must keep away, she'd insisted—well away from the alley which led to the back of the houses, and the waste ground where he loved to go with his sister. They liked to play among the rubble and weeds. But even though Fatima was older, she'd also been told not to go there now.

Fatima and he—they'd been building a house out of some old bricks and blocks of stone from a tumbledown workshop. It had taken days to build, and it was their secret. They'd found a jagged sheet of corrugated iron and dragged it bit by bit across the ground. Fatima thought it might do well as a roof, and they'd struggled with it, propping it up and tilting it into place. It was very heavy—and hot. It burned their fingers. But they were so pleased with themselves when their little house began to come together. They even made a garden in front of it—drawn a square and marked it out with pebbles. They went on a hunt for plants, the ones with flowers, then pushed them into the gritty earth. Fatima had poured a few drops from her tin of water for them. And they discovered a load of interesting feathers which they arranged in a Cola can, and a torn picture to fix on the inside wall. Under the corrugated roof there was space just enough for one of them at a time to crawl in. They planned to make the room bigger, but now, even though the house was still their secret, they were forbidden to go to the waste ground.

Mother, when she'd screamed at him, her face looked frightening. In a harsh voice he hadn't heard before, she told him of the terrible thing which would fall on him if he disobeyed. And if that wasn't enough, she said his father would come, and he would be even more angry. His father had left them weeks ago. They'd told him—his mother, aunts and uncles—he was away fighting bravely for Saddam in the desert. But he'd come flying back in the dark of night if he didn't obey his mother. But Jamil was getting bored in the house. The thought of his father flying in through the bedroom window was terrifying, yet it was broad daylight now, midday, and his mother and sister were taking a sleep in the shade. If he didn't *exactly* go up the alleyway, but quietly slipped out and down the street to the corner, he wouldn't be disobeying, and he thought he could find his way around the back of the other houses. He was curious about another pile of rubble he'd seen over the neighbour's fence. It couldn't do any harm to just take a look. He quietly lifted the door catch and peeped outside, hesitating on the step. But the street seemed empty, so, noiselessly, he crept out and sped past the front of the houses to the corner.

It had a special feeling, this being alone, and it grew as he realised he'd got himself into a deserted back yard where he'd not been before. He could see a pile of rubble and garbage and began poking with a piece of stick. He wanted to loosen that big packing case so he could reach the corner of an old carpet he could see buried under it, but the whole pile, sand and masonry, started to shift. He scrambled away, fast, out of its path, as it rolled down pattering and clattering. There was a bad smell and a lot of dust. He froze, expecting someone to come and yell at him. But it all stayed quiet.

The dust settled, but the smell got worse. He took a cautious step or two back to the rubble pile and tugged the rotten carpet again. He jumped with surprise as it tore. And that's when he saw the legs. A man's legs, big and swollen, and strange in colour. He picked up his stick from where he'd dropped it and slowly, one foot then the other, holding the stick out in front of him, he approached the corpse again. The stick shook in his hand, but he pointed it at the leg and nervously touched, wondering what would happen, if it would kick. There was a buzzing sound. Scared but fascinated, he looked closer and poked again at the flesh. Then he saw the maggots, a mass of them writhing and glistening. He flung the stick onto the ground and fled.

'Human flesh! Twisted strands of Creation. Now there's an interesting subject,' Finn thought he'd heard Gaia whisper in his ear.

'Biology and consciousness, Finn. Spirit woven into matter, that too,' echoed the voice of his mentor.

'The history of mankind when you really look deep into a person... All of human evolution's there,' Finn heard his own reverberating, hollow-can voice say.

'Like a carpet unrolling,' said Gaia. 'Remember? Your sacred mission unfolding.'

'I think I'm remembering,' Finn said. He was drifting into and out of layers of consciousness. 'Am I dreaming, Mandy?' he called. 'Are you there, Mandy?'

'I'm here, Finn,' he heard Mandelbrot's familiar voice say.

But now there were other sounds, other voices. It seemed as though a crowd was gathering. Although 'crowd' seemed too solid a concept for what he was sensing. A veil of beings, a throng, maybe, he wondered.

'Who are you? Who's there?' he asked, tremulous and confused. He couldn't see in this swirl of light and mist.

'We are all here. Always here, Finn. Remember?' A multitude of gentle voices answered. The sound was as though the air itself sang. It was utterly beautiful.

'All of us were there,' they chorused in waves of strange, ethereal harmony which seemed to shimmer around him.

'In the beginning, we were all there, remember?' they sang.

Then a sound Finn hadn't heard for many a long day, distinct and utterly recognisable, came forward from the veil. Tears welled up in his eyes and joy in his heart. 'In the beginning I was there,' sang the wonderful voice of his mother, Cléa.

'And I,' said his father. 'Both of us were there, my son.'

'There was darkness, then there was light,' sang his mother. 'At last we could see what had been there all along.'

'Yes, wife, there all along, hidden in the darkness,' his father said.

'In the heart of darkness,' said his wife, 'there sat Love dreaming and weaving.'

'Dreams are mysterious things...' echoed Mandelbrot's voice. 'Dreaming *was* my pet subject.'

'Weaving and dreaming life into being,' said Cléa softly, speaking to him now as if she was telling him one of her bedtime stories again. 'Weaving consciousness out of the cloth of light. Look with your heart, Finn, my darling, then you will see the Creator nurturing thoughts of Planet Earth. A new beginning was in mind, and Gaia herself was being conceived. See Love seated in her chamber spinning her cloth of light and dreaming her weave into being. Thoughts were becoming particles and a beauteous fabric, a cloak of mineral life was beginning to cover the earth, flowing and cooling into crystal cups and basins, waiting for the waters of the stars to condense. And you will see a billion years of consciousness passing before you, out of which came the second weave, the mantle of plants. Simple forms at first, but they trembled to the dance of evolving, and their forms grew, reaching up, rooting down, spreading, fanning out into a million forms. And then another spinning brought the winged ones, insects at first, then birds, fanning evolution even further afield as seeds of life were carried through the air. And the seas also awoke, and life swam and moved, dancing itself into being.

'And then the creator thought more deep thoughts, and these became particles imbued with greater consciousness, and the stars sang to this new planet Earth, and Gaia's consciousness sang back, welcoming that which was to come. The souls of animals stirred. They were being called to make their home on Gaia's breast. Softly she called a welcome. I will begin my weave of biology especially for you to inhabit, she sang. And, stirred with fear and excitement, they felt themselves being drawn into the peculiar structure of a great adventure, and they began parting and paring off from their home in the far galaxies to begin the new way of being, uniting with Gaia.

'Are you seeing this, Finn, do you see? Do you remember? We were there; we were all there. There we all sat in the Council of Love, preparing for the emergence of a great civilisation of gentle beings who would come in a hundred million years, and who also would join the adventure, learning to live within the strands of biology. Learning to sustain themselves on flowers and leaves.'

'I'm remembering, mother,' answered Finn.

The mist-like quality of the light seemed to swallow him up—at least as far as any consciousness he still possessed could grasp.

HIS NEW BIRTH DAY

Finn rubbed his eyes. Instinctively he breathed in and felt air, wonderful air filling his lungs. The clarity and sheer beauty of it all! Tears began welling up, brimming his eyelids, and his hands automatically lifted and started to wipe them away. Then he let them drop. As they fell to his side, his fingers touched the ground he was sitting on—bare rock with a fine, gritty covering. He trailed his fingers making small circles in the sand, as slowly—he almost resorted to pinching himself—he took in the realisation that the sensations he was feeling were physical. His body had weight and a sense of physical power.

He'd been dreaming, and now he'd woken up. That was it, wasn't it? Everything before this was a dream and now he was awake. He swivelled his head from side to side then up and down, as if to stimulate the little cells inside, get them to spark into action, firing off messages which would remind him who he was, where he was, where he'd been, where going. *If* he should be going? He felt he had something important to...

A bird, quite a large one, had taken off from a pinnacle even higher than his own, spread its wings and risen into the overhead blue where it circled before swooping down towards him. 'Good morning,' it called as it passed his face. It had flown past him before; it seemed like an old friend. He had no other friend as far as he knew. He looked around, listening. Down below in the tops of some trees, faintly, other sounds drifted up. Unknown birds chattering among themselves, busy, but not in the least concerned about being watched and listened to by the solitary being on the rock shelf. He noticed other, tinier sounds; creatures busying themselves too among the roots and the small green-leaved plants clinging to the rock in places. Busy, busy. Important.

'Good morning Finn. What a beautiful day!'

His head jolted and he shuddered. 'Gaia?' he heard himself whisper. He looked around but could see no-one. This voice had come from the ground too, but it was a much louder, larger, resonating sound than the little creatures.

'Yes, here I am at your feet. Happy birthday, Finn. Congratulations, dear child.'

'Is it my birthday? It certainly feels like a birthday. But what am I supposed to do with it? I think I'm meant to be doing something.'

'Be happy, Finn.'

'Are you sure? Is that it?'

'That's it. Do whatever you like. Find your feet.'

'That's all?' he asked, puzzled. 'Shouldn't you be telling me what to do?'

'That's what I'm saying. Do whatever you like. Find your feet and see where they take you. I'm very pleased with you Finn. I adore birthdays and this is a beautiful day for a birth. I'll leave you to enjoy it.'

'Find my feet? Oh! Sure, OK then.' They were dangling in front of him a few inches from another flat slab of rock. He slithered his bottom forward, whereupon they touched the ground, so he stood his weight on them to see what it felt like, and took another great breath. It was strange, felt wobbly, but good. Good to be alive. 'I'm enjoying this, Mother Gaia,' he sang. The bird flew past him again and soared into the blue air, circling, wings outspread. Finn leaned forward rocking on the balls of his feet, and spread out his arms like the bird. Tilting his head up he called, 'You enjoying yourself too, are you?' The bird paused its circling and hovered directly overhead.

'Mwee-o' it cried, looking down into Finn's eyes. Then another bird appeared, and the two began circling round together, calling, mewing and yelping.

'Happy birthday,' Finn called to them, and raised his arms wide out and took another deep breath. He thrust his chest out and felt more of the delicious air pouring into his lungs and his heart. His whole frame wobbled as he stretched up on the tips of his toes, reaching towards the birds. His centre of gravity tilted forward, and his head bobbed, chin on chest, gazing down. There was a lot of drop below him, and his arms widened out again and stretched as far as his fingertips, and the next time his wobble took him forward he leapt out into the space between him and the floor of the ravine.

His body plummeted. There was a rush of air, but he was going down and not up to where the birds were. Except suddenly they were there beside him, one on either side, one wing of each under his wildly flapping arms, lifting him gently and steering him into a glide. They soared together, out and over, towards the sea and round and back and over the green tree tops, until they gently deposited him on a step of rock part way down the gorge. 'Thanks guys,' he said. It seemed a strange thing to say, so he added, 'I love you, thanks.' They flew around a few times, dipping a salute, before flying off, calling, 'You're on your feet now. Goodbye! Good luck!'

The ground was steep so he wriggled his toes, digging them into the sparse earth on top of the rock. He sniffed the air as scents rose up from the ground, and from leaves too, and barks releasing aromatic oils, and delicate florals drifting in clouds from tiny pollen-filled blossoms. He could smell other things as well. Some creature had recently passed this way; he could smell that warm musky odour of creature. It excited him; he could smell female as well as male, and his body shivered again, wondering, tremulous. His heart bumped in his chest, and his mouth opened, smiling. He knew these smells. These were friends, so he had friends after all; friends with the same form as himself. Everything in him seemed to be trembling, coming alive, excitingly, disconcertingly. He wanted to hold it back, because it threatened him, threatened to engulf him, overwhelm with memory. Too much rushing upon him all at once made him feel odd, so he sat down quickly.

He knew now what he had to do: that *thing* he must do—apart from the feet, that was; he'd found those. And now all the rest would follow, he felt sure, if he took it a step at a time, and in that way he wouldn't be overwhelmed. 'Keep it simple,' he told himself. The birds had shown him that he could fly. Now he must discover how to use his feet to best advantage. The ground fell steeply, rock in places, skittery stones in others, and skimpy grass of a kind. Scents all around him; root, plant, flower scents, as well as those enticing animaly-human ones. He must follow those, particularly the female scent; she who had recently passed this way. He knew that one all too well, and could, if he needed to, put a name to her. But that would pull in too much memory and information, and he was keeping things simple just for now.

He stood up, positioned himself, ready to go. One of his feet lifted itself off the ground and pointed forward and down. He sprang. The energy in the spring took him a leap of a couple of metres before his feet touched the ground. He leapt again—and again—arms outspread, leaping and winging until he'd covered a hundred more meters downward through the air, touching earth, and leaping over and over. He gave a whoop of joy, loud enough for anyone for miles around to hear. This was even more exhilarating than flying, he decided, his breaths coming short and fast with wetness running down his skin. So he sat down again, thinking the blazing sun would dry him, but it seemed to make him even wetter.

As he sat, a strange sensation arose in his stomach, and he remembered the three potatoes in his pouch. He felt all over himself, hunting for them, discovering in the process that the stuff clothing him was unfamiliar. Exploring now with some urgency he thrust his hand between his legs. No potatoes there! But something even more important was. Reassured, he let out a sigh. But where had his holding pouch gone? And his leggings, and his wonderful tunic, for that matter? He felt again. The garment of strong, blue cotton clothing his legs was clumsy but intriguingly fashioned, engineered almost, with metal rivets, fastening devices and big stitches. He ran his hands up the outside of his thighs and there at the top of his right leg were three more bumps. He slid his hand into a slit in the material and pulled out the potatoes. He stuffed them one at a time into his mouth, chewing and mixing the chew with saliva which came flowing under his tongue. They tasted delicious. "They'll earth you," he remembered, and noticed for the first time that everything he was wearing smelt earthy. He pinched and smelled the cotton on his legs, taking in the indigo blueness which seemed to be incorporated by some means into the fabric. He remembered too that indigo had been one of his favourite colours of an evening. He'd drawn the most mysterious tones and undertones from storm clouds, or pulled dark blue jewels from the oceans to illumine his mood, whereas this rough cotton was second cousin to those corded jobs his old friend Mandy... 'Oh Kripes!' he gasped. 'They haven't given me *his* wardrobe, have they?' and his hands went to his chest, where he was relieved not to find that ridiculous museum-piece of a shirt, but a marl-coloured vest with enough skin exposure to show off his musculature to advantage.

Then he noticed animal scents around his feet, and bent to remove a leather sandal which he held to his nose. The warm mix of human sweat and bovine skin stirred sensations in him which hitherto had been locked away. If only he'd known what taking on a late twentieth-century body would be like, he'd never have hesitated so long.

Fortified by his meal, Finn set off in a series of winged leaps and reached the vantage point of a mound of dead roots and stumps not far from the floor of the gorge in time to see a dilapidated truck boneshaking its way along the coastal strip. As it drew closer he could discern the shapes of two males in the front. One appeared bearded, the other clean-shaven, although his features were shaded by a straw hat. Otherwise the two men were almost identical; same height and breadth. It seemed imperative suddenly to keep out of sight. Crouching, he waited, quivering with shock and anticipation as the vehicle lurched towards him. Then swerving past with a crunch of gears and a flurry of dust, it turned off the main stretch and onto an even more rutted and potholed track, and headed inland. He must keep them in view, yet stay out of sight himself until he'd had time to assess the situation. Both men were visible to him, and by the same law of physics he had to assume he was visible to them. He had no doubt about the identity of the bearded one; it was definitely Mandelbrot. Obviously there was a lot of catching up to be done, and the sooner he had a word with him the better. But how to handle this new set of circumstances? Run after them? Hardly! Yet he needed to find out where they were going, and if possible listen in to any conversations, while at the same time staying unobserved. At least until he'd got a handle on how the other might react to seeing him. There were drawbacks to having this new body after all, he was beginning to realise. Yet strangely he wasn't finding the need to question the new and extraordinary powers which seemed to have come along with it as part of the package. Like a babe fresh from the womb he seemed to have no background with which to compare—for the moment, at least.

He had an idea. He'd take a sounding on the vehicle's probable route and maybe find a shortcut and head them off. Luckily the track was circuitous, forced into winding, climbing and dipping by the nature of the terrain. Finn raised his head and half closed his eyes, concentrating on a cavity behind his nose. It filled with light which he focused into a beam, sweeping it from side to side across the landscape, seeking the probable path of the vehicle. A geometric pattern of lines and co-ordinates began to form. Observing, he noticed certain lines standing out as others faded. Then he asked for a pin-point of the truck's destination, and in an instant a picture of an old farmhouse nestling between a group of trees and an outcrop of rock appeared in the space behind his eyes. With his own route clearly mapped out, he set off like a lynx in sight of its prey, striding and leaping, all the while taking advantage of the plentiful cover. He arrived minutes later sweating and breathless as the truck drew up in front of an ancient farmhouse. He managed to dodge behind a screen of vines just as the driver was climbing out.

The man removed his hat and stood, wiping his hot face. His passenger likewise got out, but with rather less effort, it seemed to Finn. He wasn't exactly sure but he thought he'd seen *him* sidle out without bothering to open his door.

Without question the passenger was Mandy, and Finn, unable to contain his joy, stepped out from his hiding place. In spite of himself he began to run forward, arms outspread, ready to give his old friend a hug. But Mandy lifted his hand with an urgent 'stay where you are' gesture. The one holding the hat seemed dazed as he made his way unsteadily over the cobbles towards the door of the farmhouse. Finn recognised him now, but Mandy signalled again to wait until Manfred had gone inside, then beckoned Finn to follow him round the back of the house where stood a large wooden table with the remains of someone's lunch still on it.

Mandy drew out a couple of chairs and sat down. 'Great to see you, lad. Go on, Finn, have a seat. We'll be alright, I think. They'll be busy for a while, so we might as well help ourselves to what's left of this food. You do eat, I suppose? Then we can eavesdrop later. They've got plenty to sort out between 'em, but there'll be enough news left over for us. We must do some catching up too.'

'I must say you're playing this a bit cool, Mandy.' Finn sounded put out. This reception wasn't quite how he'd imagined it. Not sure he *had*

225

imagined it, but if he had... he was sure it would have been somewhat warmer that this.

'What did you expect, Finn—fireworks, birthday cake, popping corks?'

'I...' didn't say that aloud, he'd almost said, but Mandelbrot's grin made the rest of the sentence redundant.

'Don't want them to know we're here, not yet. So, quiet as ghosts. Right?' Mandelbrot offered, by way of explanation.

'OK Mandy, enough of this,' Finn demanded with a rasping whisper. 'You'd better let me in on the joke.'

'More cheese? Or a plateful of this,' Mandelbrot asked, ignoring Finn's irritation and helping himself to the remains of an aubergine salad, and dipping a discarded crust into the oil. Finn, in spite of his annoyance, was following suit eagerly. Mandelbrot nodded approvingly. 'My word, your appetite has improved! We'll soon have cleared the lot between us. Maybe we should show our appreciation and wash up. What you think? Second thoughts, that might spook 'em more than disappearing food. We'd better play it by ear then,' he said, casually picking up Xena's empty glass. A drop or two only of red wine remained in the bottom. Mandelbrot studied it, swirling what remained of the liquid, then passed his hand over the glass a few times. Finn watched the performance, impatience rising to the point where he had to keep himself from kicking Mandy's shins. The older man calmly replaced the glass on the table. Red liquid began to bubble up from the bottom of the vessel and filled it to the brim. All this while the irritating grin had hardly left his face. He picked the glass up again, slowly savouring its bouquet before taking a noisy slurp. 'In my day,' he sighed, dreamy eyes half closed, and beads of red glistening on his lips, 'a vintage like this would have set you back a few hundred quid.'

'That's it!' Finn yelled, tears of rage starting in his eyes. 'I've been all the way to the origins of the earth and back again. Got myself stuck in a billion year long fog... Eaten alive... Squashed and shrink wrapped and rolled up in my own juices, sucked dry like a spider's dinner... Spat out... Shat out looking like a dogs breakfast... And all you can do is sit there an—'

Mandy cut him short. 'Oh! Is *that* where you went!'

'You *know* where I went. You were *there*, damn you!'

'So! It's all coming back, is it?'

Finn was trembling now, and sniffling as the tears came down his nose.

'Here! A sip of this my boy. Do you good,' Mandelbrot said, holding out the glass. 'And, I know! Wait a minute.' He took a plate and did a few theatrical passes over it. The most stupendous cake complete with birthday candles rose up. 'How about a slice of this?' The candles flamed into life, and Finn burst into something between a roar of laughter and a howl. Then, clapping his hand over his mouth he remembered about noise.

'Come lad.' Mandelbrot stood up and leaning over Finn gave him an almighty hug, half lifting him off the chair. 'Lots of catching up to do, hey! Tell me what you want me to tell you, and then you can fill me in with your news.'

Between sniffles and munches of cake, Finn fired a non-stop salvo of questions until Mandelbrot held up his hands, pleading for him to stop. They'd covered the business of that cloud, and the billion year trip to Gaia's conception. His glimpse into the mysteries of Lemuria, and how the material necessary for life had travelled from the vastness of the star colonies, and gathered according to plan. And how they'd all been there at the original planning sessions. 'A lot to take in, you'll agree,' Mandelbrot said, solemnly, 'and I don't expect you to have mastered it all at once. No-one ever does. But what your questions point to is you trying to get a bearing on where you are now. Is that right?'

Finn nodded. Still munching, he insisted that he could remember only snatches—and those mainly the unpleasant ones—of what he'd experienced.

Mandy raised his eyebrows. 'We were all there, remember?' he said, in a sing-song sort of voice, hoping it would refresh his memory. But Finn only looked back at him dazed. 'OK, you're overwhelmed and bewildered, and I'm not surprised, lad. But we only have to take it a step at a time, as you realised for yourself as soon as you got back. I'm just here as prompt—a mirror, if you like, to help you see yourself more clearly. You've been on a journey to Lemuria, and reawakened that in yourself which was there all along, in your DNA. You've done what you came to do, brought back buried and forgotten material on behalf of Humanity, and you've completed your mission—or part of it.'

'Part? Only part?' Finn gasped, spluttering crumbs. 'You mean I'm not finished yet?'

'We're never finished, Finn.'

'But...'

'But we never have to repeat an experience, not unless we didn't learn its lesson the first time.'

'But how do I know? I don't know what I learned, do I? Or why would I be asking all these questions?'

'That's why *I'm* here, I suppose. *Of course* you learned, Finn. You're just suffering from a bit of jet-lag. Haven't caught up with yourself yet. But not to worry, it'll all come back in due course. You did all you were required, and everyone's proud as hell with you.'

'Everyone!'

'We were all there, remember?' Mandelbrot repeated, the slightest touch of impatience creeping into his tone now.

'But what about Annya? And all the others, for instance.'

Mandelbrot sucked his teeth. 'That's going to be a bit difficult to explain, so I won't bother. Just wait and see, hey?' he said, helping himself to cake.

Finn's frustration was growing. 'That's about as helpful as Gaia with her cryptic comments,' he exploded.

'You see, you *are* remembering, Finn. And it won't be long before the rest comes back. You've returned, I have to tell you, with a sackful of gifts which you're using already. Without a second thought, too, because they're second nature. And that's why you don't yet realise you have 'em.'

Finn restrained his emotions and considered this for some minutes. 'But look,' he said eventually. 'I might have done all you say, but the fact is I don't know the most basic things. For instance, can they see us or not, those in the house? You told me to keep out of sight, not make a noise, yet you got out of that truck and the fellow driving didn't seem to have a clue you were there. Or did he? Have we got solid bodies, or what? I'd better know that at least, or I'll not know whether to scarper out of sight if one of them comes out suddenly.'

'We'll be fine. They'll be busy a while yet, but I see what you mean. I'm trying to explain, Finn. There are no rules. It's different for everyone. I shift from one dimension to another in my own peculiar way. I discovered my gift by chance. Serendipity. Happy Accident. Remember? You've taken another route. Your primitive body underwent corruption and rebirth, something even more extraordinary in the long run. What's important is that the lost Lemurian strands in your DNA have awakened, and you now have the ability to move between worlds at will—just like our long-ago ancestors. I think you called it 'the knack', right? Well you just got it, OK? But haven't had much practice with it yet. Or a chance to have some fun. I guess I'm having all the fun. That it?'

'You mean this birthday cake thing?'

'How about some fruit?' There was no fruit to be seen on that table, and Mandelbrot's non sequitur provoked another scowl from Finn. 'Come on, I'll show you,' he said, waving Finn to follow him. Through the back garden, out of sight of the house, they came on an orchard comprising a banana, a straggly fig or two, and a few citrus. Casually Mandy went over to a tree and stood deep in contemplation, then quietly beckoned. 'Come and pick a peach, Finn,' he whispered.

'Another damn joke?' grumbled Finn. He was still muttering, 'What's he up to now? It's obvious, there *are* no peaches,' as he came over.

'Pick me a peach,' Mandelbrot calmly repeated. 'Just there! See it?'

Finn looked. As he did the green of the leaves changed, at first subtly, seeming to shimmer. He noticed it was only the stem he was focused on which was behaving this way, the one bearing two or three leaves and an axial bud. Then the tiny bud began to swell, and out from it a cluster of white flowers burst. Caught by a gleam of sun one of them too began to shimmer with a strange luminescence, while its sister blossoms faded and fell. The petals of the shining one opened wide then curled back revealing a tiny green fruit, which also swelled as it began to shape into a small green peach. Colours of orange, pink, amber and russet came and went, washing across its surface. In an instant a fully formed fruit glistened on the stem.

'Pick it then. Don't be shy! Let's know how it tastes,' Mandelbrot told him dryly.

Finn picked it, holding it to his nose and breathing its warm, ripe fragrance into him. He turned it round in his hand, stroking it and feeling the soft hairs like down on a kissable cheek. Then he held it out. 'It's a present for you,' he said.

Mandy took it. 'Thank you Finn, but let me do one for you then, and we'll compare notes.' They were both biting into juicy fruits moments later, grinning and smacking their lips.

'Success?' inquired Mandelbrot. 'I'd say not short of perfection myself. How about you?'

'Perfect,' agreed Finn.

A TASTE OF ATLANTIS

'But Mandy,' he said later, 'peaches aren't even in season!'

The sun had moved a few degrees towards evening, but no-one seemed to be stirring in the house. While they waited for signs of something worth listening into, Mandelbrot and Finn lazed around in Xena's little orchard taking advantage of the shade. Finn's question and answer session had taken up a lump of the afternoon, and now Mandelbrot was filling him in with his own latest news when Finn interrupted with his remark. Mandelbrot had been relating how he'd had this surreal conversation in the truck, with his friend the doctor, and how they'd done a bit of sharing—both of them witnessing Annya's dream. At this point Finn had begun to sit up and take notice as the details unfolded. 'I don't think I've seen you *this* concerned before, not about Annya, at least,' Mandelbrot told him. 'This trip to the origins of the earth and back seems to have sharpened up your empathy? Pity your ideas about multi-dimensional reality are still a bit woolly though. We *made* the peaches, Finn? Don't be so pedantic. It wasn't even a peach *tree*. Or didn't you notice that? We created them out of mind. Everything arises out of mind. Flows in and out.'

'But the food on the table? Their food. We didn't create that.'

'No. They created that, dumbhead, out of their beliefs. The belief system that tells them tables, and chairs and food is solid matter— delicious, but solid.'

'But we ate it. Ate solid food—that is until you did your cake and wine spectacular. Then we ate that.'

'Yes.'

'But?'

'But *what*, Finn? Answer it yourself.'

'We flowed, I suppose. In and out,' he answered, still looking uncertain.

'Got it! Now you know what to do if they suddenly come out of the house. OK?'

'Glad we got that settled then,' said Finn.

'Good!' said Mandelbrot. 'Then can we get back to Annya now?' But sounds of stirrings in the house put a stop to any further consideration of Annya, her dreams or her problems. The door opened and Xena came out with a tray and began clearing the table, and laying it with fresh cutlery. Voices and accompanying sounds and smells of food preparation in the kitchen soon followed. 'Fade-out time, I think, Finn? Manage that, can you? Let's give 'em time to get settled with their meal. We'll make ourselves comfortable close by, and do a spot of eavesdropping.'

He was beginning to get the hang of it. It had been a long journey to Lemuria and back, and he'd returned with a body; a body in which he had the capability of moving at will into and out of a variety of modes and dimensions. In terms of the day he had returned to, this was a Super-body. It had, he saw, all the characteristics of a contemporary physical and biological job, while at the same time it now incorporated many of the virtues and gifts which had belonged to those far off descendants from the stars. It included the instinctive nature of the animal race, as well as the gentle intelligence of a child of the Central Source where the Lemurian race originated. And all of this gracefully melded with human frailty and greatness. Yet, as he and Mandy sat, discretely out of sight, listening to the table-talk, Finn was

232

all at sea at first, not quite getting the drift of the conversation, and Mandelbrot had to fill in and translate.

'They seem to be having the same kind of trouble as you Finn, sorting out their realities,' he told him. 'I can see you're all het up about Annya, but it's poor old Manfred I'm worried about.'

'But Annya's the one most disturbed by that dream, isn't she? She's convinced that her Simon is dead. She saw him, his throat cut, dumped, screwed up and thrown away with the garbage. It's absolutely barbaric! I can't imagine what he did to get himself butchered like that. No-one could deserve that kind of treatment, Mandy. I was sick to my stomach just to hear you tell it. So I can only guess what it's doing to her.'

'You realise it's still a potential, I hope, Finn. Hasn't happened yet.'

'Maybe not yet, but energy has its own momentum, and in this case it's so powerful it's causing it to happen. Even I can see that.'

'But happening in a parallel reality, Finn.'

'But still... happening, Mandy. It's in the process of being created, because the necessary factors are all coming together. Simon is already in the centre of a whirlwind of violence and hatred. The conflict is on its way, unstoppable—if it hasn't begun already.'

'Yes,' Mandelbrot agreed, 'but maybe we've time to pause it. Not the conflict. Humanity is set on that course, but Simon's fate. That's the beauty of living in the Fifth Dimensions. That's the world you were born into Finn, and it was so natural to you that you hardly realised what powers you had. But now you're learning about it from the ground up, and helping humanity at the same time to ground that knowledge. Our friend, the good doctor, is having to do a spot of learning as well. See him? Staring at the tablecloth wondering where he's been?'

Drifts of mist blowing up from the coast were beginning to veil the sinking sun at the point when Annya threw her arms around Manfred, and Xena shepherded them all inside.

'What do you want to do now, Finn? Follow them in?' Mandy inquired.

'Not sure. You're not going to bugger off and leave me to it again, are you?'

'I'm not planning to.'

'That's *really* set my mind at rest, Mandy. As I remember it, that's exactly what you said last time you disappeared... What's that sound? Well?'

'Well what? That sound? Is that what you're asking me?'

The whine of approaching engines was impossible to ignore. In moments two cars had screeched to a halt beside Xena's truck, and Manfred charged out of the house, quickly followed by Annya. The driver, a short legged, short neck Spaniard in oily dungarees, got out of the first car, while the second sat back and rolled a cigarette. Finn, who'd been hoping for reassurance on Mandy's forward plans, and possibly some pointers about his own next move, was caught up in the general kerfuffle, though not too distracted to grab Mandy by the arm. He wasn't going to let him get away so easily this time. Baffled by the gabble of Spanish, German and English, he tugged Mandy's sleeve.

'Oh, it's nothing, Finn,' he explained. 'They've brought Annya's car. Apparently she's offering it to Manfred so he can get back home. She's staying the night with Xena, but he's not ready to go yet.' They watched as Manfred began drawing notes from a wallet. He handed them to the first driver, who jumped in the second car, slamming the door. The other chucked his lighted butt out of his window, and amidst more screeching, whining, and dust, the second car was gone, while Annya and Manfred made their way back inside. 'Let's join them then, OK Finn?'

Still holding tight to Mandy's sleeve, Finn gave a gasp of frustration. Mandelbrot had dissolved into thin air, closely followed by the piece of sleeve Finn still held in his hand. He spun round to face the house, noticed a lighted window, and was peering in before he'd time to worry about being seen. Luckily Manfred and the two women were sitting with their backs to the window. The room looked cosy, the candlelight mellow. Then he spotted a couple of easy chairs in an unlit corner. With knees apart and glass in hand there sat Mandy, large as life. Finn felt a tug on his hand, the one which had been holding the sleeve, and the next moment he found himself occupying the chair beside him.

'What do you fancy, my boy? Cognac, wine, coffee? Or one of my Atlantean nightcaps?'

'Krise Mandy! How did you do that?' he hissed.

'No need to whisper. I've turned off our volume. Or rather I've isolated our field. Easy to do if you have the knack. And in this case it's for Annya's benefit. She's still a bit overwrought you know, and we don't want any more hysterics tonight. They're trying to decide what to do about Simon. She's insisting they're keeping something from her.' He handed Finn a glass of dark multi-coloured liquid.

Past caring about the hows or whats, Finn took it, and after sniffing and sipping, decided it must be the Atlantean brew.

Seated opposite, Finn's eyes were drawn to Annya's face. Her skin, as the candle-light flickered over it, seemed translucent and fragile. Her lips, beautifully soft, moulded and delineated in a way he'd not been aware of before. And her eyes, large, luminous and tragic. He wanted to stretch out his hand to touch her cheek, his arms longed to hold her. He knew how she felt. Her desperate need to rescue Simon from his fate, because in her heart she also knew that his death was suspended. He, Simon, was calling for her still, waiting for her to save him. Yet although she knew this, it was a reality which didn't compute in their world.

Manfred was telling her he'd heard snippets of news via his satellite receiver. The Americans were gearing up for another invasion—other nations too—the British. Something hot about to burst in the Middle

East. What exactly was Simon involved with? he was asking her. Why was this mission of his so hush-hush? 'Contact Peter again, phone him. Surely he'll have something by now. Insist, Annya. He must tell you how things stand.'

All the while, talking over him, Xena was busy telling her she must decide whether to decamp and move in with her, or pack her bags and leave the Island all together. After all she could do little from here. Back home with her family—who knows—maybe...

Manfred chipped in again. 'You need a plan of action, Annya. If you phone Peter as soon as possible...'

But Annya was interrupting him. If it was bad news, she said, or something inconclusive, that would only make things worse. Simon may be dead, in which case... Or he may *not*. It was no longer, as far as she was concerned, a case of 'no news is good news.' In fact, as far as the Amsterdam office was concerned he may already be on the 'no news, possibly disappeared' list. Or if it turned out to be good, they could all relax, forget the dreams and all that nonsense—put it down to one of those inexplicable things, call it a day, wash it out of their hair and get on with their lives.

But even as she was saying it, she seemed to realise she didn't want to face up to what might be staring her in the face. Perfectly aware of the risk he'd voluntarily signed up to, the likelihood was he'd been kidnapped or blown up. Manfred was still demanding action, but Xena voted they sleep on it, see how things looked in the morning when they had clearer heads.

'Any idea, Finn,' Mandelbrot in the dark corner enquired, 'what Simon is up to in Iraq?'

Finn looked at him. 'You know something, don't you, Mandy? I can tell by your expression. My guess is he's involved in some way with this invasion they say is on its way. He's a newsman or something, isn't he? An image capturer.'

'You've picked up that much then, Finn.'

'OK Mandy, I can see you're onto something I haven't seen yet. That's it, isn't it?'

'Not sure Finn. This may or may not be important, but I think he's doing something far more interesting than a spot of battlefield reporting. My feeling is... Give me a moment... He's been sent to retrieve some of the most culturally valuable artefacts... pieces of antiquity... Assyrian... It's to do with a hidden city. I'm getting it clearer... Irreplaceable sculptures about to be uncovered, then looted or destroyed quite soon. And there's something else I'm picking up.' He stopped and peered into Finn's eyes.

'Well? Come on Mandy. What else?'

'I'm not sure. You'll think I'm interfering, being tactless.'

'You've got to tell me now, damn you. *What?*'

'Well, I, that is, my feeling is, Annya. I think you should... perhaps...'

'*Mandy!* What?'

'I think you already know, Finn. Look, she's about to retire to bed. Why don't you .. In you own inimitable way... Oh!'

He'd been trying to say, why don't you follow her. But Finn had already gone!

Seems he's got the hang of that knack thing, at last, Mandelbrot chuckled wryly.

This time Finn hadn't needed a tug on his arm. It was a tug on his heart-strings which had whisked him away.

Annya fell into bed. She was immensely tired but her mind still churned with the dilemma of what next to do. Obviously she couldn't stay here. Simon's apartment needed to be cleared of her stuff. Those holidaymakers would be arriving soon. That phone call had to be made, and whichever way it turned out it would be sensible for her to go back home. Yet it was the last thing she wanted. Something held her here. Just this evening, sitting in the cosy glow of Xena's sitting room, she'd switched off. Closed her eyes for a moment. And when she opened them again she was sure... She'd glanced across the room and imagined, in the half-light, that the two chairs opposite were occupied. She'd smiled to herself. Whether it was the fact that Manfred and Xena were present, protecting her, or maybe too tired and past caring, or whatever it was, a couple of extra guests sharing a glass or two of something or other seemed congenial and suddenly natural. Strange what the mind gets up to, she thought. I don't think I'd be too worried if that incredible guy with the blueish sheen to him was sitting right over there. Right now. In that bedside chair. In fact I'd almost... Was that my imagination too, but hadn't his outfit changed quite a bit? He's actually rather... I'd almost....

Sleep was overtaking her.

I'd almost welcome his advice. Maybe *he'd* have something worth listening to. I wonder! Could I talk to him about Simon?

Finn had waited discretely outside the half-open bedroom door as Annya removed her clothes. He'd observed. He might have been admiring a tree or an exquisite piece of alabaster sculpture. She must be really tired, he thought, to give so little attention to her toiletry needs. A quick wash-down splash and rub, oversize tee-shirt pulled on, and she was between the sheets in seconds. He sat down on the chair, making himself invisible to normal physical eyes again, while he allowed things to unfold. It was all completely natural, he knew now. No carefully thought-out plan needed. Things fell into place. Today he'd been born—reborn with everything intact—and in the body he was always meant to have. One in which he could move at will into and out of all dimensions. The hidden codes in his DNA were now fully awake, thanks to his reconnection with his roots in the mists of Lemuria.

* * * *

Little Jamil was still under his mother's banning order about the alley-way. He'd kept absolutely silent about seeing the dead man, though holding the secret to himself was bringing him awful nightmares. He'd cried out in the night—Fatima had told him. But she hadn't told mother, and now they were allowed to play ball with the other children in front of the houses. But the older boys got bored with him. They were into real football. And Jamil didn't want to play ball with his sister either, that would be too embarrassing, in the street. So he'd begun to wander off on his own. He'd been doing this for a few days now and his mother hadn't seemed to notice. He'd gone further afield, as far as the shops. His uncle, a weaver, had a workshop somewhere nearby. Though, according to grown up talk, trade was bad. No-one wanted his craftsmanship these days. But Jamil liked this uncle, his mother's brother. Today he ventured just that little bit further up the street and discovered he was opposite an open doorway which looked very much like the entrance to the workshop. Nothing was coming, so he ran across the street and peered in. He couldn't see anyone about. There were looms, but their clattering was still. The smells and rich colours of the wools were the same, though, as when he'd been there with his mother just after his father left. He called out, Uncle Ahmed, are you there? But no-one answered, so he went outside again to search for him.

There was a passageway between Uncle's shop and the one next door. As it wasn't exactly an alley, he thought his mother wouldn't count it. It might be sort of OK too as it probably belonged to his uncle. It felt dark and dank, one or two closed doors, windows with iron grills, then another passageway to the right with sun shining at the far end.

Jamil found himself on a patch of waste ground where two houses had been demolished. He glanced up. Cooing birds perched on some rotten-looking rafters spanning broken walls were wafting flakes of plaster off with their wings. Green leaves with flowers trailed down.

They must be rooted in the cracks between the stones. Fatima would love this. They had a sweet smell, but in the corner he spotted another pile of garbage and another kind of smell. This time he knew he was going to be in trouble because he just had to investigate.

He had no stick with him, so he poked about with his hands. But the stuff didn't turn out to be all that interesting. Disappointed, he went behind to see what was between the pile and the wall. This was more like it! What he'd expected. Another man! Jamil stood fascinated and transfixed. This one was tied up like a parcel. And a lot of runny blood. His fingers reached out. He would just give him a touch and run away. That was all he'd do.

Jamil prodded the body gently. It moved. His own body tightened, his stomach went like a ball of knotted string, but he touched again because this one felt different, not wooden and dead. Not cold either—although he hadn't felt the other with his fingers, he knew his skin had to be cold. Flies were buzzing around. Maybe they liked the trickling blood. Something about it alerted him that he must tell. Telling his mother was out of the question, he'd get himself beaten, and no waiting till his father came home this time. But his uncle? Maybe he could trust him.

Finn moved from the chair to the bed. Annya, he was sure, was asleep now. He looked at her more closely. Yes, deeply asleep. He perched on the mattress weightlessly. Maybe she was already dreaming. He lay his new body beside hers and buried his face in the covers. He drank in the lavender and blue skies of the sheets, and the oily, dusty, blossomy scent of her hair. He held her in his arms and she moaned and turned her body to him. Putting her arms round him, she buried herself in him and murmured, 'Who are you?'

'Finnegal,' he told her. 'Emissary of the Galaxies.'

CRADLE OF CIVILISATION

Finn lay patiently. They had merged, and Annya in her breathing and moaning was breathing him, as he breathed her. It couldn't be like this for long. The intensity of their emotion was rising to flood-tide and she would soon beach on the shores of wakefulness. But he knew that for her to find him so intimately encircling her would be too much shock. She was still in her dream, yet half aware, in that betwixt and between dawn where truths are seen sharply, only to fade as rapidly as they are perceived, back into the forgetfulness of night the moment consciousness breaks in. There had been no violation; her assent was fully given. Neither had there been a physical penetration; that would have been inappropriate to the occasion. What there had been was so sweet a union of spirit that they were now as one in their purposes. Yet those purposes needed still to unfold in a timely and natural manner.

In the throes of her moanings she'd pleaded for his help in finding Simon. Now he must wait for her to ask in her daylight awareness. Meanwhile... He could leave Mandy to take care of himself. Annya and her friends would settle something between them in the morning, no doubt. It didn't really matter, life's performance would go on, one way or another, and all would unfold.

As to Simon, Finn had already got hold of a thread. A carpet thread as it happened.

* * * *

241

In a muddle of anxiety and guilt, Jamil made his way back to the workshop. Everything seemed quiet, just as he'd left it. He crept around nervously exploring. One of the looms seemed to have a part-finished rug set up, with a shuttle ready to resume weaving slotted between two loose warp threads. He climbed onto the bench in front of it and perched, swinging his legs so he could think. He fiddled absently with the rusty pink wool hanging from the shuttle. Without a light on, the workshop was dim, but as he sat he began to take in the many-coloured patterns in the piece of completed work he could see rolled up on the loom. His mind began playing, making patterns of its own. Then he noticed several more shuttles attached to the weave separately threaded with sapphires, indigos, russets and ochres, and he began adding more colours to the patterns in his head. He was getting so interested in his game that he hardly registered, among the other street sounds, the voice of his uncle outside the door talking to another man.

Suddenly, his uncle's silhouette filled the doorway.

Startled, he let drop the blue shuttle he'd idly picked up.

'Jamil!'

The little boy's eyes grew large. 'I'm sorry,' he wailed.

'Jamil, what are you doing here?' The astonished man rushed over to the loom to see what had happened. 'What is it? Why have you come?'

'Sorry, Uncle. I'm sorry.' Jamil stammered again.

'No need for that,' Ahmed said, resting both his hands on Jamil's shoulders, and gripping them gently. 'Dry your eyes, boy. I'm your uncle. No need to look that way at me, is there? Now, how did you get here alone? Does your mother...?'

'No, Uncle Ahmed. But...'

'But what, boy? I'm sure whatever it is, you can tell me. Can't you? What makes you so afraid? Here, I've just bought this bag of cakes. Take one and get your breath. Come!' he said, holding a hand out.

242

'Let's go sit in the back room and I'll make us some coffee. Then you can tell me all about it.'

'But it's a secret. I'm not sure I can. I might get beaten.' Jamil had taken his uncle's hand, but his eyes were still wet. He brushed them with the fist clutching the cake as they squeezed past idle looms and boxes of wools.

The space was cramped. Ahmed switched on a light and reached for the gas ring under a metal coffee pot. 'Who beats you, boy?' he asked quietly, turning to look into Jamil's face. 'Is that why you're here?'

It took some minutes before Jamil could begin. The sniffles and hiccups as he munched bites of cake had to be allowed to die down first. At last he managed to get out the story of his discovery. The man, and how he had moved, and how the flesh had been warm to his touch. Ahmed's reactions went through several stages. Complete disbelief; the possibility that the boy was fantasising, dreaming, playing tricks with him. But the fact that Jamil's face was so troubled and the boy so obviously shaken drove him to the conclusion that he should at least investigate for himself. 'I'll go and look,' he promised, 'but no-one must see me. We can't afford that. And I must get you back home—as soon as possible. We must do that first.'

'But, Uncle. The man. Something might happen to him before... And my mother. She will be so angry with me, she'll shout, and I get frightened. I can't tell her. Please, you must promise not to tell her.'

'I will take you back and make up a good story. You can trust me. But we must do that first before you get into further trouble. So! Are you ready? Eaten all you can, huh?'

Khalid, the man Ahmed had been speaking to outside his workshop, walked briskly back to his car. He drove south a few streets, then, eyes flickering watchfully in the rear view mirror, turned left and left again to the bridge. Half an hour later he was on his way to Mosul in the north.

Khalid Al-Rahman worked for the Iraq Department of Antiquities where he'd been for the last twenty-five years. Regarded internationally as a leading authority on Assyrian narrative decoration, and palace relief sculptures from Nineveh, his work was his passion. But he was a troubled man. The feeling he had for the land of his birth went beyond patriotism or nationalism; it ran in his blood and in the cells of his very bones. And although his president had made it his proud objective to protect and display the treasures of his empire—and built a lot of Saddam museums into the bargain—the many artefacts still scattered in the smaller sites, not to mention those which lay under the sands, had always been vulnerable to the worst kinds of desecration. Now, in the last decade of the twentieth century, the scramble for booty was worse than ever. The Sack of Nineveh almost fourteen hundred years ago was equalled only by the vandalism and rapaciousness taking place in the desert today.

It wasn't so much the common thief making a little extra cash in the market flogging fragments of tiles and ceramics which bothered him. This must have been going on down the centuries. But the smuggling of historic art had become an international trade lately, with thousands of dollars, yen and pounds changing hands. And now, with this new invasion, in spite of the official rhetoric and Saddam's bluster, Khalid's land would soon be swarming with U.S. tanks. No-one dare say this, not to his closest friend, but everyone knew.

A small team of Europeans had been expected. Khalid and a few dedicated colleagues had been engaged in secret negotiations with them for some time. The team were on their way to make a documentary. They would visit some of the remote and still unknown sites which he and his colleagues had unofficially excavated, and the idea was to carefully film the relief covered walls, and record all the stunning and surprisingly well preserved artefacts they had uncovered thus far. These would then be reinterred until such a time when it would be safe to reveal these new treasures to mankind. Who knew how long they must remain in the dust. As long as it took, he thought ruefully, for mankind to respect and value the art for its own sake, and not for what could be gained by its sale.

Having invited these Westerners to carry out such a sensitive project, he was left with mixed feelings. These lands between the Tigris and the Euphrates had nurtured some of the most skilled artists the world had known—or forgotten!—and pride in his Mesopotamian heritage was fierce. Yet it had been on a visit to London in the fifties that its true grandeur actually hit him. But this was where his mixed feelings were at their most acute. He'd been allowed into the basements of the British Museum, a warren of a place, floor to ceiling with sculpture from every corner of the world, and among them a whole room lined with these exquisite Assyrian narrative reliefs. So much stuff! So much booty! And never to see the light of day in the galleries above ground. He was only viewing this now because of his 'privileged' position. Privileged! Allowed to view his own heritage! But even so, the public would never see it at all! Yet these magnificent works would never have got this far if some European back in the nineteenth century hadn't unearthed them.

He remembered now, driving across the familiar flat desert, how he'd stopped, transfixed, before one particular relief. The detail astounded him. And not only the carver's skill, but his humanity. He'd walked past panel after panel marvelling at the scenes of domestic life from three thousand years ago; military campaigns, warriors returning triumphant, hunting scenes in all their gory detail. Then suddenly this! A lioness struck by arrows. The artist had carved the beast snarling with pain, and with such loving care that the creature lived and died before you. Khalid had put his hand on the stone. He remembered stroking the surface and tracing the exquisitely drawn lines with his fingers. He'd swept his hand over the beast's flanks, paralysed now by the two arrows. The animal vomited! And he, in a flash, had, it seemed, just put down the chisel with which he'd been working to stroke the loose dust off his finished work. It had been such a curious sensation—transporting him into the past. It had been this experience in London that had fired his desire to dedicate his life to his present work.

But over many years he'd come to realise that the men who'd lived in Iraq thousands of years ago had also studied the heavens and produced astronomers of the highest quality. Many ancient cultures had observed the activities, the cycles and seasons of the stars, but no-one, he believed, had made such connections between the heavens and life on Earth. Yet the World in general failed to understand the connection between modern Iraq and ancient Mesopotamia. Or seen it only as a honey pot, a target for their despicable modern campaigns of rape and pillage over the recent centuries. Saddam at least had restored some of his people's self-esteem, he'd give him that! Hadn't Byron said, in his poem "The Destruction of Sennacherib", 'The Assyrians came down like a wolf on the fold.' Well, it was the West now which slavered after Iraq and her buried treasures.

And yet, once again, wasn't he, one of its most devoted heritage keepers, turning to the West for its expertise and help? Acknowledging, albeit grudgingly, the respect certain of its people had for that great Past? And wasn't he, Khalid Al-Rahman, even now in the process of arranging a little bit of art smuggling?

Annya lay there. Dawn had broken, but the walls of the room were so thick and the window opening so tiny that, as yet, only one pale grey slant of light had crept in across the floor. Shapes didn't seem ready to emerge out of the shadows yet, and Annya hadn't opened her eyes. She was still immersed in a glorious cloud of sensation in which her body glowed and her mind, for the moment, was still. As though she'd taken some powerful tranquilliser, her anxieties were quelled, and her thoughts anaesthetised. But unless this happy state had indeed been induced by a drug, it would have been surprising if it had lasted.

And in seconds, the moment evaporated, her bliss burst like a bubble, and her eyes opened.

The first thing they fell on was the chair on which Finn was sitting—an old fashioned upholstered chair with arms. He'd moved there in his usual discrete fashion after disengaging himself from her sometime in the middle of the night to have a chat with Mandy. A pale blur of movement from the depths of the chair startled her into a sitting position. She fell back again with a cry of dismay. But landing prone must have felt altogether unsuitable, as she sat bolt upright again.

From the shadowy depths of the seat, Finn smiled a sweet smile. Whether she caught the expression or only sensed it, she found herself smiling back.

'Finnegal?' she whispered.

'Finn. Call me Finn. Everyone does.'

Hearing the soft voice she narrowed her eyes and peered into the misty blue shadow. She could see him growing clearer. 'I can't. I've dreamed you, conjured you up. You're some sort of wish-fantasy or a psychological quirk, and I shouldn't be talking to you at all. I should be ashamed of myself, particularly ashamed for what I dreamt.'

'Then I should be ashamed too,' he said, 'because I also dreamt we made love.'

This had her stumped for a moment. Was this the sort of thing a dream lover would say? She wasn't sure. She'd never had a conversation with a dream before. Not while she was awake, anyhow. And she *was* awake. 'What do you mean, you dreamt me?' she asked.

'I mean, you invited me into your dream and I obliged. I invited you and you... came,' he said.

Annya's cheeks flushed pink. I'm talking to a phantom, she thought. He's sitting on my chair, and he's making me blush! This can't be happening.

'But it is,' he said, giving her an even more bewitching smile. He was clearer than ever. His face, which had always struck her as beautiful, but indefinable, as she looked closer seemed some strange hybrid of angel and faun.

'Finnegal? Emissary of the—*what* did you say? The Galaxies? Am I completely doolally? Did I actually hear you say *that*? Galaxies?'

He nodded.

'And did I plead with you to help me? Find Simon?'

He nodded again.

'This is nuts! A fairy story, and you've got me acting like I believed it. Talking to you as if you were real. I think you should go. Maybe when it gets lighter you'll disappear anyway. But I can't wait till then, someone might... You'd better go before someone comes in.'

'And sees me?' He looked at her quizzically.

'No! You're not here. They *won't* see you,' she told him. 'They'll hear *me* having this crazy conversation with a piece of furniture.'

His laugh rang in her ears like glass and silver.

Annya's voice rose. '*Go!*' she said in a tone reminiscent of one declaiming an incantation against the Evil One. Catching the sound of her own voice, she hastily modified her, 'Depart, hence!' command to, '*Please!* They'll hear you.' Then realising how ludicrous the whole situation was becoming, she began to laugh too.

Gauging this to be an opportune moment, he asked, 'Do you mind if I come and sit on the bed?' Her mouth dropped opened, but as no sound came from it, he went on, 'We could talk more comfortably.' Still she stared at him in open-mouthed silence. 'Simon.' he said. 'I know, Annya. I can see how racked with anxiety you are. Don't you want to tell me about it?'

'I, oh, I,' she stammered. 'Oh! What the hell.'

He was suddenly sitting at the foot of the bed. Annya squirmed, but said nothing.

'OK. You want me to help?' he asked, gentle but matter-of-fact. 'Then you'd better give me the full picture, tell me how *you* see things.'

His manner was so disarming that, setting aside her scruples about

248

the sanity of conversing with a mirage in blue jeans, her fears and doubts poured out. Hesitatingly at first, she told him how she only had that terrifying dream to go on. Yet to her surprise, as she filled in more background, Finn seemed to know as much as she did herself. Even the phone calls to Amsterdam. But the struggle to find words for her feelings on seeing Simon's mutilated body, dream though it had been, were too much, and she threw herself down, burying her face in the pillow. Yet, as she felt Finn's hand stroking her hair, and his face pressed to the back of her head, she turned towards him sobbing, and put her arms around him.

The sensation was extraordinary. This body she was holding had neither substance nor weight, yet it had warmth and it had—*presence.* His breath was the scent of the outdoors, of herbs. His body smelled of sun on lichen-covered rock—and of things she couldn't even put a name to. A tang of sensuality and tenderness?

'Good God, Finn!' she said between sobs. 'For a ghost, or whatever it is you are, you're remarkably alive.'

He'd moved to her side. 'Hushhh,' he whispered, his fingers stroking strands of hair from her damp face. 'And one thing you *can* be certain of, I'm *not* a ghost. But learn to believe in miracles, Annya. They happen. I shan't attempt to explain, but... Can you trust me?'

'All I know is,' she sobbed, 'that I'm desperate and you seem to be the best hope I've got. Whether what I saw was real or not, I've no way of knowing. But if he's dead, it's already too late. Only Manfred thought it might not have happened yet. In which case someone has to get to him in time, and there isn't a hope in hell I could do that. Even if I rang Peter, what would I tell him? I've had a *dream?* He'd, well, Annya's got a touch too much sun, is what he'd think. As for your miracles. Listen!' she said, disentangling herself from him, 'I can hear them moving about already. I must get up before Xena comes in. We have to make decisions this morning, and I *still* don't know what I'm going to do.'

249

'If I told you that you don't *need* to do *anything*, that whatever decisions you make now cannot prevent the pattern from unrolling, could you live with that? The weave and the warp are already in place, my earthly, earthy girl. We just need to fill in the colours.'

Strangely enough, this piece of incomprehensibility was reassuring. It seemed more the kind of other-worldly gobbledegook she'd expected from an Emissary of the Galaxies. More authoritative, somehow.

'You mean, I just...?'

'Just live in the moment,' he told her. 'Believe me; from experience, that's *all* one has to do.'

Khalid opened the door to his office. A message lay propped up on his desk. Ring Ahmed. Urgent!

'I've just left the fellow,' he muttered. 'What can it be?'

He went to the wall safe and tapped in the digits to unlock it. Glancing round, he took out a glass and a bottle, then with thoughts furrowing his brow he walked over to the fridge. The place was silent, the staff had gone home and his other colleague didn't seem to be about either. He poured whisky into the glass, added a drop or two of iced water, returned the bottle to the safe, re-set the lock, and took off his jacket. Throwing it over the back of his seat, he sat down at the desk. His left hand stroked the phone as he took a gulp from the glass in the other hand. He'd promised himself a leisurely evening after that drive back from Baghdad. He finished his drink and banged the thick tumbler down, then picked up the receiver.

After Finn had slipped away from the sleeping Annya during the night, he returned to the sitting room where he'd left Mandelbrot. He found him lounging full length on the sofa holding an empty tumbler. Another one, full of luminous, multi-coloured liquid, stood on the coffee table.

'I've poured you one, Finn. Thought you might need it,' Mandy had said with a wink and a jerk of the head. 'How's Annya?'

'Oh, you know! Fine!' said Finn, minimally, as he seated himself on the chair opposite. He'd reached for the drink. 'What is this, anyway? More of that Atlantis brew?' he asked, picking it up and sipping.

'Like it?'

Finn was half way down the glass already. 'What's in it? And what's this all about, Mandy?'

The older man sat up. 'Just a spot of preparation for your next trip, a taste of things to come. But you've still got a lot of processing to do from your last jaunt, I'd guess. Also, I'd bet you've something in mind you want to do first. Am I right?'

Dismissing Mandy's hints of further time-travel, he'd said, 'You may be right. Annya needs me now, and I think I've got hold of something. A thread of some sort. She's asked me to find Simon. She believed she was dreaming when she told me, but the fact was, we were so merged that our communication was without the usual barriers that come with consciousness. Singing from the same sheet, I think they say, these days. Anyhow, I got hold of this link and if she can ask me again when she's awake, I think I can locate him. Although he may be dead already, I'm not yet sure.'

'And what will you do if he is?' Mandy had asked.

ANOTHER ROLL OF THE CARPET

It was late afternoon by the time Ahmed arrived back at his workshop, and there was something he must attend to before he went to check on his little nephew's story. He'd had quite a time with Jamil's mother. His sister had given him the sharp edge of her tongue, and it had taken more time than he could spare to talk her out of giving the boy the slapping of his life. He'd never seen his sister in such a state. He put it down to the stress of the times. Husband away with the army. Shootings and kidnapping on the increase. He could understand her behaviour—the fear and insecurity, shortages, breakdowns, children left in her care to worry about. But he had concerns of his own, especially this commission from Khalid. And if he wasn't careful he'd be nursing a slit throat of his own.

That was why he'd not ridiculed Jamil's tale. It could well be true. The 'commission' was well hidden in the workshop awaiting collection, but Khalid's agent hadn't turned up when expected, and there were rumours. Always there were rumours. They ran like rats through street-sewers, but many turned out to be as real as the rats themselves. He hadn't been told the name of the agent, only that he would be European, British possibly, and that he would come to the workshop with an order written out in a certain manner. Ahmed had memorised it. He was to give the agent the flat box—a distinctly heavy and unusually well-sealed box, he'd noted. He'd been asked to secure it, carefully disguised, inside the folds of one of his carpets. All the documents for taking the carpet out of the country were provided, and the agent would take a taxi straight to the military airport. Everything would be taken care of. Khalid's friends at the Air Ministry would see the Brit onto the plane—and away! No fuss!

But there was no sign of the man. And now, with the promise to Jamil that he would check out his story, Ahmed was scared. Yet a promise was a promise.

Ahmed was wearing an old djellaba he found in one of his cupboards, hoping that would be disguise enough. He usually wore Western shirt and trousers. The pile of rubble had been easy to find. All he had to do now was look behind it. Car horns blared streets away, dogs barked, but the alley was quiet and the dilapidated yard was empty. He moved soundlessly. A form, no doubt that it was human, a man, but trussed, slashed and twisted just as Jamil had described, lay half hidden under rubbish. He could see the congealed, dark red pools on the ground. Taking care not to get blood on his hand he cautiously felt the nearest part of the body. It was faintly warm. (That discovery shocked him more than the sight of it—which, if truth be told, hadn't shocked him at all.) So! The fellow was still alive! It seemed impossible. From the skin tone the man was almost certainly a Westerner. Ahmed wasn't going to search his clothes for identity—it would be surprising if there was any. And anyhow, he wasn't inclined to avail himself of that knowledge. He'd phone Khalid immediately and tell him his suspicions.

Khalid remembered how he'd gazed long and lovingly on the gold disk before packing it, and how his fingers trembled when they first unearthed it and painstakingly brushed the dust from it. They'd trembled even more when that strange and intricate delineation upon its surface gradually revealed itself. He spent evening after evening after his colleagues had gone home wondering, doubting, yet in the end believing—a belief beyond the wildest shores of hope and reason— that the object in his hand was an astronomical map. What he held was an accurate depiction of the heavens, sun, moon and stars, and it was, he believed, more ancient by far than the ruins of that hidden temple in which it had been discovered. After months of secret study, poring over pages of photos and records, from the latest available high-resolution camera shots to carefully drawn sky maps from earlier times, his conclusion that the constellations depicted on the disk could be verified and named, astonished him. Astonishing, because it revealed stars which could only be seen from space, or by powerful modern telescopes. But being convinced himself was one thing: quite another to be able to obtain verification from international experts.

And another thing again to know that the disk, if his plans went to order, would eventually be placed in some respected overseas museum secure from the World's avarice and corruption.

With a despairing gesture, Khalid spun the card, with its 'Urgent, phone Ahmed' message, into the bin. He sat slumped at his desk, receiver in one hand, head in the other, with sweat trickling and heart-beats fast and uneven. Ahmed had just given him the worst possible news.

Annya had made her decision. Manfred's repaired car was delivered before breakfast, leaving her free to go or stay, and she'd decided to go back to the apartment after all, and bite the bullet. She would phone Peter and face whatever news she could drag out of him. She was ready for the worst, though unsure how she'd react if it came to that. She would also pack her things and leave the apartment tidy for the paying guests. After that, it would depend on the news she received. Xena had extended an invitation to return to the finca until she found her feet. But she knew in the end she'd have to go back home to England. She'd said a temporary goodbye to Manfred as he got into his car, and now it was time to thank Xena for all her hospitality. As his car drew away, Annya turned towards Xena, but before she could get her words out they fell into each other's arms.

'Xena, I...' Annya dabbed at her wet eyes.

'I know, I know. Come back soon, won't you?' Xena said, her voice cracking with emotion. 'Come and tell me how it goes—whatever it is. Won't you?'

Annya nodded. Unable to trust her own voice, she climbed into her car.

Meanwhile, Finn, having got hold of a certain thread, was seeing where it took him. It led him, in fact, to the dilapidated courtyard in a warren of streets and alleys somewhere in old Baghdad just as Ahmed, dressed in his old, striped djellaba crept up to the pile of rubble. From the rafters where the pigeons were roosting, Finn watched as the man looked warily around, but without looking up. It took only seconds for the Arab to find what he'd been seeking. Pulling his garment tight around him and shuddering, he crept away.

Finn floated down from the rafters and stood over the body. It was clear that the poor man's life was ebbing away fast. The neck wound was the most grizzly—a botched attempt to slit his throat, which along with a dozen or so other wild stab wounds added up to a brutal, and inevitably fatal assault.

Annya unlocked the door to the apartment. Warm, stuffy air met her again. But unlike before, that day Simon had left her—alone, with all the stuff that followed—this time she crossed the threshold calmly. Leaving the door ajar she went round opening all the vents. Maria must have been in; the place was extremely clean and tidy. She walked into Simon's room and sat on his bed. It was as near as she could get, intimate, the closest thing she had to the real person. She leaned down to smell the smell of him, a trace left on the pillow. But the linen was fresh. It was as if he... She couldn't bring herself to say her thoughts.

As if he'd... He'd never been! Feeling her resolve melting into tears, she got up and walked back to the sitting room. Before her determination abandoned her all together, she phoned Peter.

'Peter!'

'Oh!' A long pause. 'That's Annya, isn't it? I thought—I recognised your voice. How are you, Annya?'

His voice sounded flat and awkward. Before another long pause could develop she said, 'I want to know. I'm insisting, Peter. What's the news?'

'Well! Well, Annya. It's not good.'

'Then tell me.'

'If you're sure... You *are* sure, are you?'

'Tell me, Peter.' She was surprised at how firm her voice sounded. How calm she felt.

'He's disappeared, Annya. So nothing's for sure, but... Well, there's been a sort of... Three of our team have been taken, one shot, but Simon doesn't appear to have been with them at the time. But we've received no report from him and he's been gone a week now. So, it doesn't look good. He was on a special assignment, and didn't turn up. I still can't give you details, but until we hear one way or the other there's still hope.'

'But, it doesn't look good, you said. You must have a reason for saying that, Peter. Is it something to do with the nature of this assignment?'

'Yes. I can say *that* at least. But we mustn't give up.' The pause again. 'Annya. Wouldn't it be best if you came home, love, as soon as possible? Will you be OK? We'll send someone out to escort you, but that would take a day or so.'

'No, Peter. No thanks. I'm OK. I'll think what to do and act soon. But there are things out here. People and *things*. I'll ring you again. Thanks Peter, thanks for telling me. OK?'

She rang off abruptly and made her way slowly back up the hibiscus path.

Stooping over the near-lifeless body, a stab of pain went through Finn's heart at the sight of the inflicted savagery. He had set Simon in a state of suspended animation where only his spirit had the power to decide whether to depart the flesh or remain. But at least he could give his body first aid. Finn passed a hand over him, and the bindings immediately fell loose. He straightened the limbs, then held both hands over the body while he imparted enough energy to heal the wounds and staunch the faint trickle of blood which still flowed. He fashioned a glass of water and moistened the open mouth. Then, with much satisfaction, he swept him clean of maggots and filth.

Thinking fast, he flew to Ahmed's workplace and with seconds to spare took down one of the weaver's best carpets from the wall. He returned to the body before Ahmed reached the shop. With the greatest care he rolled the cleansed, healed and unconscious man inside the carpet, then elevated it, lifting it up between the broken rafters and laying him gently on a flat, sound area of roof. He could almost hear Mandy chuckling. That's my boy, he'd be saying. Learns fast, that one—with a bit of tuition from Yours Truly, of course. Those lessons in alchemy haven't been wasted, I see. And that journey to the healing temples of Lemuria hasn't gone to waste, either.

Finn paused to let the last remark sink in. I told you. It's all coming back, my boy, Mandy would be saying. And so it was. Even though parts of his cloud journey were still shrouded in mystery, he seemed to have absorbed its lessons, and, piece by piece, the memory of his experience did seem to be returning. But at this mundane level he still didn't know quite how to proceed. More bits of the puzzle needed to fall into place yet. He'd watch over the roll of carpet until he could find another thread.

* * * *

258

Annya dug her fingers into Simon's pillow, weeping uncontrollably. It grew dark by slow degrees, yet the tears still flowed. Night came and she could cry no more, but neither sleep nor numbness descended to soften the blade-thrusts of pain in her heart.

ARRIVALS AND DEPARTURES

His roll of carpet safely wedged in the shade under the roof tiles, Finn gazed down on streets of traffic. Conveyances of every kind, from cart to glossy limo, vehicles military and vehicles utilitarian, passed into and out of the city. His eyes fell on a white pick-up truck. There were a thousand such vehicles on these streets, and the only thing which distinguished this particular jalopy was the amount of smoke it was emitting from its rear end. But also, as it drew nearer, he noticed the dirt on its windscreen and the excessive rust and discolouration of its bodywork. He lost sight of it as it turned off the highway and disappeared into the network of narrow streets. Seconds later, however, it reappeared in the street below, and came to a halt outside the door of the very same workshop Finn had borrowed the carpet from.

Sun slanting on the dusty glass made it impossible to see inside the cab, but Finn's curiosity was kindled. He watched fascinated as a cloth began wiping a small circle of windscreen clean, and as the circle grew the head of the cloth-wielder became visible. The beard had gone, but the driver's face was unmistakable—Mandelbrot!

Mandelbrot climbed out. He gave his khaki slacks a brisk dust-down, tucked his crisp white shirt into his waistband, and, briefcase in hand, went smartly into the workshop.

The astonished Finn, like a stunned stoat in headlights, was unable to move. What in all the Worlds was going on! Faintly the sound of men's voices inside the shop drifted towards him, but he could only guess at what they were saying. Not for the first time in recent days he experienced the frustration of minutes ticking by like hours. Eventually, Mandelbrot emerged carrying a folded carpet tied up with tapes and stuck about with labels and red seals. He sauntered round to the passenger door, opened it, and placed the heavy-looking parcel on the seat. Then he casually glanced up to where stood the immobilised Finn and winked at him, then with a palm cupped to the side of his mouth, he called, 'See you in Arashid Street.'

If any of the passers-by heard or saw this exchange, it was not apparent; not a single head turned. But Finn heard it clearly. One problem though; he had no idea where this Arashid Street was.

Xena's old truck, now as recognisable to Finn as the man who'd emerged from it, drew away with its usual crunch and clatter—and with an unusually black fart of smoke. Ah! thought Finn, all I need to do is follow that. He sped across the rooftops with his eyes glued to the trail of smoke which pothered up between the rows of buildings. Moments later, for the truck had only gone a few streets before coming to a standstill again, Finn arrived to find his old friend on the pavement beside the vehicle.

'No time to lose, my boy. Let's roll!'

'Krise' Mandy! What you up to now? And If I can believe what I'm seeing, you've managed to rejuvenate yourself by at least fifteen years—and up-dated your wardrobe to boot!'

'No time for all that,' Mandelbrot said with a sharp wave of his hand. 'And if I was being personal—which as you know is not my style—I'd point out you'd *matured* somewhat. Let's find that carpet of yours and get out of here fast. We've a tricky bit of performance to get underway. That Simon's been in suspense long enough. Annya too. We've got to get this show on the road, and there's a lot of manoeuvre and negotiatin' to get through before we're out of the woods.'

'Where're we going then?' Finn wanted to know.

'As soon as we've loaded that carpet—oh, by the way, Ahmed hasn't noticed that gap on his wall yet—we're off to the airport.

How long Annya had lain on Simon's bed she'd no idea. Somewhere in the last twenty-four hours a ghost of herself had maybe wandered to the fridge; she could see a half-eaten yoghurt. Only gradually was she beginning to pull some rational thoughts together. Her brother. He must have heard the news by now. He'd also be worried—shit worried. Simon after all was Gideon's best friend—like brothers, like Simon and herself, he was part of the family. She stopped herself thinking again, remembering. The physical sensation of it would overwhelm her. She felt limp, stuffing all gone, but couldn't just lie here any longer. Strange though. Lying here in the apartment wasn't frightening any more. Even if she were to glance up—right now—and catch sight of that amazing face in the mirror... Even if she found him sitting on the bed—that creature with the strange name... 'Finnegal.' She said it under her breath. 'You don't scare me, Finnegal of the Galaxies. You're impossible to believe in, but you don't scare me.'

While she'd lain there weeping, and afterwards, after all the tears, when her mind and heart had become empty and dried up, like a stony bed of a stream, the one she'd descended with Manfred; that gorge down which centuries ago water had flowed; after all that night-long catharsis, pictures had begun to fill her mind. Simon kidnapped by the road-side, forced into a car, driven to some far away deserted place and... She'd tried to shut them out, but her mind defied her with a succession of grotesquely brutal images each more graphic than the last. Sickened, she turned on the light and waited for morning, eyes wide open. Had the Simon she'd seen calling for her in that first dream been nothing but her fear-distorted imagination too? But after a while, lying there, she was sure that Simon was real; her dream a glimpse into a kind of truth. It wasn't a particularly comforting discovery. His actual situation may be just as terrible, but there was a difference. It was having something to deal with, even if that meant living it and facing it, trusting without knowing.

Together, Finn and Mandelbrot lowered the carpet with Simon inside and set off.

'I'm bothered, Mandy. I only gave him first aid. How long's this plan of yours going to take?' Once again, pleased as he was to see him, Finn was beginning to feel a bit miffed that Mandy seemed to be taking over.

'Not to worry, Finn. It's not *my* plan. I've just set up a few technical details. I've a better idea how things work down here, wouldn't you say? We're back in my home territory again, my era. But it's *your* show. Yours and Annya's. And *his*. Simon. You've done a great job so far.'

'But I didn't want him to be suspended longer than necessary, Mandy. It won't be at all difficult to revive him, but it's not my place deciding if he lives or dies. It's his choice.'

'Agreed. But I think you'll find he's already made his decision. When we get a good safe distance from this place, we'll stop for a breather, and we can do the necessary. But we have to get through all the official rigmarole yet. And he stays in the carpet till then.'

Finn noticed the ride becoming smoother with each mile. The vehicle seemed to be undergoing a respray and refit. Mandy, too, as they cruised along with the benefit of a newly acquired overdrive, seemed slimmer, younger by degrees. And his clothing. By the time they stopped for the breather, Finn no longer recognised him. This cool, casual guy with the golden locks, and slung about with camera gear, was beginning to piss him off. The youthful good looks the old man had appropriated were upsetting his equilibrium. The ex-Mandy gave him a blue-eyed smile full of innocence. 'I don't think you ever met Simon, not at his best anyhow,' he said, holding out a hand to be shaken.

Finn, ignoring the invitation, and with a picture in his mind of the filthy, blood covered body he'd rescued, gasped, 'Simon! You're Simon now?'

'For the moment.'

'But isn't he in the carpet?'

'I've just stepped in, taken him on as a temporary measure while we go through customs.'

'Customs? Stepped in?'

'You'll see Finn.'

Khalid stared dumbfounded. His fax machine had just printed off a message. *'Dear Professor Al Rahman, esteemed colleague,'* it began. *'The professor and myself,'* followed by the names of two experts from the department of Assyrian and Babylonian antiquities at the British Museum, *'would like to express our satisfaction at having received your very interesting but unfortunately relatively unimportant fragment of limestone panel, an item for which you recently requested an opinion. We shall send you our report in due course by the usual means. In the meantime we thank you for consulting us, and we remain grateful for the trust you have placed in us in times past. Yours etc...*

They'd got it! What kind of miracle was this? The message spelled out in terms already agreed between them the fact that the gold disk was now in safe hands.

Khalid wasn't the only one needing an explanation. Finn, who by the time the fax arrived had witnessed all that had taken place in the run-up to the hand-over, was still bemused by the speed of the operation, and by the many changes of appearance it seemed to have required. They'd driven up to the military airport in an official-looking four-by-four. Simon, aka Mandelbrot, produced a stack of official looking documents, first for the guard at the gate, and then again as, escorted by two gold-braided and moustachioed Iraqi Air Force officers, they'd walked up to the steps of the plane. Finn was given the job of carrying the heavy, taped and sealed parcel, while a trolley was produced for the roll of carpet. There had been some fuss when 'Simon' insisted it be placed on the floor next to his seat, and not stored in the hold. But, on the production of yet another sheaf of papers, even that request seemed to have been officially approved. As had also a seat permit for Finn himself. Again, Mandy had thought of everything.

After Finn had got over his excitement at this novel way of flying, their conversation, mid-air, consisted of him bombarding Mandy with a hail of questions. Something which particularly intrigued him was this 'stepping in' business. Mandy explained how it was a relatively simple procedure, when the soul of the person concerned gave permission, to borrow the physical body for a time while its owner was transferred to a therapy room on the other side, on the astral plane. Back in the days of Atlantis for instance, it would have been a healing temple.

'The other side? On a Plane?' Finn asked. 'Is that where we're landing?'

Mandy laughed. 'No, for Chris'ake, we're not *landing* on some multi-dimensional plane. We're on an *aero*plane heading for London Heathrow. I'm talking jargon Finn. Like people who believe when they die their spirits go to someplace they call "the other side", or "the astral plane". But Atlantis...'

'Isn't Atlantis under the sea?' Finn sounded bewildered again. 'A sunken civilisation, like Lemuria?'

'Just another misconception, Finn. These continents—they didn't sink, they rose. And that's where your Planes come in; multi-dimensional levels.'

'But I've heard them talking about remains, actual physical structures.'

'Off the Turkish coast and such? Well, yes, but Atlantis itself, the greater part of it, just like Lemuria, existed at a multidimensional level, so only a fraction of it was three-dimensional physical matter. Though *unlike* Lemuria, Atlantis was a more technological society, more mental. Lemurians were always gentle and childlike, more feeling and intuition based. But this they had in common: they both developed the magical arts of healing and rejuvenation.'

'So you're saying he's in one of those multidimensional healing temples right now?'

Mandy grinned and ahemmed. 'You got it, Finn. However, as these Atlantean guys evolved over time and regrettably left behind their original innocence, their magicianship became infiltrated. The technology bug took over, cut them off from their innate wisdom, and they began all sorts of clever stuff, creating satellites, moons, space platforms, then de-creating them again just to see how it went. That was the problem, it all went out of cosmic kilter so they ended up destroying the whole shebang. They got a taste for power, became addicted, and forgot the wisdom of the heart was the reason behind their whole existence.'

This set Finn thinking, and he didn't speak for some minutes. As usual, Mandy's explanations left more questions than answers. And if he'd started asking why he was being sent off to Atlantis for the next bit of his mission, that would distract him from more immediate concerns. His promise to Annya for one.

The patio door swung open. Half awake, Annya wondered if she'd left it ajar. Suddenly Simon was sitting on the edge of the mattress. His bag and camera equipment dropped with a clatter. He threw a rumpled cotton jacket he'd had over his arm after them onto the floor, then leaned back, arms lifted, palms behind ears, ready to flop backwards onto the bed.

Annya jolted upright. They stared at each other, disbelieving, aghast. She struggled to free her legs from the sheet, and both of them shot onto their feet, facing one another. 'Annya? What are you doing here?' he said, as she said, 'Simon? What... you? Why...? Oh God!' And then, 'Can I touch you?' And he, ashen, gaunt, backed away from her. 'No. Don't. Please, Annya, please,' he was saying.

It was Magdalen and the risen Christ in the garden all over again, except she, Annya, was more the Doubting Thomas. She began to cry. The only possible thing to do.

Simon sank onto the bed, his face contorting with the emotion he seemed to be struggling to force back. He slumped forward, head in hands, and she saw tears oozing between the fingers. Then his head drooped between his knees and she thought he was going to faint. But so was she. Her ears droned and buzzed, the room swam, her thoughts raced. He didn't want her near him. He needed her. She was hallucinating again. Desperate for air she glanced up, ready to rush out of the open patio door he'd come through. But even more she needed the proof of her fingers to tell her if the person before her was real. 'Simon, look at me.' Her arms reached out.

He lifted his head slowly. 'Make us a cuppa, will you,' he said with a thin smile.

A pot of English Breakfast and two cups. She poured; she was mother with a shaking hand. She'd angled the yellow umbrella so the early morning light wouldn't get into their eyes, like that first morning, except it had been coffee then. He sat with his hand round the cup, but his legs weren't sprawled, and today his arms were inside shirt sleeves buttoned at the cuffs. Unlike before. Before, when the gold hairs on the back of his arms shone in that patch of sun, when in his absence he'd been so real. And now in this reality she wasn't sure.

'I don't understand,' she said. 'There's so much I don't understand.'

He stared into his cup, swirling the last few drops. 'That was so good. I haven't tasted anything that good in a long time.' He was looking right into her eyes. 'Thank you, Anns.' She lifted the pot, asking if he wanted more, but he shook his head. 'I think, if you don't mind, I'd like to go back indoors, love.' He seemed to be asking her permission. So she nodded. He grabbed hold of the table as he stood up, and she didn't know what to say or do. To help and steady him would be to steal strength away from him rather than lend it. And she didn't know what he needed from her—or if he needed anything at all.

But he was holding his hand out to her. 'Come with me?' It was a question, but also her answer. 'Lie down with me, let's lie on the bed?'

They were still drawn, the curtains, shutting out the day, all those helpless weeping days which had dimmed the room with the motes of her grief and terror. But now side by side on the bed they began to breathe, taking in breaths like they were one being, or twins; breaths of an air that felt increasingly new and fresh. They lay entwined, inside of knee against inside of thigh, the warmth of her breasts bursting against his chest like opening buds. But still her fingers held back from touching him, and his hands, even as he grasped her tight to him, awkwardly managed to keep hers from feeling his flesh. Frustration overtook her as bewilderment vied with her mounting passion; her desire, to know, to have, to feel. Was he punishing her for that time she'd frustrated him? Yet as the thought broke into her mind he seemed to sense it, and pulled her more fiercely into the melting fire where their bodies pressed together so that her longing for him to begin unfastening and unbuttoning her spilled out of her in moans. Then, 'Annya,' he gasped, clasping her each side of her face, his mouth seeking hers until their tongues found each other.

'But why? Why can't I touch you?' she asked when their lips pulled apart.

She felt him withdrawing again, and again the image of their last time together came to her, the day he'd left and she'd pulled away from *him*. But this wasn't that kind of withdrawal. He was fading from her, going into some other space where flesh and blood bodies couldn't exist. He was going to disappear, his presence seemed that fragile, like he was in a curious state of quarantine. Then she knew why she shouldn't touch him; knew not in words, but in some other, just as real, way. Intuitively. But she couldn't let it happen now, couldn't let him slip from her now. She must hang on to him somehow.

'Can't you tell me? Simon, I love you. I thought—we *all* thought, you were dead. Nothing's adding up. Help me understand, because otherwise I'm just going crazy.'

His sigh was heavy as if dragging up weights from a deep well. 'I'll tell you all I can remember, love, but nothing's adding up for me either. You see—there are these gaps—and, I'm possibly crazy too. That's what they're thinking at Amsterdam apparently. I've been... some kind of hospital. No, I think... No, I'm sure, that's definite.'

Beads of sweat glistened on his brow, and the eyes which sought her face looked out from shadows. Again that vague, wordless sense of quarantine dropped into her mind; an astronaut. An old picture she'd seen once, or a newsreel? A woman's face, a wife, her days filled with steeply rising anxiety while her man in space remained beyond contact. And now at last returned to Earth, she's prevented from touching him by a sheet of glass. Incongruously separated, they struggle with telephones while press cameras flash around them.

'Let me get you another drink,' she said, 'and a pillow.'

'Later,' he said. 'I'm OK. But these gaps...' He shuffled into a sitting position as she put a pillow behind him. 'So, where was I? Good question! Well, I'm in intensive care all of a sudden, this fantastic hospital. But first there was this little boy. Tiny chap, sweet little Arab fellow, must have been playing. I don't know, but he found me somehow, and it seems he fetched his uncle, and, sorry...' She was listening intently. 'Yes, the hospital. How they managed to get me in there, must have cost someone the earth. State of the art, air-conditioning, aromatherapists, quiet music, soft lights. It's all a bit of a blur I'm afraid, and it seems I lost my memory altogether around that point. Must have been going through the paces on automatic because apparently, so they tell me, I delivered. Someone got me on a plane to London. Mission accomplished. Then I came straight here, to the Island. Insisted, big fuss, they say. But had to go out the back way or the men in white coats would have spirited me off to the Ministry loony bin.'

Finn felt he could allow himself a sense of achievement. He'd delivered him safe and sound as promised—or as sound as possible, taking into account how a physical body needed time to catch up with the radical surgery which had gone on in the healing temple. Yet bodies still presented a challenge for him personally, present-day ones with their weight and density, at least. Although he'd created an updated version for himself, a super-body which he could manifest, leave and enter at will, he was finding that the closer he became drawn into Gaia's energy-field, the more pull this Earth was having on him. His new-found pleasure in sensations, from tasting and touching—earth under his feet, textures at his fingertips—to the various delightful rattlings and jolts of its mechanical transport methods, not to mention his admiration for the skills required to control these ancient vehicles, was increasing all the time. And now, having grown so close to Annya, the peculiar scent of her essence was seeping into his heart, too. Yet living in a body, even one as advanced as his, was hard work. And it was having a disconcerting effect on him. A new fear that if he let physicality really get a hold he might find himself caught up in nature's rhythms, its cycles of birth, death and rebirth, and not be able to return to his homeland again.

What if he could never get back to Li-Ona except through the long drawn-out process of dying a physical death? His longing for her pierced him at times like shards of glass. Yet he was contracted to carry out his mission, and one way or another he'd become involved in an adventure too exciting now to forgo. He'd never heard of anyone from his own times travelling bodily back to this present

271

world—except Mandy of course, who seemed to have done it in both directions. It came to Finn, probably not for the first time, though he hadn't allowed it to form words before, how lucky he was to have been assigned Mandy as tutor. His magic often just seemed to have rubbed off on him—effortless learning.

'Simon?' Annya sounded tentative; the mundane reality of their situation was creeping up on her. They'd lain warmly curled into each other for some moments making quiet adjustments, renegotiating that propinquity thing, discovering each other afresh. 'I hate to drop this on you now, but you realise, don't you, we have to be packed and out of here by tomorrow? Unless you know something I don't.'

'Do we? I'd forgotten,' he said wanly, clearly still struggling with where he was and why. 'I suppose we could go to a hotel. How long've we got?'

'Tomorrow morning at the latest, and we'd need to bribe Maria to do another clean. Don't worry though... I can...'

'Anns, I'm so sorry. I've really messed up, but we've still got time, haven't we? Your body, your presence... it's so healing. Be with me now, and in the morning I'll sort everything, I promise.' He shifted to look into her face, seeing something for the first time, or he'd seen it before but not in real time, in the flesh. 'I was lost and you came. You saved me. It was you.'

'What do you mean?' she asked, her voice trembling.

A sudden flash of light, and Finn's smile beamed at her across the room. '*We* saved him, Annya; we did it together,' he whispered.

Simon was holding her, drawing her into him, kissing her again. Passionately she kissed him back, and her arms wound round his waist and torso. He didn't flinch from her touch this time but began pulling her top over her head and peeling off her skirt as she moved her hips to wriggle free. He made no protest as she took his damp shirt and crumpled it to her face. Then her hands were caressing, running all over his body, her fingers digging into the hard muscles of his back, delicately and carefully feeling the wound marks there. Eyes closed, she could sense soft, pink-white gatherings of healing skin, finger-sized holes and longer slashes where there'd been unblemished, golden tan before.

'Oh, God! Simon. These are real! And your throat?' But her courage failed so she didn't touch the scar. It would have been sacrilegious to probe it. So she kissed his mouth again, and he turned, struggling with the effort, raising himself until he was above her. His arms were shaking and she feared they might fail him, even though his naked body with its thin, unfamiliar feel had little weight as he came into her. But his strength, far from fading, miraculously seemed gathered into a hard, single power thrusting and rising through her body. Her consciousness flickered, out, then back in. Her eyes opened, and her mouth too, with an ecstatic cry. It was joy—then unbelief. The infinite blue gaze looking out of Simon's eyes into hers was *Finn's*. Finn of the Galaxies had taken her to somewhere out beyond the realms of Earth, and she was kissing him in pleasure and with the most extraordinary sensation of wonder. She grasped his hand, and he took hers and held it to his mouth. 'I think I'm leaving, lovely earthy, Earthly Annya,' Finn whispered. 'Think of me and I'll be there. Need me and I'll come.'

Simon moaned and rolled onto his side. 'Are you still there?' he asked faintly, reaching for her hand, and locking his fingers into hers. 'Sleep now, my love. Tomorrow morning. Promise.'

Finn felt a shiver of light pass over his skin. And a hand touching him. The light, so bright he could barely see her face—but her voice was unmistakable. 'Darling Finn,' Li-Ona whispered, her breath kissing his ear. 'Come, beloved one. There is somewhere we must go; something we need to do. Atlantis beckons us.'

From her multidimensional plane, Cléa smiled at her husband. In some incomprehensible way she saw the seed her son had brought back, his Lemurian DNA, safely planted in the body of Annya, the woman who, as this World crosses the threshold into the Twenty-first Century, would become Cléa's own mother.

www.ingramcontent.com/pod-product-compliance
Lightning Source LLC
Chambersburg PA
CBHW020608260626
47157CB00003B/910